# WILDE FOR YOU

He'd gotten used to these magical little spots on the ranch. But now . . . "Through your eyes yesterday and right now, I guess I kinda see the ranch anew. I appreciate that you did that for me." Because as the loneliness grew, so did his discontent with where he was in his life. He loved the ranch. But it had grown stale. Until she made him see the wonder of this place again.

Her warm smile told him she understood what he meant.

"Come on. It's even better from the bottom looking up. I'll show you."

She reached back and put her hand on the outside of his thigh. "Wait."

His leg burned with heat where she touched him. He wouldn't move for anything at this moment, not if it meant she took her hand off him.

She glanced up at him.

He was so close, if he dipped his head, he could kiss her.

# By Jennifer Ryan

*Stand-Alone Novels*
SUMMER'S GIFT
THE ONE YOU WANT • LOST AND FOUND FAMILY
SISTERS AND SECRETS • THE ME I USED TO BE

*The Dark Horse Dive Bar Series*
WILDE FOR YOU • WILDE LOVE

*The Wyoming Wilde Series*
MAX WILDE'S COWBOY HEART
SURRENDERING TO HUNT • CHASE WILDE COMES HOME

*The McGrath Series*
TRUE LOVE COWBOY
LOVE OF A COWBOY • WAITING ON A COWBOY

*Wild Rose Ranch Series*
TOUGH TALKING COWBOY
RESTLESS RANCHER • DIRTY LITTLE SECRET

*Montana Heat Series*
TEMPTED BY LOVE • TRUE TO YOU
ESCAPE TO YOU • PROTECTED BY LOVE

*Montana Men Series*
HIS COWBOY HEART • HER RENEGADE RANCHER
STONE COLD COWBOY • HER LUCKY COWBOY
WHEN IT'S RIGHT • AT WOLF RANCH

*The McBrides Series*
DYLAN'S REDEMPTION
FALLING FOR OWEN • THE RETURN OF BRODY MCBRIDE

*The Hunted Series*
EVERYTHING SHE WANTED
CHASING MORGAN • THE RIGHT BRIDE
LUCKY LIKE US • SAVED BY THE RANCHER

*Short Stories*
"Close to Perfect" (appears in SNOWBOUND AT CHRISTMAS)
"Can't Wait" (appears in ALL I WANT FOR CHRISTMAS IS A COWBOY)
"Waiting for You" (appears in CONFESSIONS OF A SECRET ADMIRER)

---

# WILDE FOR YOU

## A DARK HORSE DIVE BAR NOVEL

## JENNIFER RYAN

AVON

*An Imprint of HarperCollinsPublishers*

WILDE FOR YOU. Copyright © 2024 by Jennifer Ryan. All rights reserved. Printed in the United States of America. No part of this book may be used or reproduced in any manner whatsoever without written permission except in the case of brief quotations embodied in critical articles and reviews. For information, address Harper-Collins Publishers, 195 Broadway, New York, NY 10007.

First Avon Books mass market printing: March 2024

Print Edition ISBN: 978-0-06-331976-9
Digital Edition ISBN: 978-0-06-331974-5

*Cover design by Amy Halperin*
*Cover image © Rekha Garton/Arcangel*

Avon, Avon & logo, and Avon Books & logo are registered trademarks of HarperCollins Publishers in the United States of America and other countries.

HarperCollins is a registered trademark of HarperCollins Publishers in the United States of America and other countries.

FIRST EDITION

24 25 26 27 28  BVGM  10 9 8 7 6 5 4 3 2 1

*For you. The ones who get lost in*
*the story, in the beauty of life,*
*in someone else, in love, and all the magical things.*

# Author's Note

Dear Reader,

It's not unusual for me to tackle tough topics in my novels. Life isn't easy. Everyone has struggles and things they have to deal with and overcome. Sometimes those issues are easy to spot, other times they're hidden beneath the surface, silent and unseen, even to those closest to us.

This book contains references (no graphic details) to abortion and suicide and may be triggering to some.

If you or someone you love is struggling and need help or support, please contact the National Suicide Prevention Lifeline by dialing 988.

Ask for help.

You are worth it.

Because you deserve your own happy ending.

With love,
Jennifer Ryan

# WILDE FOR YOU

# Chapter One

Layla Brock stood in the middle of her empty home feeling as still, quiet, and waiting as the house surrounding her. She'd lost her husband a little more than a year ago. His death was the last of the losses she'd suffered during their marriage.

But she didn't want to think about those dark times right now.

Somewhere out there was the new life she wanted to make for herself.

She was more than ready to move on.

The house was just a place. What she wanted was a home again.

A real one this time. Not one built on a lie she hadn't even known she'd been living.

Christopher had wanted a home with her. And it had felt real and true. But it hadn't been enough. *She* hadn't been enough. And although she'd made mistakes, pushed him away when they needed each other the most, it still hurt to discover the man she'd loved had turned out to be someone she didn't recognize.

He hurt her. He hurt others. That wasn't the kind, generous man she knew at all.

And now all she had left was the knowledge that she could love someone, faults and all, even with a broken heart filled with his secrets.

"Where do you think you're going?"

She jolted and glanced behind her.

Michael stared at her with the same pine bark–brown eyes as Christopher but without all the joy and tenderness of his older brother.

She hadn't heard him come in. He stood behind her as she turned back to the massive windows that overlooked the Pacific Ocean.

She loved this house and the view. But the space held her sadness, and the beautiful scene didn't bring her joy anymore.

She needed a new view.

She needed to find the beauty in life again.

It hurt to look at Michael and see glimpses of Christopher in his features. Her mind wanted to play the what-if game, but she shut that down. She couldn't rewrite the past. She could only move forward.

"I accepted a commission." She didn't explain further.

Michael cared little for her artistic talent, except when he could use her name to brag to someone he wanted to impress.

She didn't play those kinds of games.

Christopher hadn't needed to use such tactics to gain people's attention or trust either. He charmed everyone with his easy smile, gentle heart, sharp brain, and witty humor. She'd fallen in love with him because of all that and so much more. His depth of character, the ability to let the little things go and live in the moment, the love he showed not only her but his family and friends, it drew people to him. He owned up to his mistakes, said sorry when it needed to be said, and when he hurt her, or anyone really, she knew it hurt him just as deeply.

All those things made him complex and special.

She still had trouble reconciling who he'd been to her and what he'd done. Not out of spite but selfishness . . .

Michael was nothing like Christopher. And Michael resented Christopher for the life he'd built, the successes he'd achieved, anything and everything that Christopher had and Michael wanted.

"How much?" Michael demanded an answer that was none of his business.

She'd been a working landscape artist when she met Christopher, selling her paintings in a local art gallery in town. Barely known, she spent the night of her gallery showing worrying no one would buy any of her paintings. He came in looking for something to brighten his new office. A gift to himself for his recent promotion at a high-end furniture import company. The scene that captured his attention: Maya Bay, Koh Phi Phi, in Thailand. He loved the blue ocean and light sand-colored cliffs with the rich and vibrant green vegetation. One of the most beautiful beaches she'd ever seen. He fell in love with it. And when she made a point to thank him in person for the purchase, he couldn't take his eyes off her and asked her out on the spot. She fell just as hard and fast for him. They honeymooned in Thailand a year later.

She'd come a long way since those early showings where she waited with bated breath, hoping someone bought her work. Over the last few years, her career had skyrocketed. Her paintings were sold in many high-end galleries. The prices for her landscapes went up and so did demand, until she couldn't believe the amount of money people paid for her creations.

She loved painting. That she made a living doing it had been the dream all along. It felt lucky, and sometimes unreal, that she got to do what she loved most. It still felt more like pleasure than work even after all these years.

Michael wouldn't understand any of that. For him, life came down to what you had and what you wanted.

She finally turned to him. "What are you doing here?"

Michael took a step closer. "Looking out for my brother's interests."

"As you know, I have them well in hand." What was left of Christopher's things anyway.

"You don't deserve any of it."

She raised a brow. "Christopher and the judge disagreed with you."

Michael folded his arms over his chest. "He told me you asked him for a divorce."

"Everything I had to say on the matter is part of the testimony I gave when you contested the will. Now, if you'll excuse me, I have a schedule to keep."

He stepped into her path, blocking her from showing him out.

Angry and bitter, she tried to hide both because she didn't want to give him the satisfaction of seeing her lose her composure.

All she wanted to do was say goodbye to the ghosts

in this house and this part of her life and take that first step toward the future. She wanted the chance to leave with a clear head and heart, knowing that she'd never forget Christopher, but she was ready to move on and live her life without him. It had taken her a long time to grieve and accept the part she'd played in the downfall of their marriage and learn from her mistakes. It took even more time to understand that not everything that happened was her fault. Though sometimes, she faltered on that when she thought of the aching hole in her heart.

Her hurt and anger had been an anchor weighing her down and stealing the light from her life for far too long.

So she'd found a way to forgive, if not forget.

Michael leaned in. "Do you really think I'll let you just walk away?"

She met his gaze and held it, confident that she'd executed her husband's last wishes to the letter. As per his will and in the spirit in which he'd wanted her to handle things with the ones he loved. All of them.

Michael simply couldn't accept that Christopher chose his beloved wife over his blood. The law was also on her side as far as that was concerned. It should have been a simple matter of executing the will. Angry, grieving Michael complicated the matter.

And now he wanted the money he thought she didn't deserve.

She simplified things for him once again. "After all that's happened, the one thing I know, and you refuse to accept, is that Christopher loved me, and he knew I loved him."

"And yet, you were planning to leave him."

She didn't confirm or deny, because she'd promised Christopher she'd keep his secrets. "Whatever you think you know about me, Christopher, or our marriage, you don't. So don't stand there and say things that aren't true simply because you want things that don't belong to you."

He glared down at her, his arms rigid at his sides. "He's gone because of you!"

She knew that was his grief talking, but still . . . it hurt. "You're angry. So am I. You can't direct it at him so you're lashing out at me. But I didn't do anything but love him."

"Bullshit. You ended things, and he wanted nothing to do with you."

"That's a lie. Now get out!"

He fumed, his chest out, eyes narrowed. "This isn't over."

"But it is. You even gave up what Christopher did leave you and got a judge to tell you it's done."

Since he'd contested the will, Michael lost his portion of the inheritance. "He didn't want *you* to have anything." Furious, bitter words.

"And yet he left it to me, and I'd give it all up to have him back." Not as her partner. That bond had been fractured too badly to be fixed. But she didn't want him gone. Not from this earth. Not even from her life. They had too much history, too many memories shared to let what happened tear them completely apart.

At least that's what she'd thought.

She never suspected that his mistakes and losing her would send Christopher into a deadly spiral.

She wished she'd seen it coming. She'd have done anything to save him, even if she was angry and hurt. She'd have helped him.

In time, they'd have found their way back to being friends again.

Now that she had distance and a chance to see their life without all the emotion but with perspective, she believed that.

"More bullshit." Michael had made her the enemy in his mind. He believed the worst of her, so he could justify his behavior.

She'd simply been trying to get through a difficult time and do what Christopher would have wanted her to do in his stead.

She shrugged and frowned because his conduct and beliefs made her sad. "I wish you the best, Michael. I really do. I hope you find a way to move on, the way I'm trying to do." She wished that someday they could reminisce about Christopher, but Michael would have to give up his anger and resentment for that to happen.

"Always so fucking placating and pleasant," he snarled.

"You should try it," she shot back. She wasn't weak. She wouldn't be cowed. But she didn't have to stoop to his level. It would only make things worse. "Maybe you'd find people aren't so put off by you if you led with kindness."

If he could glare laser beams, she'd be toast.

She pointed toward the door. "If you'll excuse me, I need to lock up the house."

"You never said where you're going." He didn't need to know.

She pointedly looked at the door. "After you."

He sneered at her. "If people only knew what you're really like."

"You're the only one who seems to bring out this side of me." She raised a brow. "Perhaps it's not me."

Michael actually growled in the back of his throat. "You will not get away with this."

She lost her temper and snapped, "I didn't get away with anything. I was his *wife*!"

"But he wasn't the only one in your bed."

She shook her head, so over him throwing out a line, hoping to catch something, because he didn't *know* anything. "That's a lie."

"Then why was he so fucked up at the end?"

"It's in the record."

"Fuck what you said to the judge. You lied. Don't give me that 'couples have issues' bullshit. You were leaving him. Admit it. Tell the truth. Or do you just not want to own up to the fact that his death *is* your fault?"

"If you don't go, I'll call the police and have them escort you off the property." Sometimes you just had to cut people off and walk away to stop an argument.

"I will find out the truth. And when I do, I'll take everything from you." He stared hard at her for another ten long seconds, then turned on his heel and walked out.

It took her a few minutes before the anxiety faded,

and her annoyance dissipated, and she found the calm and a goodbye in her heart.

"I'll miss you, Christopher."

This time tomorrow, she'd be waking up in a new state. *With a whole new state of mind*, she promised herself.

And maybe she'd meet someone interesting. Someone she could be herself with again.

# Chapter Two

Jax Wilde walked into the barn of his Wilde Wind Ranch and found his sister Lyric brushing her horse, Bruin. "Where's tall, dark, and scary?" It was a joke.

Mason's head popped up behind Jax's sister.

Jax raised a brow. "I do not want to know what you're doing in there."

Mason held up the pick he'd been using to clean out Bruin's hoof. "I won't tell you where my other hand is right now." He turned his gaze to Lyric and, like every other time Mason looked at the woman, his eyes filled with want and so much love, no one could deny they were connected by an unbreakable bond.

Lyric squeaked and jumped like Mason had pinched her ass.

Jax rolled his eyes, envious his older sister had the kind of all-in relationship he wanted, but he was also happy for her. "Please, for the love of God, stop."

Lyric gave Mason a sultry kiss that was short and sweet but potent, then turned a brilliant smile Jax's way. "What's wrong?"

"Nothing." Everything. He was tired of being alone.

His sister sized him up with one sweeping, too perceptive glance. "Someone hasn't had a date in too long."

"Someone"—Jax pointed a finger at his face—"has had nothing but bad or boring dates lately." It wasn't anyone's fault. Not his. Not the women's. The spark of interest on his part simply fizzled out before the end of the date. Most of the time, the women flirted for more, but he was long past casual affairs and one-night stands. Though his body wanted him to get over that, and quick.

He just . . . wanted something more. Someone special. Someone who looked at him the way Mason and Lyric looked at each other.

Lyric studied his face. "You're working too much. What time did you get home from the bar last night?"

"Around eleven." It wasn't unusual for him to work sixteen-to-twenty-hour days. Between the ranch and the Dark Horse Dive Bar he owned along with his three sisters, there wasn't enough time in a given day to do everything that needed to be done. On the days he worked twelve to fourteen hours, he squeezed in a date here and there.

But recently, he found himself falling into bed—alone—only to rise still tired and feeling unfulfilled. His days fell into a pattern, feeling the same way over and over again.

It had become such a habit that it was rare he found the time to even think something was wrong with this picture, let alone figure out how to change it.

"And you were up at dawn." Her gaze narrowed with concern. "Have you even eaten breakfast yet?"

He didn't need to look at his watch to know it was nearly ten and he'd already put in five labor-intensive hours finishing the glass house project, feeding the cattle they raised and sold, and fixing a downed fence line. "I'll eat soon. Our special guest staying in cabin ten just arrived. I need to go make sure we've met all her demands." He didn't mind that guests sometimes wanted to set up something special for their stay. A proposal to end all proposals. A wedding on the property. A romantic picnic. A secret getaway for lovers.

He'd personally scouted out a couple of very private spots on the ranch to accommodate guests.

But he'd never been asked to build something so specific on the property for someone to use exclusively on an open-ended visit.

But hell, why not add more work to his life. It seemed that was all he was good at lately, anyway.

Lyric eyed him. "Mom told me about the famous artist. What exactly did she want?"

"A studio. She had the prefab building delivered. Dad and I spent the last two weeks putting it together in the evenings." He had no idea the cost of the building, but it couldn't have been cheap. He didn't know much about artists and what they needed to create their work, but this one wanted a place she could go and lock herself away. A place with light. A place she said they could keep when she was done with it. She'd sold his mom on the idea when she said it would make a great space to rent out to guests who wanted to feel like they were outdoors but still enclosed. A place where you could sleep under the stars.

He had to admit, the small building would be an amazing getaway.

Right now, it was in a convenient spot for the artist who sent it, but it could be moved to a more private spot on the property later. Tucked in the trees, they could promote it as a fairy-tale-like glass house in the woods. Couples would love it.

And because it was good for business, he hadn't minded the extra hours of work it had taken to build it for their peculiar customer.

"I want to see it." Lyric opened the stall gate and walked out, Mason right behind her.

Jax shrugged. "Come on, then. We'll take my truck."

They all piled into the front seat, his sister between him and Mason. The lovebirds reached for each other, putting their hand on the other's thigh like it was the most natural thing in the world. Like it anchored them.

"We've set a date for the wedding," Lyric announced, joy and excitement in her voice. "It's in less than two months."

Jax had never seen his sister this happy. The fact that the man beside her looked just as ecstatic about marrying his sister only made him like Mason more. The man was gone over Lyric. He'd do anything to make her happy. Including moving to Wyoming to be with her, because Mason could see that Lyric was tied to her family and the bar they worked together. And while Lyric was a rising star in the country music business as a singer-songwriter, it was here that she wanted to make her life. She had big dreams, but a down-home heart. And Mason was the center of her world.

They'd bought a place not far from here. A place he'd thought about buying himself. But what did he need with his own place when he spent most of his time working the ranch and the bar and only used his room in the big house to sleep?

Besides, the ranch would be his sole responsibility one day. Not that his parents hadn't already stepped back and let him run things, so he'd be ready when they were gone. It was a big job that sucked up all his time and took blood, sweat, and tears.

He really needed to get a life.

*You're avoiding getting hurt again.*

He didn't need the reminder from that little voice in his head. After Helen knocked him on his ass, he'd shut down.

No one knew the true story behind the breakup. He didn't let anyone see the destruction of his heart.

Not because he'd lost the girl. No, his pain went deeper. He'd lost the dream of a future he'd seen so clearly. It shattered his heart and left him with nothing but broken pieces of what might have been and dreams of someone he didn't even know.

Now only his family got his heart. They wouldn't crush it. They handled it with care. But with others . . . he kept it locked down tight. And though the women he went out with tried to get it, he never found himself willing to take a chance. He was too afraid they'd smash the broken pieces under their heel.

It wasn't fair to them that he'd been waiting for someone to prove to him they deserved his trust and devotion, but that's how he felt.

He wanted the connection that somehow magically snapped into place the way it had for Mason and Lyric. The instant they met, something had just pulled them together. It took a hell of a long time for them to finally get together, but that had more to do with Mason's job than anything else, because the two of them had known they were meant to be from the moment they laid eyes on each other.

At least it seemed that way to Jax. He'd watched from the wings at the bar as the two pretended the other didn't exist. But he caught the longing-filled looks, the way Mason always kept watch over Lyric in the rowdy bar.

Once they were free to be together, it was like they'd been a couple forever. The love between them . . . undeniable.

"Oh my God, I want one," Lyric blurted out as they drove past the line of rental cabins and stopped at the end of the dirt lane. "It's a glass hothouse. I could grow herbs and vegetables all year round." Of course Lyric was thinking about growing food. She was probably creating a menu in her head right this second.

"Or you could set up a recording studio." Mason supported Lyric in both her careers. He stared at her in open adoration every time she sang at the bar.

Jax turned to his sister. "If I have to build one for your place, Mason is helping me."

"It's really cool." Mason grinned. "If you want one, I'll get it for you. I can already taste the omelets with fresh tomatoes and basil."

Lyric lightly jabbed her elbow into her fiancé's gut. "You just want me to cook for you."

"I love it when you sing to me, too. And dance in

the kitchen." The suggestive look in Mason's eyes made Lyric blush.

Jax pretended to gag.

Lyric jabbed him in the arm.

"You can give me another private dance later," Mason murmured, kissing Lyric on the side of the head. "Come on, I want to check out the inside."

They exited the truck and walked to the glass-and-wood shed that could be used as a greenhouse, studio, or guest room, depending on how you set it up and outfitted it.

Lyric stopped just before the only door into the rectangular structure and turned back to him. "If you use this as a guest space, you should put some potted flowers out front. Maybe a bench or Adirondack chairs outside. Some string lights or lanterns. It would be so pretty."

Jax thought so, too. "Still need to figure out the bathroom situation though. It's just one open room." Which was why he'd built it near the last cabin, so the artist could go between the fully furnished rental to the studio without a long trek.

The door to the cabin twenty feet behind him opened. He turned to greet their guest for the first time as she walked down the steps and approached him.

Pretty, slender, petite. And married, the ring on her finger announced. Not that he was looking for a date. He'd very rarely dated guests over the years, knowing they were short-term fun without a long-term attachment. That was fine then. Now . . . not what he was looking for anymore.

"Mrs. Brock." He held out his hand. "I'm Jax. Welcome."

The brunette's warm smile dimmed. "Sorry, I'm April, Layla's agent. We spoke on the phone." April took his outstretched hand and shook. She'd been his point of contact for everything included in Layla Brock's stay here. "She'll be here any second. She arrived last night and stayed at a hotel in town since she got in so late from California." As if on cue, a four-door Jeep pulled up behind the cabin and parked next to the van April must have driven in. "That's her."

Jax felt Lyric and Mason join him, but he couldn't take his eyes off the beautiful blonde who climbed out of the Jeep. She wore a pink boho-style sundress that stopped a couple inches above her knees and showed off a pair of gorgeous tanned legs. She didn't look at any of them, but walked past her cabin and straight for the field in front of her and the hills beyond, nothing but blue sky dappled with fluffy white clouds.

The look of wonder and joy on her face caught him by surprise. He saw how much she appreciated the simple beauty spread out before her.

"I'm going to paint this." The smile she beamed at her agent socked Jax right in the gut. "It's glorious." She turned back to the view. "I love it here." Her cheeks flushed with excitement, and he thought it was the most adorable thing he'd ever seen.

"Someone else is loving the view from here," his sister whispered, catching Jax staring at Layla.

Even his sister's teasing didn't make him turn away from the stunning woman.

"Come meet your host." April held her hand out to Jax.

He found his voice. "Welcome to Wilde Wind Ranch."

Layla took another few seconds to admire the view, then her gaze found his. For a second, she went perfectly still, their eyes locked, then she glanced at April. They shared one of those looks people who know each other really well share, one that said something without them speaking. Then she turned back to him and he felt her stare like a warmth spreading through him. "Thank you." She looked past him, her eyes going wide and appreciative again. "Oh, it turned out so perfect." She rushed past him, spread her arms wide, and pressed her hands and body to the building like she was trying to hug it. "I love it so much."

Again, adorable.

All the labor-intensive hours it took to build the studio seemed well worth it now.

Mason chuckled behind him and teased Lyric. "I thought you were the only one who hugged inanimate objects."

"Have you seen my professional six-burner stove?" Lyric's love for her new kitchen, and that of the man who'd shelled out top dollar for the appliances, knew no bounds.

Apparently, Layla loved her studio that much, too.

And he had to admit, it felt damn good to know he'd pleased her.

April grinned at her client. "Layla, seriously, you can lock yourself away from the world and lose yourself painting soon, but first, look. There are people here."

Layla bit her lip. "Sorry. I sometimes get caught up by pretty things. The view. This sweet little building that's all mine." She brushed her hand over the door like she was petting it. "I have wanted something like this forever. I mean, I had a nice studio space before, but this . . ." She looked at the building, then at the view again. "Out here. With the light and the hills and the . . . everything." Her joy held Jax captivated.

Just being near her had a strange and pleasant effect on him. He could just watch her for hours.

Not in a creepy way.

In a she's-just-so-damn-nice-to-look-at way.

"Layla." April shook her head. "Say hello to Jax."

"Hello, Jax."

His name on her sweet voice made his gut go tight. "Hi. I'm glad you like the place."

"Jax built it for you," April pointed out.

Layla's grin brightened. "Thank you. A thousand times, thank you. I know it was a huge ask." She scrunched her lips and narrowed her eyes. "And probably a little weird, right? My asking you to build something on your property."

Jax shrugged that off. "You paid for it." He'd earned extra for putting it together for her. And they'd keep it when she left. That thought made him feel something unexpected.

Disappointment.

He'd just met her. But he knew he'd miss her when she was gone.

She'd take all this lively energy with her.

"Hi. I'm Lyric. Jax's sister. This is my fiancé, Mason. You have to tell me where you bought this amazing thing. I want one."

Layla scrunched her lips again. "Oh, this was a

late-night, like, predawn online-search thing inspired by lack of sleep and dreams of painting outside, but in a place with no dust or bugs, and that's not too hot or too cold."

April stepped close to Lyric with her phone. "Layla often texts me random stuff at random times. I have the link to the manufacturer who builds these. I can email it to you. They have several versions available, depending on your needs."

Jax left Lyric and Mason with April, scrolling through the variations of the building on the website. He walked toward the beautiful woman he couldn't seem to stop staring at. "Want to see inside?" He pulled out the keys and unlocked the door. He stayed back and let Layla go in ahead of him.

She stopped just inside the door and stared at the bare wood floor. The wood ran up the walls about four feet before it met the tall glass windows that surrounded the rest of the room and made up the pitched glass ceiling. Right now, the room was empty. Nothing but the hills on one side, the forest on the other, and up above, all brilliant blue sky. At night, with the stars overhead, it would be another amazing view. "It's gorgeous. Small, but perfect."

His stomach rumbled. He really needed to head up to the house and get some food.

Layla dipped her hand in her bag, pulled out a granola bar, and absently handed it to him, then walked into the center of the room and looked out the windows to the field and hills beyond.

"Thanks," he said, biting into the chocolate, cherry, and oat goodness.

"Uh-huh."

He still didn't have her full attention. And he wanted it. "What is it that captivates you? The scenery? The colors? The light?"

"Yes." Wonder and joy filled that simple response.

He didn't know anything about painting or being an artist. But he could see that this place spoke to her.

He liked that, because he loved it here, too.

This was home.

This was where he was meant to be.

It also sometimes felt like the loneliest place in the world.

Not that he was ever actually alone on the ranch. He lived here with his parents. His sisters were in and out all the time. They had seven full-time ranch hands and three part-time workers during the busy summer season.

Still. He spent his days working this place and the bar. He did so with lots of others pitching in. Any free time he had, he mostly spent thinking about all the things he was supposed to be doing.

But nearly every night, he went to bed alone.

"You're good company."

Jax stared at the woman who finally looked back at him. "I am?"

"I find that most people feel the need to fill the silence. You let me enjoy the peace of this place."

"You'll get a lot of that here. Except when you do all the activities April signed you up for."

Both her eyebrows shot up. "What?"

"Horseback riding, campfire cookouts, archery, apple picking, that sort of thing."

She looked aghast. "You're joking."

"It's a working cattle ranch. People come for the experience. April said you're here for the scenery. We've got lots of that."

A thoughtful look came over her. "I see. The orchard. The river. Horseback riding in different landscapes." She bit her bottom lip in a lopsided smile, then she looked out the windows again. "It's lovely. You'll be my guide and help me find the perfect scene."

He wanted to tell her he had a hell of a lot of other things to do besides shepherd her around the property. That's what the hired ranch hands who worked with the rental guests did. But the words wouldn't come out of his mouth. He wanted to get to know her better, this strange—in a good way—artist, who lost herself in the beauty around her.

He had an odd thought that if he didn't keep track of her, she'd get lost wandering around looking for that perfect scene to paint.

"We start tomorrow."

Pure delight shone in her moss-green eyes. "Excellent. The sooner I find that perfect place, the sooner I can start painting." Her fingers moved, like she needed to fill them with a brush and paint palette. She looked around the empty room. "But first, I need to get set up. Because once I start, I kind of forget about everything else."

"I'll leave you to settle in." He held up the granola bar wrapper. "Thanks for the snack."

She gave him one of those warm smiles, even though there was a shyness in her eyes. "You're welcome."

"You don't remember giving it to me, do you?"

She tried to hide a grin. "Sure I do."

He didn't know if she was telling the truth or not, but he also didn't want to embarrass her. "Do you want me to show you the cabin?"

"She'd love that," April said, stepping into the room with another one of those telling looks at Layla.

Layla mock-glared at her agent, who seemed more like a close friend than just a business associate. "I'm sure Mr. Wilde has a lot better things to do."

"It's just Jax. And I'm happy to show you where you'll be staying."

She held her hands out wide. "This is most definitely where I'll be spending most of my time." She caught herself. "Except, yes, I'll sleep in the cabin. Probably." Her eyes narrowed. "Most likely."

April rolled her eyes. "Don't mind her. She tries to tell the truth, but she also knows sometimes all she sees is the potential on a canvas and forgets the outside world."

"It's a thing," Layla said conspiratorially.

Like she wanted him to be in on it with her.

It made him feel like maybe he had a shot at getting to know her better.

"Well, you can lose yourself here, just don't actually get lost out in the wilderness. Bears, coyotes," he warned her. "Bugs," he added, because she'd wanted this place so she could be outdoors but inside at the same time, away from insects.

She did that thing again where she tried to hide a grin but failed miserably. "April and I have everything well in hand. Please don't feel like you need to babysit me."

"Someone should," April said under her breath.

Layla acted like she didn't hear her friend. "I've got a lot to set up in here."

Knowing when he'd been dismissed—he had three sisters—he headed out to find some real food and figure out how he was going to rework his schedule so he could spend time with the beautiful woman who'd captured his attention the way the ranch had snared hers.

# Chapter Three

Layla stared at April blocking the exit. That look on her friend's face said she wanted Layla to listen, but Layla probably didn't want to hear what April had to say. Especially since she'd been struck by not just the view but Jax.

She'd never seen a more rugged, handsome man in her life. She'd never wanted to touch someone more just to make sure he was real. He was probably warm. And hard. And had rough hands from working that would feel oh so good against her softer skin.

Never in her life had she seen a man and immediately wondered what it would be like if he touched her. Or known that he could talk her into an orgasm with just the sound of his voice.

She shook the thought out of her head.

Something wild had come over her.

"He really got to you, didn't he?" April's knowing smile didn't help at all.

Layla tried to change the subject because Layla wasn't the type of person who ogled men or had dirty thoughts about what he could do to her with those big hands. Not normally. But right now she feared those thoughts were showing all over her overheated face.

"Horseback riding?" She couldn't believe her friend and agent had signed her up for that.

"Forget the horse. Ride the cowboy." April wiggled her eyebrows and grinned.

She burst out laughing, but said anyway, "Not funny." She turned to the view, hoping April didn't comment on the blush she couldn't hide.

"Come on, he's gorgeous. That dark hair. Those wide shoulders. His blue, blue eyes. And the way he looked at you." April made an approving humming noise. "Damn, Layla."

She glanced over at her friend. "I'm going to tell Donte you said all that."

"My man is gorgeous and knows I adore him."

Layla had to agree April's half African American, half Japanese husband, with his light brown skin, warm brown eyes, tall and lean swimmer's body, and a smile that always lit up when he looked at his wife, had nothing to worry about in the gorgeous man department. The fact that he was also the kindest, most thoughtful husband to her best friend made him damn near perfect.

Which is why Layla should have listened when Donte had once looked at Christopher with suspicion after a conversation in the kitchen when they were hanging out, drinking wine, and making dinner together. When Christopher had taken the steaks out to the grill, she'd asked Donte about the look. He tried to get out of answering, saying it was nothing. But she'd pushed. And after a shared glance between him and his wife that was a silent conversation between them, he said, *"There's something off about him. I don't know what it is, but it feels like he's acting or something. He treats you well. Says all the right things. The affection is real, no doubt. But . . ."*

*"But what?"*

*"It feels like he's doing it to make up for something."*

*"I don't know why you'd think that. Everything is great between us."*

They never fought. Sure, they disagreed sometimes. But Christopher had been understanding about everything. The days and weeks she traveled to find a new landscape to paint or to attend a gallery showing of her work. As a businessman, he traveled to meet clients and prospective business partners. But when they were together, it was . . . easy. Two best friends who loved each other. Maybe there wasn't a wild passion, but there'd been tenderness and caring.

And this conversation had happened long after she and Christopher suffered a devastating loss. The dinner with close friends one of the many steps back to normal they'd taken in the healing process.

At the time Donte's words hadn't made sense to her. They didn't feel right. And then she'd learned the truth. Looking back, his words made perfect sense.

But she didn't want to think about Christopher.

She wanted to focus on the future.

*Ride a cowboy.*

She blushed again, thinking about the handsome stranger with all those honed muscles and a look about him that said he could deliver on one hell of a ride in bed.

April brushed her hand up and down Layla's arm. "Come on, Layla, don't lie to me or yourself. I know you. The second you looked at him, something hit you. Just like that view, he made you feel something."

It was true. She sometimes didn't know what to do with all her feelings. Especially the ones that slammed into her when she saw Jax. It was like her hormones exploded.

Yes, she'd desperately wanted to touch him. She wanted to trace the line of his strong jaw with her fingertips, feel the softness of his hair, sculpt those toned muscles in her palms. But it wasn't only that. She wanted to draw him. And stare at him for hours.

She wanted to know what made him laugh.

He had a sister. Did he have other family?

Did he live and work on the ranch?

What was his favorite food? What was his favorite music and movie?

One thought stopped her from wondering anything further about him. *Does he have a girlfriend? A wife?*

He hadn't worn a ring, but maybe he was married and had beautiful blue-eyed kids.

The thought made her sad for her loss, but happy for him, because he seemed like a family man.

She balled her hands into fists.

April's squeal of delight startled her. "You are so hot for him."

"Shut up." She rolled her eyes and hid a grin. "We're not teenagers. Even if he's unattached, I'm not here for a romp. I've been commissioned." She made sure the last part sounded super important and professional.

April stared up through the glass roof, sighed

out her exasperation, then pinned Layla in her gaze. "You're not dead. It's okay to live." Those gentle words hit Layla in the heart. Her friend was looking out for her.

"I know. It's not about that." It really wasn't. She didn't feel disloyal to Christopher for finding another man attractive, for wanting to touch, taste, savor, and feel again.

"Isn't it? Christopher is gone. He'd want you to have a full life. He'd hate to see you unhappy."

That brought her up short. "I'm not unhappy." She'd worked damn hard to put the past behind her.

"You're lonely. And I get that. If I lost Donte, I'd feel adrift."

"I'm fine. I'm working again." For months she'd been lost after the devastation. She couldn't find the light, the joy, in the darkness of her mind where all she did was question everything. She thought her life would always be with Christopher until the illusion had shattered just before his death.

April's gaze softened with sympathy. "You needed time to sort out your feelings. Everyone, most especially me, understands that you needed to find your way after he was gone."

She found the beautiful view again. "Nothing seemed real for a while."

April took her hand and squeezed it. "Because of what *he* did. You don't owe him anything. You can move on without any kind of guilt."

"I know that. It's just . . ."

April wrapped her arm around Layla's shoulders and stared at the view, too. "He hurt you and you don't want to get hurt again. I'm not saying marry the cow-boy. I'm just saying you should steam up the glass in this place." April tilted her head and leaned it against Layla's.

"I'm here to paint."

"Painting isn't a life. It's a job."

She knew that. "I love what I do. It makes me happy."

"I know. But you know what else is true at the same time? You want someone in your life to love."

She did.

April continued. "You liked sharing your life with someone. That part of what you had with Christopher was real. And I know you want more than that this time. You want what you lost and what was missing." True. Because she hadn't seen what had been miss-ing until the reality of her life hit her in the heart and shattered it.

"Why are we even talking about this? I'm here to do a job."

"That's what brought you here, but we both know you're searching for where you belong now, too. That's why you closed up the house."

She didn't feel right in the house anymore.

"Are you planning to keep it? Or are you going to sell it?"

"I don't know if I can go back there." It was a hard admission to make. "Everything good and bad between us happened there. I want something new. That's why I took this job."

April glanced out the windows. "It sure is pretty. A person could get lost in the view while you ignore reality. Make sure you don't hide in your art and forget to live."

Layla turned and faced her very caring friend. "It sounds like you've made sure I can't with all these excursions you've set up for me to see this place."

"You owe the buyer a single painting. Based on the way you reacted to this place, and because I know you so well, I'm betting you put together an entire series for a show."

Layla pursed her lips, not liking that April not only read her so well, but made her confront the things she wanted to leave behind. And the things she didn't want to acknowledge, like her attraction to Jax and how he made her feel when all she wanted to do was not feel that way for someone again.

It was dangerous.

April dropped the subject. "Let's unpack your stuff. You'll feel more settled when you've got your studio space set up."

"April?"

"Yeah?"

"I don't know if I can do it again. Love someone and lose them."

"What happened with Christopher . . . it wasn't your fault. Yes, you lost him, but he wasn't yours, not the way he should have been. The man you loved, that was who you thought he was. In the end, he revealed another part of himself that was a stranger to you. He never treated you poorly. And that's the thing, right? You could hate him if he'd been mean or abusive. But he wasn't. He loved you. Just not the way you deserved to be loved."

"Love wasn't enough. *I* wasn't enough for him."

"You were everything a wife should be," April snapped back at her, letting some of her anger toward Christopher spill out. "You were a partner who was supportive and protective. Open. Honest. Loving. Kind. Generous. He was happy with you. I saw it. You felt it. What he did . . . you didn't deserve that. And he was a selfish bastard for thinking he could live two lives and get away with it. He swore he never wanted to hurt you, but he did. Daily. Without you even knowing it," she emphasized. "Until you discovered his secret. That was his fault. Not yours. You kept your promises. He didn't. And when the shit hit the fan, he was a chickenshit asshole who hurt you and everyone else who cared about him. You deserve better. I hope you find the courage to take a chance on love again, because you have a beautiful heart. Someone would be lucky to be loved by you. I know I am. Christopher was. And this time, because of what happened, I know you'll find someone who returns that love with a true heart of his own. Because you deserve it. And you won't settle for anything less."

Layla wrapped her friend in a hard hug and blinked back tears. She whispered her greatest fear. "How will I know it's real?"

April squeezed her tight. "Because you won't be able to deny it. Like you can't deny the sparks between you and the man you keep looking for out the window."

Caught, Layla felt the blush heat her cheeks. "I just . . ."

April leaned back and looked her in the eye. "What?"

"I don't want to end up alone, hiding in a room,

painting the world I see but don't actually live in because I'm too scared of being disappointed again."

"Disappointed is not getting the gift you want on Christmas. Christopher pulled the rug out from under you and turned your life upside down. It's okay to be cautious. Please, make sure the hot cowboy is a good guy before you jump him. And if he's not, toss him aside and find another hunky cowboy. This place has got to be crawling with them."

They separated on a laugh.

April put her hand on Layla's shoulder and eyed her mischievously. "Have some fun. Make a friend. Just make sure you get the benefits, too, before your lady bits dry up and you turn into a hermit."

Layla playfully smacked April on the shoulder. "Ugh. Fine. I'll go horseback riding. And maybe I'll remember how to flirt with the cowboy."

"I have a feeling that cowboy is going to be hot on your trail. Let him catch you. Then hang on for the ride."

She could do that. She wasn't one to throw herself at a man. But she could definitely let herself be caught by a blue-eyed cowboy if he was so inclined to want a widowed artist who really wanted something raw and real, even if it was just a moment in time.

# Chapter Four

Layla walked out onto the porch of her cabin and stared at her studio. She desperately wanted to go in and fill the blank canvas she'd left on the easel last night with color until it transformed into the beautiful fields, hills, and brilliant blue sky in front of her.

"Don't even think about it." April stood on the cabin porch next door, looking lovely in jeans, a flowy blue blouse with tiny white daisies decorating it, and brown cowboy boots. Her dark hair streaked with golden highlights from the California sun was twisted up into a loose bun. The gold earrings with a waterfall of golden citrine polished round stones dangled from her ears. Layla had given them to April for her birthday last year. Each of the three different length strands had a stone at the end that caught the light.

"What?" Layla asked innocently. "I was just getting ready to walk up to the barn."

April eyed her.

Donte walked out behind his gorgeous wife and grinned at Layla. "Trying to sneak into the studio and not follow April's agenda?"

"I don't know what you're talking about." The grin she tried to hide bloomed on her face, because they knew she was lying. The studio and that blank canvas called to her.

After all, she had a job to do. Collin O'Brian was paying her a lot of money for the perfect Wyoming landscape. They had a meeting set up soon to discuss his vision. But being here . . . she felt inspired to explore this wild place and fill a dozen canvases with the beautiful scenery. She'd have a show and bring Wyoming to the world. She'd booked an open-ended stay at the ranch.

But now . . . maybe she'd rent out her California house and stay awhile.

This place felt special.

Her studio was all set up. Once April and Donte left this morning, and she finished the horseback riding excursion, she'd get to work.

Donte wrapped his arms around April's shoulders from behind and kissed her on the side of her neck with sweet affection.

Layla's heart yearned for that kind of warmth in her life again. "I'm going to miss you both."

Donte had been fighting a migraine yesterday when Layla arrived. But after a nap in the quiet cabin in the dark, he'd joined April and Layla in the studio to help them finish setting up. Mostly, he did the heavy lifting. They'd rolled out a thick rug, then a canvas sheet to cover most of it so that Layla didn't ruin it with dripping paint. And while she and April had carried in the table and chaise lounge together, they'd needed

Donte's help to bring in the large cabinet that she used to store her paints, brushes, and everything else she needed to create her paintings.

Last night when April and Donte headed into town for dinner at a local place and picked up groceries for Layla, she'd organized her blank canvases and paints just the way she liked them. It took a couple of hours to have everything just right, but by the time April came in and ordered her to eat dinner and get some rest, she'd created the perfect workspace.

Now all she needed was the beautiful scenery to paint.

And he was headed toward her riding a gorgeous dark brown horse and leading a white-and-gray one behind him.

"You were right. She lights up when she looks at him." Donte's words startled her out of staring at Jax.

She glared at her best friend's husband. "Don't encourage her."

"I'm encouraging you." His smile wasn't all amusement. Behind it was a knowing look and subtle nudge. "It's been over a year. I watched you at the last gallery showing. No less than a dozen men stared at you. Half of them flirted with you. Two asked you out. You politely got out of hurting their feelings by simply changing the subject. You didn't look at any of them, the way you just looked at him."

"I'm here to work." And she wanted to get to it before Jax got close enough to hear any of this conversation.

April frowned. "You've spent the last year trying to figure out who you are now after Christopher. You took this commission because it was a good opportunity to get away from your past and do something new and different. He's both those things."

"What happened, happened," Donte said, bringing up the past like it was over, even though it was still so much a part of her life. "You had nothing to do with what Christopher did and why he did it. You were more than he ever deserved. Any man would be lucky to have you by his side. And you've earned the right to be happy."

She snuck a quick glance at Jax. "I don't even know him."

April waved as he approached and whispered, "All we're saying is let yourself have some fun and see where things go."

She eyed the cowboy and the horse that was much larger than she realized up close. "If I break my neck, it's your fault," she admonished her best friend. "And then there's no more commission or girls' night where I bring the good wine."

"What kind of wine do you like?" Jax asked.

She hadn't expected him to be interested but answered anyway. "It's a Moscato from a small winery in California." She named the winery. "You probably can't get it here."

"I own the Dark Horse Dive Bar with my sisters. I can get anything from our supplier."

Donte came down the steps. "Does your wife mind you working late at the bar?"

Jax dismounted the horse, held the reins in his hands, and answered Donte's question while still looking at her. "I'm not married or seeing anyone."

Donte pet the horse's massive shoulder, then shook Jax's hand. "Donte. April's husband. It's nice to meet you. Sorry we can't stay longer. You've got a beautiful place here."

"Thanks. It's home."

Layla wondered for a fleeting moment if Jax was trying to tell her this was where he belonged, like it wasn't as obvious as his gorgeous blue eyes, but dismissed it because she was seriously losing it if she thought every little thing he said was directed at her.

April joined Donte by the big horse. "Layla's all set up. Once she starts painting, she'll be easy to find and hard to draw out."

Layla glared at her friend. "I'm not that bad."

April rolled her eyes. "She's amazing but loses herself in the process sometimes."

Jax looked at Layla.

She couldn't deny it. "It's true. I don't mean to forget about the world."

"I know it's asking a lot," April began, "but if she's supposed to be at one of the events you have set up here and she doesn't show, will you please text her and encourage her to attend? Otherwise, weeks will pass and she won't even realize she hasn't seen another living soul."

Jax held Layla's gaze. "Even 'the best working landscape artist' in the country needs an escape from her art now and then. I'm sure there's got to be something compelling enough on the ranch to draw you out."

"Or someone." April pointedly looked from Layla to Jax. "And thank you for all your hospitality and going above and beyond when it comes to Layla's stay here."

"It's no trouble." Jax's deep rumbly voice said he could be trouble for her.

Layla had paid extra for the added accommodations, but she didn't think the money motivated Jax. He seemed to mean what he said. She liked that.

Donte came to her for a hug. "Don't be trouble, but get into some."

She laughed and hugged him back. "We'll see."

He stepped away so April could take his place. "Don't forget about the client meeting. Once you have the image settled, you can paint until your heart's content. Or at least until you pass out because you forgot to eat."

Layla rolled her eyes. "You stocked the fridge. I'll eat. I promise. I'm not totally helpless." She gave Jax a look, letting him know she really wasn't. Mostly.

April squeezed her shoulders. "You're just single-minded sometimes. And I won't be here to nudge you."

"Stop worrying. New place, new me. I'll be fine. And soon, you'll have a bunch of paintings to sell. Now, go. Spend time with your adoring husband. Get lost on some back roads. Find something you want me to paint for you. And I will see you soon."

"Be careful," April warned. "Explore. But don't get lost."

"I won't. Promise."

April glanced at Jax. "You have my number."

"Anything happens, I'll call you."

Donte handed Jax the keys to their cabin. "This place is amazing. If we hadn't promised my family we'd be in Denver in a couple days, we'd stay here longer."

April started backing away. "I have a feeling we'll be back soon."

Layla waited for April and Donte to grab their overnight bags off the porch, then head to the van they'd unloaded yesterday, which they were taking for the rest of their trip.

"You're really close to them," Jax said as she waved goodbye.

"April and I met in high school and stayed friends all through college, even though I went to an art school and she got a degree in business and accounting. I thought she'd be the CFO of some Fortune 500 company. She hated the corporate job she took because her parents pushed her in that direction. And although the art world wasn't really her scene, she came to every one of my shows and to every gallery I wanted to check out. Along the way, she made connections with my other artist friends. Every time we walked into a gallery, I got lost in the art. She talked to the gallery staff or owners and talked me up, showed off my work on her phone. It wasn't long before we'd leave those galleries and she'd tell me they wanted to display one of my paintings, or do a full show. And while I was painting, those pieces were selling, and April was handling all of it for me."

"And those other artist friends became her clients, too." Jax caught on quick.

"She's so in demand now, I'm surprised she puts up with me."

"She loves you. She worries about you."

"Yeah. Especially the past couple of years." She

caught the inquisitive look on his face and changed the subject because she didn't want to talk about the past. "So I'm actually supposed to sit on the horse."

Jax chuckled. "I take it you've never ridden."

"Nope. I grew up in suburbia with my parents and brother. After school and summers I spent with my grandpa. He taught me how to paint, not ride a horse."

He didn't look at all worried about her lack of experience. "I've got you. Don't worry. It's a big ranch. You want to see all the good parts, best to do that on a horse instead of trying to walk it yourself. And Moon is a sweetheart. You'll love him." Jax pulled a carrot out of his back pocket and held it out to her. "Want to make friends?"

She took the carrot and pointed it at Moon. Before she knew it, he chomped down and broke a piece off. The brown horse next to him swung his big head over and snagged the other piece out of her hand. She gasped in surprise and jumped back.

Jax chuckled and her stomach tightened at the low, deep sound of it. "Sorry about that. Capi loves carrots and he doesn't like to share." Jax gave Capi a nudge to get him to move his big body away from Moon. "Let's get you up in the saddle so we can join the others about to ride out."

She eyed the cowboy and held his steady gaze. "Are you sure this is safe?"

He met her stare with utter confidence. "I won't let anything happen to you. Promise. You're safe with me."

She didn't know why, but she believed that solemn vow.

"Left hand on the saddle horn. Right hand on the back of the saddle. Lift your left foot into the stirrup, and lift and swing yourself up."

She followed his instructions and found herself in the saddle, an even better view from up high. Then Moon shifted his weight, and she yelped and held on to the saddle horn for dear life.

Jax's hand settled on her thigh. "Relax." He seemed to catch himself and removed his hand. "Horses are empathic creatures. They sense your emotions and fear. If you're relaxed, he'll be nice and calm. If he feels that you're scared, he'll think he should be scared of something, too." Jax ran his hand down Moon's neck. "Give him a pet. Let him know everything is okay."

It took her a second to unclench her hands and run them down the horse's long neck. "He feels like velvet almost. And he's warm."

"He loves to be pet, so indulge all you want."

Her mind made her think he was talking about her petting him, but she chalked that up to the long dry spell she'd had and that this man's presence woke something inside her. She could feel it stretching, the need growing.

"Let's get the stirrups adjusted and I'll go over the basic riding instructions."

She moved her left foot out of the way while he shortened the stirrup and helped her put her foot in it.

"Feel good?"

She liked his soft touch, but focused on the fact that he wanted to know if her foot was secure. "That seems right."

Jax moved around the back of Moon and adjusted the other side. "Stand in the stirrups."

She did and felt balanced and even. "I think that's good."

"Okay. Now press your right heel into Moon's side."

She did and Moon shifted a few steps to the left. She grinned, then pressed her left foot into his side and Moon responded by taking a step to the right.

Jax grinned. "You're a natural." He draped the reins over Moon's head and handed them to her, showing her exactly how to hold them in one hand. "You can use the reins to guide him, too. Whichever way you pull the reins and turn his neck, is the way he'll go. He's used to just following the leader, so you shouldn't have to do too much to keep him on the path. Once you've got the hang of it, and if there's something more you want to see than the planned route, then we'll head off on our own."

She gave Moon another pat and smiled. "Sounds like a plan."

Jax rose up onto Capi beside her and turned the horse around so they were facing the same direction back toward the stables. "Okay, now let's practice how to walk and stop. Give him a gentle kick with both heels in the side."

She did and Moon started moving forward. It took a second to get in the same rhythm as him.

"Now pull back on the reins, not hard, but enough to get his attention."

She pulled back gently, not wanting to hurt the poor thing.

"That's good. But if you don't use a firm hand, he'll

catch on that he can do whatever he wants and he won't mind you. So give him a kick to get him walking, then pull the reins a bit harder and make him stop."

She did so, Jax right beside her.

"There you go. Remember, you're in charge."

She eyed him. "What happens if he decides to bolt?"

"Moon's more likely to be ornery and stop and chomp grass than bolt, but if he gets spooked, keep a firm grip on the reins, pull back, and make him stop. And I'll be close. If I have to ride up on you and grab him, I will."

She felt confident that she could do this. The longer she sat on the horse, the more comfortable she felt. Moon was strong and powerful below her, but also calm. He minded her small commands. And Jax exuded so much confidence she knew he wouldn't let anything bad happen to her. "Let's ride."

An open smile split his lips and transformed his gorgeous face into an even more devastatingly handsome one. She didn't really know how that was possible. "I knew there was some adventure in you."

"Who knew?" Not her. But she liked this feeling of freedom and excitement. The most adventure she had was traveling and experiencing other cultures and landscapes. This was something different. Something wild.

At least for her.

"Ready to go?"

She turned back toward her cabin. "Shoot. I forgot my backpack."

Jax turned Capi around. "I'll get it. Stay put." He

rode the short distance back to her cabin, slid off Capi
like a man who rode often and didn't mind the drop,
grabbed her pack, boosted himself back up in the saddle like he'd been born in it, and made his way back to
her. "It's kind of heavy. Want me to carry it?"

"That's okay. My camera is in it and I'd like to take
pictures along the way if that's all right?"

"Sure. Just be mindful of keeping Moon under you
and in your control. Don't worry about the group. Stop
when you want to and I'll stick by you."

"I'm not totally unable to take care of myself, despite April's concerns."

"I promised her I'd look out for you, so that's all I'm
doing." Jax nudged Capi to start walking and Moon
followed along without her prompting him.

With Jax a little in front of her, she could watch the
way he rode, how he held his reins and moved with
the horse. She matched him and found it comfortable,
easy and amazing all at the same time. She felt connected to Moon and wondered why she hadn't adopted
a pet as an adult. She'd had a dog and a cat growing up
and missed the companionship.

"What is it?" Jax asked, glancing back at her.

She caught herself lost in thought and focused on
him. "What?"

"That sad look on your face."

"Oh. I was just thinking that it's been a long time
since I had a pet. And I don't know why. I loved my
dog and cat. They felt like family, and it was nice
to come home and they were always there." And
then they passed away after a good long life and she
never got another. Because the heartbreak had been

overwhelming. And she'd gotten lost in her art to ease the pain.

Was that what she was doing now? Using this trip and her commission to hide away from what hurt?

She blinked back into focus and found Jax so close their thighs were nearly touching. He held one of her reins in his hand and stared at her with concern. "Do you need a minute?"

"No, I—"

"It's fine," he quickly assured her. "But you need to pay attention. While Moon is a good horse and minds well, you're still sitting on an animal that can knock you off and hurt you." No anger, just concern resonated in his words.

"I'm sorry." She didn't want to seem incompetent.

"No apologies. Just stay here with me and everything will be fine."

She wished it was that simple. But the past wouldn't let her go. And she had a feeling it wasn't done with her. Not when Michael wouldn't let it go either.

# Chapter Five

Jax had a hard time tearing his gaze away from the beautiful woman cuddling Moon like he was her favorite new pet. They'd stopped at the barn to join the other group. He'd made her dismount because he didn't trust her to stay present and not let Moon just walk away with her.

She held the big horse's head and planted a line of kisses down Moon's nose. Moon liked most people, but the way he nuzzled into Layla's chest, the horse was in love. And Jax was jealous as hell. Of a horse.

Jax rolled his eyes and tried to focus on Zac, who was running the trail ride today.

"What are you doing here?" Zac asked, trepidation in his voice.

"We have a special guest." It was the best excuse he could come up with for why he wasn't taking care of his usual duties, which today included dealing with the farrier and vet, along with the hundred other things he oversaw at the ranch.

Zac glanced past him and whistled. "She's gorgeous. I get why you want to pay close attention to her."

"It's not like that." The growl in his voice made Zac stare even harder at him. And it should have told Jax something that he didn't like Zac, or anyone else, thinking Layla was just some casual fling waiting to happen. She had class and style and something oddly wonderful about her he couldn't define.

He'd spent a good long time last night on the internet looking up everything he could find about her. Though her art took center stage, there were a few personal bits and pieces that didn't have to do with her education and meteoric rise in the art world.

He looked at her now, knowing that she'd lost her husband a year ago, and wondered if she was using this getaway for exactly that, a chance to escape her loss and grief, or if she'd healed enough to be looking for something new.

He'd like to be that someone.

Zac glanced from him to Layla and back. "Then maybe I'll see if she wants to go line dancing at the bar tonight."

"No you won't," Jax ordered, like he had a right to tell his employee how to spend his personal time and who he could ask out. Like he had a right to speak for Layla in any way when they'd barely spoken to each other. They hadn't shared any personal details. Maybe she'd like to go dancing. How the hell did he know? But he knew he didn't want anyone taking her but him.

And that's why he was going on a trail ride and not doing what he was supposed to be doing today. Because he couldn't stay away from her.

They made no sense together. He lived and worked

here on the ranch. She painted masterpieces that sold for hundreds of thousands of dollars. She would never want to be tied down in small-town Wyoming.

And he had no desire to leave and be something he wasn't. At the heart, he was a rancher. This place, the land, the animals, all of it spoke to him like the landscape had spoken to Layla yesterday.

This place was his home and future. His responsibility.

But that didn't mean he didn't want her.

She kissed Moon again, when the horse nudged her for more pets. Jax wanted to be the one those slender fingers brushed over as her lips pressed to his skin and made him burn.

Zac chuckled and gave him a gotcha grin. "Just so you know, every time you're not looking at her, she's looking at you. A woman looked at me like that, with those deep green eyes, I'd be claiming her, too."

Jax turned to Layla and caught her abruptly turning her head back to Moon. Something warm in his chest stretched like a lazy feline. Just as he thought he was in so much trouble, Layla pulled out her chiming phone and read a text that made her frown and her eyes go cold before she stuffed her phone back in her pocket.

He walked over to her. "Everything okay?"

She ran her hand down Moon's nose. "Ever had someone in your life who just couldn't let something go?"

"I think we've all known someone like that."

She pursed her lips like he'd seen her do yesterday. It seemed to be an unconscious gesture. "I suppose you're right. And I should probably be more patient, but in this case, it's time to let it go."

"This have something to do with your deceased husband?"

Her eyes went wide.

He rubbed his hand over his neck, uncomfortable he'd blurted that out and revealed too much. "Yeah. Sorry. I googled you after we met yesterday."

"Read anything interesting?"

"I find everything about you interesting." *And I should shut up now.*

That shocked look came back into her eyes. "Um . . ."

He didn't acknowledge that little truth bomb he tossed at her and went back to finding out what had bothered her. "Why did that text upset you?"

"My husband's brother is still grieving and upset about how things played out after Christopher passed away."

Her husband hadn't just died. He'd committed suicide in their home. Layla found the body. He couldn't imagine how she must have felt in that devastating moment. He didn't know how her husband could do that to her. But of course, the circumstances hadn't been publicized. He bet Layla's best friend and agent, April, had had something to do with keeping it private.

"I'm sorry for your loss." He meant it. Losing someone you loved like that had to be really hard, especially after years of marriage.

"Thank you. Sometimes it feels like it just happened. Other times, I feel like he's been gone forever."

He could see that in her eyes. "You loved him. You remember him. He will always be a part of your life and story."

Everything about her softened, and the peaceful

look in her eyes when her gaze settled on him was filled with gratitude. "Yes. That's exactly it. Right? And this is a new chapter for me. I just wish Michael could turn the page, too."

"Everyone eventually does when they're ready."

"I don't know why, when April has been saying all those same things to me, that your understanding seems to have solidified it for me."

"Maybe this is just the right time and place for you to accept and believe it."

She glanced past him to the fields and trees spreading out across acres and acres of land. "There's something special here. I felt it the moment I arrived." Her gaze fell on him, then quickly turned toward Moon again. But for a fleeting second, he thought he caught a glimpse of something that looked like desire and a wanting so deep, if she'd held that gaze on him, he'd have fallen into it and lost himself in her.

"Everyone saddle up," Zac called to the group of ten riders waiting.

He stepped back so she could move to Moon's side. "You need a hand?"

She grinned with excitement. "Nope. I had a great teacher." And in a fluid motion, she was up in the saddle, leaning over, and hugging Moon's neck. "I love you, baby."

And just like that, he fell a little in love with the woman who loved a horse with a childlike enthusiasm and wonder.

Not for the first time, he marveled at where this woman came from and whether she was for real.

Jax mounted Capi and waited beside Layla as the

others rode ahead of them. They settled into the back of the line. Jax kept Capi next to Moon so he could be side by side with Layla.

She rode with her head on a swivel. It seemed like she couldn't get enough of the view. But there was also something in the way she looked at things. And he got another glimpse of how she saw the world when she said, "It's so alive. The sway of the tall grass. The drift of the clouds. The hawk floating. The cows ambling. The trees standing sentry, their tall backs and arms spread out, offering shelter or a blockade. And there's the music of it all. The birds chirping, the tiny squeak, squeals, and buzz of bugs. The whisper of the wind a hum in the background."

He enjoyed her interpretation. "You and Lyric should write songs together."

"Your sister is a musician?"

"Singer-songwriter. Mostly country music. She's sold a bunch of stuff. A few have even made it onto the top one hundred."

"She must be so proud. Does she tour?"

Jax shook his head. "She lives and breathes this place. It's home. For all of us. She spends time in Nashville writing with her partner and other artists. She wants to hear her songs on the radio, but she doesn't want to be the superstar."

Layla nodded, understanding in her green gaze. "It's a lot of pressure. I started out just wanting to do what I love. Then it turned into a business. Everyone wants you to do what they want you to do. Without April, I probably would have given up painting." She frowned. "That's not exactly true. I'd have ten storage lockers filled with paintings no one ever saw but me."

He got it. "You have to paint, like Lyric has to make music."

She gave him a gentle smile. "I would love to hear some of her songs."

"She's got a YouTube channel. I'll text you the link. Or you could just come to the bar. She sings there often. Lately, all she sings are love songs to Mason. It's getting old." He was kidding, and let her know with his smile and a shrug.

Layla smiled at him. "You secretly like it."

*I do.* "She's happy in a way we all want to be. So I'm happy for her. Even if it makes me cringe every time I see my sister sucking face with him."

Layla laughed. The sweet sound drifting on the light breeze. "Do you like him?"

"No one will ever be good enough for my sisters. But Mason comes damn close. He loves her. It's in the way he looks at her, in everything he does, and how he sees her for who she is and wants to just make her happy every second of every day."

"They sound perfect together."

"They are."

He caught the haunted look in her eyes. "Hey, sorry if I've made you remember your husband and what you lost." He never wanted to make her sad.

She frowned. "I bet a lot of people thought that what Christopher and I had was perfect. For a long time I believed it myself."

"Did something happen?"

"Yes."

# Chapter Six

A half an hour later Jax was still wondering what Layla might have said if he wasn't practically a stranger to her. Every second and minute that ticked by with her silence only made his curiosity grow.

He had his own bad memories and secrets and wasn't ready to lay them bare to her either.

But something was happening between them. Something that made him think he could tell her anything and she'd understand.

Moon suddenly stopped.

The rest of the group was about twenty yards ahead of them and moving toward the creek. He was happy to hang back with Layla and let them go.

Jax caught the rapt look on Layla's face and dismounted beside her. He took her reins. "Swing your right leg over and slide down."

It took her a second before she tore her gaze from the idyllic scene and focused on him. "It's beautiful."

"One of my favorite spots." The creek ran along a hillside and into the trees up ahead. "We'll water the horses here. Give Zac ten minutes to do that with his group up ahead and we'll stay here awhile. Once everyone else is cleared out, you can take some pictures and we can explore."

"Really? You don't mind?" She sounded so hopeful.

"I'm your tour guide."

"I overheard Zac. You don't usually do the trail rides."

He wondered if she'd overheard him cutting Zac off from any attempt at asking her out. He didn't really care if she had. At least she'd know he was interested.

"I do the trail rides and fishing trips sometimes. When April and I spoke about your stay, I understood you'd need someone to show you around."

She narrowed her gaze and put her hands on her hips. "You were going to pawn me off on one of the other ranch hands."

He didn't deny it. Him being here told her what she needed to know. That he wanted to be with her. "I was going to make sure you got what you paid for. Then I saw the way you looked at the ranch yesterday and . . ."

"What?"

"I guess I understood what you needed." It was the same thing he found here.

"What do you think I need?"

"Inspiration. A jaw-dropping view. Something so ordinary, some might miss that it's extraordinary."

He pulled two apples out of his saddlebag and handed her one.

"Thank you." She bit into it and brushed away a drip of juice.

He chuckled and she grinned at him.

"That's for the horse," he pointed out, making her cheeks flush with embarrassment.

"Oh." She held the rest of the apple out to Moon, who took it without begrudging her the bite she stole.

Capi ate his apple and Jax pulled a bag of pretzels and peanuts from his bag. "Here. Snack on this while I water the horses."

She took the bag he offered with another sweet smile and pulled her backpack off and set it on the ground at her feet.

Zac's group was just heading out when he reached the creek and let Moon and Capi drink to their heart's content. When he turned to check on his guest, he found her sitting on the soft green grass that matched her eyes with a long-lens professional-looking camera pointed right at him.

She took the camera from her eye and stared over it at him with a look that was direct and hinted of speculation. Like she was trying to figure him out.

He didn't mind the scrutiny. He hoped that, like him, she felt something building between them.

"Do you want to get a shot of the creek from up there without the horses?"

She nodded.

He walked the two horses back to her and farther away so she could decide what she wanted to shoot and from where.

She took a couple of shots, then moved closer to the creek and off to the left where she had a different angle, one that looked into the trees as the water disappeared and the banks became greener and carpeted in tiny purple wildflowers.

When she seemed content to simply stare at everything before her, he walked the horses to a couple of trees, tied off their reins so they could graze and stay put, then waved Layla closer. "Come. I'll show you a spot I think you might like. It's not the wide-open spaces you usually paint, but it's pretty."

Ten feet into the trees and along the bank, they were picking their way over rocks and dodging trees while the sound of the creek tinkled and sang its song as it wound along the land.

"You know, my mother always told me not to go in dark places with strangers or boys."

He held out his hand to help her over a tricky spot. "Come with me, Layla. I promise, it's worth it." He gave her a mischievous grin.

She pinched her lips, holding back a smile. "Promises, promises." But she took his hand. She caught her breath as the sizzle of energy shot through both of them.

He squeezed her hand to let her know he felt it, too, then he helped her navigate the rocks and a fallen tree.

Even when it was safe to release her hand, he kept hold of it, walking in front of her and enjoying the feel of her skin against his, the electricity sparking through his fingers and up his arm.

And when he looked back to check that she was managing the rough terrain okay, she kept her hand in his and gave him a shy smile.

He never expected something so simple could feel so good. He wondered what kissing her would feel like. "It's just around this next bend."

"The water is getting louder."

He hid his own smile this time. "Just another few feet." He stepped out of her way and let her pass him so that she'd get the full impact as they reached the cascade of waterfalls and pools ahead.

"Oh. Wow. That's just . . ." She went quiet for a moment, the only sounds the trickling water and the birds chirping. "It's beautiful. Like a hideaway."

He closed the distance between them and stood right at her back and brushed his hand up her arm. "I thought you'd like it."

"I'm going to paint it." Reverence. Pure and sweet on her tongue.

He'd gotten used to these magical little spots on the ranch. But now . . . "Through your eyes yesterday and right now, I guess I kinda see the ranch anew. I appreciate that you did that for me." Because as the loneliness grew, so did his discontent with where he was in his life. He loved the ranch. But it had grown stale. Until she made him see the wonder of this place again.

She turned her head just enough for him to see her warm smile. One that told him she understood what he meant.

"Come on. It's even better from the bottom looking up. I'll show you."

She reached back and put her hand on the outside of his thigh. "Wait."

His leg burned with heat where she touched him. He wouldn't move for anything at this moment, not if it meant she took her hand off him.

She glanced up at him.

He was so close, if he dipped his head, he could kiss her.

Her breath hitched. "I want to take a picture of it right here. Just like this."

He brushed his hand over her soft hair. "Anything you want." He meant it.

She caught her breath for a moment, and for a brief second her fingers squeezed against his leg, then she exhaled softly and picked up the camera hanging around her neck.

He didn't move from his place behind her, their bodies close, but not close enough for him.

She wasn't short. Tall enough for them to pair up nicely with the top of her head fitting just below his chin. He wanted to turn her around, wrap his arms around her, and haul her up until all their good bits lined up and he could kiss her. She'd taste like pretzels and peanuts. She smelled like citrus and sweet flowers. Her scent went to his head.

Unexpectedly, she grabbed his hand again and tugged. "Show me more."

He squeezed her hand and nudged her forward so they could continue along the creek. When they passed the first of three pools, they stopped so she could look back up the softly sloping and curving creek route. At this time of day, with the sun overhead, its rays slicing through the tree canopy and reflecting off the cool, clear water, it was all shadow and beams of light and wonder.

"Jax. This is magic."

He had to agree that the feelings she brought out of him did indeed feel like some kind of witchery.

And he liked it.

She took several pictures, shifting the angle and moving this way and that, "To catch the light," she said.

He enjoyed looking at her and noticing all the fascinating expressions on her face as she worked and everything she felt reflected in her eyes.

"God, you're beautiful."

She went still, the next shot forgotten as she turned her head and stared at him. Then she suddenly had the camera at her eye and took his picture, up close and personal. She moved the camera out of her way and stared at him again. "The way you were looking at me."

"I can't seem to help it."

"Is it this place, or is it us creating this . . . intimacy?"

"Yes." It was both.

"Jax."

He took a step closer to her. "I love the way you say my name."

Her soft green eyes held his gaze. "It's been a long time since I let myself feel something like this."

"Me, too." He waited. The need to close the distance so strong he had to really fight it.

"I don't know if I'm ready. I don't know, for a lot of reasons, if this is real."

He wasn't usually this forward, but he couldn't let this moment pass. He couldn't let her deny what was happening between them. In one long stride he closed the distance, cupped his hand at the side of her head, her soft hair a caress against his skin, and he pressed his forehead to hers and looked deep in her eyes. He saw the fear and hope there. "You feel what I feel. This is real. And I don't want to ignore it so I can feel safe, or dismiss it because it could all fall apart. And I sure as hell don't want to stop touching you. I want more. I want to know how you take your coffee in the morning, what you like to watch on TV. What's your favorite color and song? What's your favorite food? Who do you call family and friends? What makes you happy and sad and angry?"

He softly kissed her forehead, then went back to looking her in the eye. "I want to know all that and more, so that maybe someday, if we're lucky, you'll tell me what you want for the future, and if I'm in it. But first, I just want to stand here in this pretty place, with your gorgeous self, and help you find the perfect thing to paint because I know that's what truly makes you happy, even if there's one thing I want to know more than anything else right now. And that's how you taste."

She put one hand on his jaw and fisted the other in his black T-shirt at his side. "I like my coffee with low-fat milk, but an overpriced caramel macchiato always hits the spot. Criminal investigation shows, action movies that have a little romance in them, and those shows shot at various zoos. My favorite color and song depend on my mood, the situation, the vibe I want. Tacos, pizza, Italian, Chinese, in that order. I grew up in Northern California, but my mom and dad retired in Vermont where my mother's family is from. My granddad . . . he was everything to me. My dad was a plumber, my mom a teacher. Somehow they ended up with an artist daughter and an architect son. You already know April is my best friend, but I have a close group of fellow artists. Death and endings make me sad. Lies make me angry. And you, Jax, made me happy bringing me to this special place. And Moon. I've fallen madly in love with your horse."

"I know. I'm jealous as hell."

"But maybe, like you said, we can spend some time together and you can tell me all the answers to those questions you asked and maybe you can make Moon jealous that all I want to do is be with you."

"I hope you're starting to feel that way."

"I am. Just don't tell him."

Jax kissed her on the head. "Your secret is safe with me."

"And as much as I want to taste you, I've been through some stuff, and I'm enjoying getting to know you, but I think I need a little more time."

Jax wrapped her in his arms and held her because it felt right. "Take all the time you need. I'm not going anywhere." Because he definitely wanted to spend a lot more time with her.

# Chapter Seven

Jax checked the time on his watch, stood from the desk where he'd been going over the feed inventory and placing an order, grabbed the bag lunch he'd made himself this morning, then rushed out to meet Layla at the orchard where she was scheduled to join the group apple picking. A favorite summer activity for guests.

Yesterday he'd caught her at the archery range for a few minutes and shared a laugh with her about how bad she was with a bow and arrow. He'd tried to help her, which was really just an excuse for him to get close to her. His chest to her back, the smell of citrus and sunshine going to his head, and his hands wrapped around hers. So tempting. They'd been so close, every breath she took, he felt. Heaven and hell. He'd never wanted anyone the way he wanted her. But he'd kept things light and easy.

Well, not so easy to keep his hands to himself. That had been damn hard. He'd tried to remain focused on helping her set up the shot. She'd been so determined to hit the target. She missed every time, but didn't give up. He liked her spirit and how she faced a challenge.

He'd wanted to stay and help her reach her goal, but he had other responsibilities. Later Zac told him that as soon as he'd left Layla had put away the bow and pulled out her camera to take pictures of a nearby outcropping of rocks that overlooked a small valley. If he'd stayed, she'd probably have kept trying to hit the target. To have him close to her? He hoped so.

As soon as he arrived at the orchard, he spotted her. She was hard to miss in a pair of tight jeans that hugged her perfect ass, a simple white T-shirt, and a pair of paint-splattered canvas shoes as she ran to catch up with Zac's group of guests.

"I'm sorry I'm late," she said to Zac, trying to catch her breath.

Jax walked up behind her. "Get caught up in your studio?"

She whirled around and a huge smile spread across her face and lit her eyes. "No. Yes. Hi." Her gaze swept over him.

He liked the heated feeling that came over him when she looked at him like that.

"You're here."

He held up his lunch bag. "Thought I'd grab an apple to go with my lunch."

"Oh." Disappointment dimmed her initial joy.

He didn't like that at all. So he took her hand, squeezed it, and gave her the truth. "I came to see you."

"Oh." The smile came back, full wattage. "That's nice. I was hoping to see you, but I wasn't sure . . ."

"What?"

Her lips scrunched for a second. "I thought maybe you were busy."

"I am. Always. But hanging out here with you . . . I'd rather be doing that anytime, any day."

She tipped her head. "I'm glad you made time to come see me."

Zac called the group together. "Okay, everyone, grab a basket and fan out. Let's get picking. Parents, please keep the small ones off the ladders for safety. If you pick more than you can eat, no worries, put them in the green bins. We'll be taking them to the farmers market."

Layla looked up at him. "So in addition to the cattle business, you also sell the produce you grow on the ranch at the farmers market?"

"My mom loves doing it a few times a year. We don't like anything grown on the ranch to go to waste. We also make donations to the local food bank."

"That makes sense." She turned toward the grove. "The trees are beautiful."

"You're going to take more pictures than the apples you pick, aren't you?"

She gave him that sheepish look. "Probably. Yes. More than likely. I mean, I can only eat a few apples."

He pulled out his sandwich. "Did you eat lunch?"

"Yes?" It sounded more like a question.

He raised a brow.

She sighed. "I had a late breakfast that we'll call 'brunch' about an hour ago, after I finished the final touches on setting up the studio. Then, I just had to start on a painting."

"And you lost track of time and ran out here."

"I can't miss the fifth day activity." She looked back at the trees. "Plus, the orchard is beautiful."

"And you don't want April to find out that not even a week in you started painting and forgot about everything else."

"But I didn't. And some things I can't forget." She pressed her lips tight as a pretty flush swept across her cheeks, and she suddenly didn't know what to do with her hands, or how to stand still.

So cute.

She rushed to grab a basket. "I'm going to pick some apples."

"Leave your backpack with me." He took a seat on a log and started devouring his sandwich. He worked up a good appetite on the ranch.

She put her pack beside him, then walked past several of the other guests to a tree no one else was at and picked several Honeycrisp apples.

He loved watching her. The sway of her hips, the elegant line of her neck and body as she reached up to a high branch had his gaze tracing her curves as his body grew hot with desire. He'd love to strip off her clothes and see what she was wearing underneath, because every once in a while he caught a glimpse of a pale pink bra strap at her shoulder and lace at the deep V of her shirt.

Was she wearing matching panties?

He'd like to find out.

Just like he wanted to know how soft her skin was against his hands and gliding against his body.

"Jax?"

His gaze flew from her ass to her face. "Yeah?"

"You okay? You were looking at me like . . ." She held his gaze but didn't finish her sentence because she probably figured out what he was thinking.

*I want you.*

"What can I say? I like the view." He hadn't looked away from her at all since he got there.

Her cheeks pinked again, but she smiled sweetly and headed back to him, picking an apple from her basket and tossing it to him. "Eat up. I bet you burn a lot of calories working this place."

He'd like to burn some calories in her bed.

He bit into the apple, not because he really wanted it, but because she'd given it to him. Like she cared about his health and well-being. He could get used to that.

He ate half the apple, then held it out to her. "Finish it. You must be ready for a snack."

She took the fruit and bit into it. A drip of juice ran down her chin. He snatched it away with his thumb, then sucked it off.

Her eyes went wide and filled with lust as she stared at his mouth. Caught in the act, she grabbed for her bag and pulled out her camera. "I want to get a shot between the rows of trees."

Finished eating, he put away the wrapper, stood, and went with her. "Come on. We'll go down a few rows so nobody gets in your picture." He took her hand and led the way to a row that hadn't been picked at all yet. The bright-red-and-gold-skinned apples hung heavy among the green leaves.

"This is perfect."

A lightness burst in his chest that he'd made her happy.

"You should see it when it's in bloom."

Excitement brightened her eyes. "I would love to photograph and paint that."

"You'll have to come back next year." *Or stay.*

She took several pictures, then turned to him. "Would you mind grabbing a ladder? I'd like to take the shot from a higher vantage point."

"I'll boost you up." He took her by the shoulders, turned her around, then bent and put his head between her legs.

"Jax!"

He lifted her up onto his shoulders and held her steady with a firm grip on her thighs. "How's that?"

"I'm going to break your back." She held her camera in one hand and his forehead in the other, her fingers threaded through his hair.

"Not even close, sweetheart. I do a lot of lifting around the ranch. This is one chore I do not mind." Not at all when he had his hands on her.

He tried to look up at her.

She bent forward. "This reminds me of my grandfather carrying me around. I always loved it when I got to be up high and see everything."

He squeezed her thighs. "You miss him."

"All the time. I haven't seen him in months." She brushed her hand over his hair. "Thank you for bringing back such a good memory."

He was happy to do it, but he wanted to erase the sadness and make her smile again. He pivoted to the right really fast.

She screamed and grabbed onto his head really tight.

"Do you want a picture of that?"

He turned a one-eighty.

She screamed again, this time with a big laugh.

"How about that?"

She was still giggling.

He swiveled to his original position. "This is the one. But do you need to be a bit higher?" He jumped up and down.

"Stop!" She giggled so hard she was vibrating on his shoulders. She gave his hair a playful tug. "Just be still." She took a couple of breaths to calm herself after laughing so much.

He found himself doing the same so he could be still and she could get her shot.

She took several. "Can you take, like, five steps to the right, then turn about forty-five degrees toward the left?"

He did as she asked.

She took several more pictures, then sighed. "It's truly beautiful here." She put her hand over his on her thigh. "Okay. You can put me down now."

"What if I don't want to?" He liked her close.

"It's going to be really hard to ride a horse this way."

He let out a full belly laugh. "Fine. Have it your way." He gently lowered her back to the ground, then stood behind her and put his hands on her shoulders. "I don't remember the last time I laughed like that."

She turned and looked up at him. "I'm sorry to hear that. You should have more fun and play."

"I'd like to with you." His phone alarm went off.

"Looks like it's time for both of us to get back to work." She adjusted the camera strap around her neck. "I'm glad you came. Thanks for your help." She started backing away, when all he wanted was for her to come closer so he could kiss her. "I hope I get to see you again soon."

He couldn't wait.

Layla picked up her basket of apples and her backpack and headed back to her cabin.

Zac walked up. "Hey, boss. How are things going with you and the artist?"

He didn't answer but he thought it was going well. He felt lighter and more optimistic about the opportunity to see her again and for this flirtation to turn into something more. He hadn't felt this way in a long time. And he didn't want to screw it up.

"I was just making sure the guests were having a good time."

"Uh-huh." Zac glanced over his shoulder at the others still picking apples, the kids running around the trees, then he looked back at Jax. "I think this is the first time you noticed anyone else was out here."

So what? It wasn't every day he met someone like Layla. Smart. Interesting. Adventurous. Talented. Kind. He could use some of that last one. "I need to get back to work."

Zac waved him off and returned to the group.

Jax headed back to the barn, but couldn't help walking close enough to the cabins so he could get a glimpse of the gorgeous painter, who was so engrossed in sketching something on a canvas she didn't even notice him walking by. But then just as he passed the studio, he thought maybe he felt her watching him and turned.

She waved to him.

He waved back and that tug pulling him toward her got harder to resist.

# Chapter Eight

Layla sat on a stool staring at the painting on the easel of Moon. White, gray, blue, and green paint splattered over her fingers, the backs of her hands, her bare feet, and the tarp below her. She'd finished the painting, thinking about her very first horseback ride.

*Who knew I'd love riding?*

She loved her sweet Moon. She couldn't wait to go again.

She had pictures of the creek, the pools, the beautiful orchard . . . a small glimpse of this wonderful place. But there was so much more out there for her to explore.

She needed more views to put together a show. And she wanted more time with Jax so she could learn all the pieces that made up the cowboy who looked at her like no one ever had.

She couldn't stop thinking about him and lost herself in the memories and feelings of her time with Jax. She thought about him so often she didn't get nearly as much done as she wanted to the last three days.

She thought about their time at the pools. A place

that spoke to her artist's soul. He'd wanted to show her more that day, but didn't complain when she told him she needed to get to her studio so she could pour all her emotions and the magic she'd captured in her heart onto the canvas.

She'd started with the beautiful creek where they'd watered the horses. The canvas sat unfinished on a nearby easel. She'd get back to it soon. After the moment she and Jax shared at the pools, she needed more time to reflect on how she felt and what it meant before she tried to re-create that beautiful place where her heart came back to life because of a cowboy who poured out his to her.

A lot of people found her odd.

He seemed intrigued by her quirks, so she didn't worry that maybe he thought she'd been trying to put distance between them on the quiet ride back to the ranch after that intimate interlude by the creek. In fact, she actually felt closer to him.

She didn't know what had possessed her to let him get that close so fast. She simply couldn't help herself around him. He'd looked at her with such need that she'd simply just fallen into him.

Maybe she'd lost her mind.

It felt more like she'd found something wonderful, even if she had a hard time trusting in it.

When she came to Blackrock Falls, it was with the intention of moving on and finding something new.

He was definitely a breath of fresh air when her life of late had felt suffocating.

But the way she'd reacted to him . . . That was so

not like her at all. Especially after what happened with Christopher.

And it was April's voice in her head encouraging, *Just go for it already.*

Yes, she grieved for her husband, but she didn't owe him her fidelity now. She deserved to move on and be happy and find someone who looked at her the way Jax had looked at her.

Every person deserved to have someone look at them like they mattered. Like they were everything that person wanted and more.

She stood and walked over to the other easel, which held a canvas. She'd barely started it. The rough sketch of Jax wasn't fully defined yet. But those eyes . . . his very intense gaze stared back at her.

She didn't paint portraits, but she was compelled to paint him.

That moment they shared . . . it changed everything.

As if she'd conjured him from her mind, or he'd stepped right out of the sketch and her dreams, he walked in the door, stopped short when he found her looking right at him, then grinned. Despite the exhaustion clinging to him, his happiness at seeing her shone through.

"Hi." She didn't quite know what to say suddenly.

"Hey." The sigh that came out of him let loose his tense shoulders, then his gaze went to the two paintings on the easels beside him. "Holy shit." He gaped.

She giggled. "Do you like them?"

Jax stared intently at the one closest to him. "That's Moon."

"I'm glad you recognize him."

He shook his head. "No. That's exactly Moon. Every

speckle on his coat. The soulfulness in his eyes. His gentle spirit. Even the way he holds his ears, one just slightly turned out all the time." He looked at it with awe and shock and appreciation.

The painting was an up close view of Moon's big head with just the hint of his long neck and chest. He was looking right out from the canvas. In the background, she'd painted sweeps of greens and blues to hint at the field and sky and wisps of white for the clouds. But it was Moon: front and center and staring back at you like a majestic animal who saw everything in you as you saw his wild heart and beautiful spirit, too.

"Layla." Wonder and astonishment filled her name. "I looked you up, saw a bunch of your stuff, so I know you're talented . . . but this . . . it's insanely . . . magnificent." Jax looked at her again. "I don't think I've ever used that word, but that's what this is."

She'd never painted anything like it.

"If you like it, it's yours." She wanted the people who owned her art to feel something for it. The painting spoke to him. Not just because he loved horses, but because he saw Moon's spirit in it.

Jax's eyes went wide. "Are you kidding me?" He pointed at the painting. "I can't take that. You could sell it for a fortune."

She shrugged. "It's not for sale. It's for you. I want you to have it. But if it makes you feel better, consider it a thank-you. You made me fall in love with horses, especially Moon. You went out of your way to take me on that amazing ride. It truly was a beautiful experience. One I'll never forget."

"How could you? You've painted it so perfectly." Jax stared at the painting beside Moon's, of the sweeping field that led down to the creek and trees where he'd watered the horses. She knew a lot of buyers would love the serenity of it and how, when you looked at it, it felt like the beauty just went on for miles.

"It's not finished." She grabbed a brush, dipped it in black paint, and went to the Moon painting. "I never sign them until they're done and ready to go either to their new home or up for sale." She signed the bottom right corner for him. "There. It's yours."

He stared at it again and shook his head. "Amazing. My very own Layla Brock. I don't know what to say."

Everything inside her felt light and happy, because he liked it and appreciated the gesture so much. "It's my pleasure."

He stepped closer. "Then will you make my day and come with me?"

"Where?" She didn't really care, but she'd probably need to change clothes.

"Dinner. At the bar."

Surprised by the offer, she glanced out the windows. Since Jax had set the overhead lights on a timer and they came on automatically as the sun began to set each day, she hadn't noticed how late it had gotten. "What time is it?"

"Nearly eight. I've got some work to do at the bar, but I'd love to spend some time with you. Lyric is singing tonight with one of the local bands. You can eat, have a drink, and enjoy the music while I do paperwork. I know that doesn't exactly sound like a ton of fun, but—"

"Let's go." She didn't think about it, she just wanted to spend time with him, too.

The rest of the time, she'd been in her studio painting while he worked on the ranch during the day and the bar at night.

Jax touched her shoulder to get her attention. "I should warn you, all three of my sisters will be there. When they see you with me, they're going to poke their pretty little noses in our business."

"I liked Lyric. Can't wait to meet . . ." She raised a brow in question.

"Aria's the oldest of us, then comes Lyric, me, and then Melody."

"Your mom really has a thing for music."

"It's always playing in the house, the barn, the car, wherever she is. She plays guitar and sang to us all the time when we were kids. She's got this lovely voice that used to soothe us all when we were little and got hurt or we were sad. Christmas, she'd have the whole family singing carols. Lyric inherited her talent, but all of us used to sing together as kids with Mom."

"That's really special."

"I know how lucky I was to grow up here with my amazing parents and sisters, even if they all think my business is their business."

"They love you."

One firm nod. "It's mutual, so I put up with it."

She eyed him from under her lashes. "And I guess it's not going to stop you from taking me with you tonight."

He took a step closer and she moved the brush away so she didn't accidently get paint on him. "We've both been busy the last few days, but I find myself thinking about you, that moment we shared by the creek, the fun we had doing archery and in the orchard, and the way you look at me sometimes . . ."

She tilted her head and looked him deep in the eye. "What way?"

"Like you see right into me. Like you want me. And then there's a hesitation. I get it. You lost your husband. I can't imagine the heartbreak. But I'm hoping that doesn't mean you're not willing to give whatever this thing is between us a chance."

Wow. He blew her mind. "Are you always this blunt and honest?"

"I try to be, but no. Not in a long time. I've kept most of my interactions with women casual and made sure whoever it was knew that going in. I don't know what it is about you that makes me want to be all possessive and greedy for your attention." Jax winced. "That kind of came out a little desperate maybe."

She relaxed because of his honesty. "What I heard is that you really like me and want to spend time with me."

He let out a sigh of relief. "Yes."

She really liked his candor. "Here's the thing . . ."

"Uh-oh. I'm not going to like this, am I?"

She held his gaze and said what was on her mind, because she wanted things to be clear between them. "My husband and I were very happy together. I thought we would be together the rest of our lives. And then I learned that he'd done something that made me question all those happy memories, every word he ever said to me, everything I thought I knew but didn't seem real anymore."

He went perfectly still, his eyes narrowed. "I'm sorry. That must have been devastating."

"It was. And then I lost him before we could resolve things in a way that I could still see him as the man I'd loved, the person who'd been my best friend, and not just see his mistakes and betrayal of all that we'd been to each other."

Jax seemed to catch on. "I've never cheated on anyone, if that's what you're worried about. I'm not that kind of man. If I'm with someone, she's the only one I'm with."

"I appreciate the honesty. That's what I needed to know, because I'm the same way."

"I don't want to share you with anyone."

"There's one more thing. There may be times when it's hard for me to accept that what you say and what you do are genuine. That has nothing to do with you. It's totally my hang-up."

He held her gently by the shoulders. "I know what it's like to give everything to someone and have it all fall apart because they lied and broke your trust. I hated that someone did it to me. I would never do that to you, or anyone else."

*I'm not the only one. He understands.* "I'm sorry that happened to you."

"No one gets through life unscathed."

"That's for sure. I just want you to know, that you're the first person after Christopher's death I've actually wanted to get to know better. I'm just not sure how ready I am to let someone in again. But I really want to try with you."

"It's just dinner, Layla." He brushed his fingertips

along the side of her face and hair. "And it's something more. But we can take it slow. Maybe we both need that to let the past go and move on."

She nodded. "Thank you for understanding."

Jax looked past her at the painting turned away from them. "What else did you paint?" He went to move past her to look at the canvas, but she shifted into his path, making him take her by the hips to keep her from falling backward as he ran into her.

"You can't see that."

His big hands branded her as his eyebrow shot up. "Why not?"

"It's not done. I've barely gotten started." Because she was still trying to figure him out, so she could paint him to reflect all the complex things that made him, him. "I don't like people seeing things when they're in progress." If he saw the sketch she'd done of him, he'd know exactly how she felt. Obsessed with the way he looked at her. Desperate for him, even as she held herself back to protect her heart.

He glanced at the landscape drying beside him. "You said that one's not done."

She scrunched her lips, the anxiety fluttering in her system, and her belly a riot of butterflies. "Please. Not that one. Not yet." If things went well. If this turned into something. If the look he gave her that day by the pools became their reality.

He squeezed her sides. "Okay."

"Thank you."

"Whatever you need, Layla." He kissed her on the forehead again. "What do you have to do so we can get out of here? I'm starving. You must be, too."

She had a feeling he meant that in more ways than one. Or maybe that was just her. It had been a long time since she'd been held, let alone since she'd had sex. She had a feeling the experience with him would be unbridled and nothing like anything she'd ever experienced. Why? Certainly he was the fittest and most physical man she'd ever met. But the way he was so open with her said he'd hold nothing back in bed, and he wouldn't accept her doing anything less—

"Layla?"

She startled out of her thoughts. "Yeah?"

"If you keep looking at me like that, I'm going to do something about it."

Between the wide shoulders, muscular arms, and trim waist accentuated by a black thermal, and dark blue jeans clinging to his long, toned legs, and that gorgeous face and his blue, blue eyes, he exuded sex appeal. "What am I supposed to do when you look like that?"

A laugh burst out of him and he held his hands out wide. "Have at it."

The heat burning up her cheeks didn't stop her from grinning back at him. Then she sighed and leaned her forehead to his chest. "I don't know if I remember how to do this."

Those big, warm hands threaded into her hair, pulling out the knot she'd wound it into until it cascaded down her back. He sifted his fingers through it, making her scalp tingle and her hair relax into loose waves. "All you need to do right now is come with me and eat a meal."

She glanced up at him and met those easygoing eyes. "Okay."

He grinned with a knowing look. "Okay."

She unzipped the smock she wore over her clothes while she painted and draped it over the chair at the table behind her.

Jax moved to help her gather her paintbrushes, but she held up her hand to stop him before he passed the painting she'd been working on. "Nope. No peeking. I mean it." She pointed to the door to get him moving in the other direction.

He held up his hands in surrender and stepped back.

She glanced down at her simple jeans and pink T-shirt. "Should I change into something else?"

His gaze swept over her. "You're perfect. But you might want some shoes."

"I could slip into a dress, do my hair." She suddenly felt nervous and self-conscious. She hadn't put on any makeup. She didn't want to meet his other sisters looking frumpy after a long day.

"Layla, the place is called the Dark Horse Dive Bar. No dress code. Just come as you are and have a good time. The music is loud, the food is amazing, and the bar is rowdy all the time."

She relaxed and smiled. "Okay. It sounds fun. And I can't remember if I ate lunch, so you definitely need to feed me."

"Done. Now, let's go."

"I just need to clean the dirty brushes and get my shoes." She gathered everything that needed to be washed and headed for the door.

Jax went to grab the painting of Moon.

"Leave it. It's not dry yet. You can have it tomorrow." She waited for him to open the door. "My key is in my back pocket. Can you lock up?"

Jax nuzzled her neck from behind, gave her a soft kiss, and found the key after flattening his hand on the curve of her ass. "You smell good."

For a moment, she simply leaned into him before she stepped out of the studio and waited for him to turn off the lights and lock up. "I smell like paint."

"And oranges and lime and you." He lifted his chin up toward the cabin. "Hurry up."

She dashed into her place, leaving the door open if he wanted to come in and wait. She put the brushes in a tub in the sink and turned on the hot water tap and added some soap to the bin. She made sure all the brushes were clean and laid them out to dry, then ran into her room and gave her hair a quick brush and spray to keep it neat. Then she slipped her feet into a pair of wedge sandals, ignoring the paint splatters on them, and pulled a couple of long beaded necklaces in shades of blue topaz, sapphire, and strawberry pink over her head to elevate her casual outfit. In the bathroom, she brushed on some mascara and lip gloss and called it done, because Jax was waiting.

When she walked out and found him leaning against the porch rail, his eyes went wide with appreciation as his gaze swept over her.

"Damn." He held out his hand to her. "You're so beautiful."

She took his hand and walked with him to his waiting truck at the back of her place. He opened the door for her and helped her inside, then closed her door, and went around to climb behind the wheel.

He turned to her before starting the engine. "I'm glad you said yes." Then the cab was filled with her joy, the twang of an old country song, and the promise of a really wonderful first date.

# Chapter Nine

Jax walked into the bar with Layla's hand in his and felt her jolt as the blaring music hit them. He glanced over to make sure she was all right and saw her full lips spread into a smile so big it lit her up.

"Oh, this is so much more than I thought it would be."

He chuckled as she stared at all the neon lights, customers dancing and having a good time. He stopped beside the bouncer at the door. "How is it tonight?"

"Same as every night. Everyone loves it when Lyric sings with the band." John glanced around him at Layla, his gaze sweeping over her as her body rocked to the beat thumping through the bar. "Who's the pretty girl?"

Jax grinned. "Layla, this is John. John, Layla."

She reached out to shake his huge hand and smiled that bright grin that made you want to smile back. "It's nice to meet you."

John eyed Jax, then Layla. "You even sound pretty."

Layla chuckled. "Thank you."

"Let her go," Jax ordered. "She's staying at the ranch for a while. When she's here, you keep an eye on her."

John gave him a knowing look and a nod. "Absolutely, boss."

"Thanks." Jax tugged on Layla's hand. "Come on. My sisters are here somewhere." Except it wasn't his sisters flagging him down when he neared the bar. His parents were at a table for four. Jax acknowledged them with a suspicious look, stopped in his tracks, and leaned into Layla's ear so she could hear him over the music. "Are you going to freak out if I introduce you to my parents?"

He'd told them his plans before he left the house to pick up Layla. They didn't come to the bar that often, especially during the week, so this had to be them butting into his business and wanting to get a look at the woman he'd maybe sounded a little too excited to see.

Layla's gaze snapped to his. "I'd love to meet them." Though she sounded fine with it, he caught a glimpse of hesitation on her face.

"Come on." He led the way to the table and his mother's glowing smile.

"Jax. Who's your friend?" Robin could charm anyone. She loved with her whole heart, especially when it came to her kids. And right now, she was showing him how happy she was that he'd ended his long all-work-no-fun streak.

"Layla Brock, this is my mom, Robin, and my dad, Wade."

She shook their hands and gave them an easy smile. "It's so nice to meet both of you. I love your ranch. Everyone has been so nice."

"Jax, especially, I see," his mom said, grinning at him.

He rolled his eyes. "Please stop."

"Sit," his mom encouraged, holding her hand out to the empty chairs.

And that's when Aria and Melody arrived to add to this way-too-soon introduction. All he wanted to do was spend some time with Layla. Alone.

Aria set a tall glass of beer in front of him and looked at Layla. "I'm Aria. Can I get you a glass of that Moscato Jax ordered for you?" His sister was trying to hide a smile and failing miserably.

Layla glanced at him. "You remembered. I can't believe you did that for me."

He shrugged, liking that he'd surprised her.

She turned back to Aria. "I'd love a glass. Thank you."

Melody took her turn to introduce herself, shook Layla's hand, then blurted out, "I love your hair."

Layla brushed her hand over the mass of golden strands. "It's a bit of a mess after I had it up all day, but thank you." She gestured to Melody's top. "That's one of my favorite shades of purple. So deep and vibrant. It complements your blue eyes perfectly, especially since yours are a bit darker than your brother's."

His mom leaned in. "I love your studio. I've been dying to get a closer look. Is it everything you wanted?"

"Yes." Layla turned to his dad. "Thank you for helping Jax build it."

"Of course. We want to make our guests happy."

Layla accepted her glass of wine from Aria. "Well, I am. I've already started painting."

Jax leaned on his forearms on the table. "She painted Moon."

His mom's eyes went soft. "You did? I love that horse."

"Not as much as she does." Jax took a sip of his beer. "She gifted me the painting. It's . . . unbelievable. And the one she did of the creek where we went the other day . . . it's stunning and she's not even finished with it."

"I'd love to come by and see it," Robin said.

Layla nodded. "Anytime."

Jax bumped his shoulder to hers, then looked at his mom. "If she's in the zone and ignores you, leave her be."

"Jax!" Layla's eyes widened in horror.

"Do you even remember me coming to see you yesterday?"

She did that thing where she scrunched her lips.

"That's what I thought." He settled back and took another sip of his beer.

She put her hand on his arm, her eyes filled with remorse. "I'm sorry."

He gave her a reassuring smile. "It's fine. You looked really intense, so I just let you do your thing. And if what you do is make vividly realistic paintings like the one of Moon . . . Damn. I'm just going to sit back in wonder."

The quiet in her caught his attention. And when he looked at her, something in her eyes told him he'd said something that had touched her deeply. "What?"

"Some people would be upset that I was so absorbed by my art I didn't see them."

He took that to mean her husband had not always been impressed by his talented wife.

"I'm not one of those people. I just wanted to see

you and say hi, in between the twenty other things I had to do. You were busy. I get that. But more I saw that you were putting your whole heart into what you were doing. I could have made you pay attention, but I get that for someone like you, creating what you create takes focus, and I didn't want to break your concentration just so I could have a minute. I got to see you and that was enough."

Layla's eyes glassed over.

He had an oh-shit moment where he felt terrible and thought he'd said the wrong thing and she was about to cry.

Then his mom and sisters sighed.

His dad gave him an approving nod.

Layla took a huge sip of her wine and looked at him like she wasn't sure what to do with him.

He changed the subject, knowing she needed a second. "We should order some food."

Melody handed Layla the menu. "Whatever you want, it's on the house."

Layla examined the menu and put in her order.

His sister scribbled it down and absently said to him, "I know what you want." She went off to take care of her other tables.

Aria made a hasty retreat to the crowded bar, which she was tending.

His mom leaned into the table so Layla could hear her over the music and crowd. "Jax got his first pony when he was six. He named him Sparky. He loved to ride. Couldn't wait to be up on the pony, reins in hand, off on his own."

"You mean with Dad trailing me."

Robin grinned. "Every morning Jax got up with his dad and went down to the barn to feed his pony and help with the other horses. Sometimes he'd sneak down to the barn and we'd find him asleep in the hay with Sparky sprawled out with him. That pony made Jax love horses even more than he already did. He taught Jax responsibility and love."

"He taught me that the ranch was a lot of hard work, but it was worth it to take care of my friends." Jax glanced at his dad. "I always knew the ranch would be mine someday. But if I got to be outside, riding horses, spending time with my dad and family . . . that sounded really good to me."

His mom put her hand on his arm. "Sparky isn't with us anymore, but Moon is Jax's favorite now. So that painting you did . . . I know it means a lot to him."

Layla stared at him. "I had no idea."

"The ranch is my life. The horses . . . as ornery and troublesome as they can sometimes be—"

"Most of the time," Wade interjected.

Jax nodded his agreement, then said, "The horses are my favorite thing about that place. And Moon, he's my buddy. I don't get to ride him as much. He's getting up in age and the trail rides are more his speed now than rustling cattle."

"Now I'm really glad I gave you that painting." She glanced over at his parents. "And I understand how tied you are to that place and all you take care of there."

"It's a business, but it's more," his dad said, and Jax knew that down to his soul. The ranch was home, work, and responsibility, but it was also rewarding.

Sometimes he got so caught up in the work, he forgot how much he cared about the people, the livestock, and the guests who made his life this good.

Mom and Dad sat back, enjoying their drinks and listening to Lyric and the band.

He turned to Layla just as her phone went off and she checked the screen. He wasn't trying to peek, but he caught the flash of Michael's name on her phone before she sent the call to voice mail and wondered why she ignored the call. "Everything okay?"

"Fine." The casual response made him think a call from Michael wasn't a big deal, even if a spurt of jealousy shot through him. "That was just Christopher's brother. I'll call him back tomorrow. Tonight, I just want to hang out with you."

And just like that, he put Michael in the not-a-problem category and settled in to spending time with Layla.

The band started playing a slow song. He stood and held out his hand to her. "Dance with me."

She took his hand and walked to the dance floor.

Lyric winked at him from the stage and waved to Layla.

He took the woman he couldn't stop thinking about into his arms. She fit so perfectly against him. And with those heels on, and her real close, he could look her in the eye. The green reminded him of the moss that covered the creek rocks.

They swayed to the music. He ran his fingertips down her spine, and she instinctively stepped into him even closer until his cheek brushed hers and her arms tightened around his neck.

She sighed and moved with him, their bodies brushing. "It's been a long time since I was this close to someone, let alone danced like this."

He pressed his hand to her lower back. "Anytime you want to be this close to me, I'm yours."

One of her hands slid into his hair at the back of his head, sending a shiver of arousal through him that surprised him because of the simple touch. Nothing was simple about her though. She pulled at something deep inside him. And that something was thumping out a beat that called her name.

Her soft smile held his attention. "I was not expecting you when I came here." She'd said something similar before, but the wonder in her words was the same. "You're a nice man, Jax."

"You're a sweet woman, Layla. I like the way you are with me."

She leaned back and looked at him. "What do you mean?"

"You're real. It's just you and me standing here. There's no coyness or game. Everything you say, I know you mean it. Whatever you're feeling, it's in your eyes when you look at me. And I like the way you look at me."

A shy smile and a blush brightened her face. "I can't help myself."

"Don't. Just keep doing what you're doing."

She rubbed her hand down his chest and back up to his shoulder.

That simple touch set him on fire.

"April will never believe I went to a bar, let alone danced with you, though she is definitely team Jax."

He nuzzled his chin against her hair. "I appreciate that."

"She thinks I work too much and need to have some fun."

"We had fun on our ride the other day and in the orchard. I made you laugh when I picked you up so you could get the perfect shot."

"I couldn't believe you did that. And the ride . . . that was probably one of the best experiences of my life."

He smirked, feeling incredibly happy with her. "Now you're just challenging me to up my game."

She squeezed him tight. "You're doing just fine."

He could do a hell of a lot better. "And the night's not even over." He turned in a swinging circle and made her hold on tighter so she didn't lose her balance. But he had her. He'd never let her fall.

The flush on her cheeks and the smile on her face made him smile back at her. He could certainly add some fun to her life. He could use some in his as well.

The song ended. He dipped her back over his arm for a second, then pulled her close as the band amped up the crowd with an original song Lyric wrote.

Since Layla looked out of her depth with the fast-paced groove everyone was jumping and shimmying to, he took her hand and walked her to their table.

The food had arrived. Layla immediately picked up one of the pulled pork sliders and took a bite. Her eyes rolled back in her head and she groaned. "So good."

His mom and dad stood, and though he felt bad about it, he hoped they were leaving.

"Layla, it was so nice to meet you. I hope you

enjoy your stay at the ranch, and I get to see you again soon," his mom said. With a warm smile and a look of approval at him, she took Dad's arm and they headed for the door.

Layla finished off the slider and took a bite of the mac and cheese. The look of ecstasy said she was really enjoying it.

"Your parents and sisters are great. Your mom and dad look at each other like young lovers, and like they have a history that means nothing can tear them apart."

He glanced to the door and saw his dad lean down, listen to something his mom said, then he kissed her quick, put his hand on her ass, and nudged her out the door. Jax did not let his mind wander into thinking what they were grinning about, but it did his heart good to know they were solid, in love, and yeah, nothing would change that.

Over the years, he'd seen them go through the good times and the bad. They laughed, argued, supported each other, ignored each other, told each other everything, and always respected each other. They taught him that relationships were about give-and-take and it wasn't all smiles and joy. It was a hell of a lot of work, *I'm sorry*s, sacrifice, working together, and sticking it out when things were hard.

He thought he'd had that once. But she wasn't the sticking or working it out together kind. At least not with him. She'd been the keeping secrets and going behind his back kind. And he didn't want someone like that in his life.

Layla had been married. She'd made that kind of

commitment. Though something had gone wrong in the relationship, and she'd lost her husband, it seemed she'd loved like his parents did for as long as she could.

"I'm sorry your marriage didn't work out." He picked up a slider and devoured half of it.

Her eyes went wide, then softened with regret and anger. "Me, too. It didn't have to be that way. If he'd just been honest, maybe things would have turned out differently. I wouldn't have stayed, but we could have remained friends. In the end, Christopher couldn't bear that he'd hurt me and lost me, and he left us both without a way to mend it."

Distressed and hopeless people did desperate things. He was sure Layla wished he'd asked for help. She would have given it to him, Jax had no doubt.

"I don't think you're a woman who would be easy to get over." And that meant he could be the one missing her and regretting losing her if he didn't play his cards right.

She picked up her wine and took a sip, not looking one bit like she believed him.

Maybe she just didn't want to talk about something so painful.

He couldn't blame her. He didn't want to talk about what had made him put his heart in a box and lock it away for the past few years. Until her. Because she'd somehow popped the lock on that box. He didn't know how she did it, or why it was her. Instinct told him to slow his roll, but he couldn't seem to help himself when it came to her. Things started coming out of his mouth, actions started happening without him really thinking about it, and here he was trying to start something with her with the single thought in his head that he couldn't let her get away.

*What was that?*

*When did it happen?*

The second she'd stepped foot on Wilde Wind Ranch and knocked him on his ass.

"Are you okay?" She studied him.

"No. And yes. And it's your fault."

She raised a perfectly arched golden brow. "Did I do something wrong?"

He leaned in and held her gaze. "I have a feeling you're everything right."

She finished off her wine in one gulp and set the glass on the table. "I think I'm going to need a refill to take this all in."

"You and me both."

They'd finished all the food.

He took her hand and pulled her toward the bar where Aria had already cleared out the two stools at the end for them. "Take a seat. I'll be right back." He took a single step away, saw the way three dudes eyed Layla, then stepped in close, and touched his finger to her chin. Her eyes locked with his, surprise in hers, and then he gave in to temptation and kissed her. He'd planned to wait until the end of the night, but in the moment, he wanted everyone to know she was with him.

And a desperate man could only hold out so long.

Her lips were soft. Her surprise turned to quick acceptance as she kissed him back. He kept it PG with only the slightest touch of his tongue to her full bottom lip before he ended it and brushed his thumb over her pinked cheek.

"Damn. You make me want to drop to my knees, Layla." The lyric from the Eric Clapton song rang in his head, but he didn't have visions of pleading for her to stay, only her begging for more with her legs draped over his shoulders and him licking her to climax as he worshipped her.

The lady sitting beside her sputtered out her drink, then stared at him.

He only had eyes for the beautifully blushing blonde gaping at him. He gave her another quick kiss. "Something to look forward to later. I'll be right back." He headed to the office to grab the paperwork he needed to do and his laptop, trying not to let himself think too hard about how easy it was to be with her, how deep he was falling at breakneck speed, or how, if he wasn't careful, she could cut him off at the knees and leave him bloody.

He focused on the fact that she could be the best thing that ever happened to him. And wondered if he had enough time before she left for some other place to paint to get her to want to stay.

# Chapter Ten

Layla blew out a breath, then sucked in a calming one, hoping her jackhammering heart slowed down while the woman beside her fanned her face and shook her head.

"You are so lucky. That man is *H.O.T.* Hot."

Layla stared down the hallway where Jax disappeared after kissing her like she'd never been kissed. If that hadn't been mind-blowing enough, he'd totally scrambled her brain and sent her libido into overdrive with that declaration about falling to his knees for her.

"You two probably have really great sex." The pout and slight slur to her barstool neighbor's words gave the distinct impression she was tipsy.

"We just met." Though it didn't feel that way. Something about Jax just felt right. "This is our first date." Unless you counted the horseback ride, the archery lesson, and the apple picking.

"Damn, honey, you work fast." The brunette with the glazed brown eyes turned to her. "What did you do to make him that into you?"

Layla didn't have an answer, so just said, "It just happened."

Tipsy Girl frowned and narrowed her eyes and looked like she might fall off her stool if she leaned any farther into Layla's space. "You're pretty. You don't have to do anything to make him want you."

Looks weren't everything. "Attraction only gets you so far. I think being honest and kind goes a long way to keeping people together."

Tipsy Girl sat up straighter. "I'm honest. I'm kind, too."

"You're also pretty," Layla pointed out. "So don't be so hard on yourself. The right guy will come along."

She spun on the stool, her back to the bar, and looked out at the packed crowd. "Maybe he's here tonight." Hope lit her eyes and filled her voice, revealing her lonely soul.

Layla scanned the crowd and saw a guy nursing a beer and leaning against a tall table where a couple of other guys were flirting with the girls at the next table. The odd man out. "See that guy." She pointed to him. "He's cute and standing all by himself. Go say hi and see if he wants to dance with you."

Tipsy Girl sighed and stared at the cute guy. "I love to dance."

"Maybe he does, too." Layla took the drink away from the woman and set it on the bar. "You're going to need both hands to hold on to him."

Her eyes went wide. "I can't just go up to him."

Layla nudged her shoulder. "Yes, you can, because you're brave." Layla believed everyone had it in them to do anything, even when it seemed hard or outside their comfort zone. She'd ridden a horse. "You've got this."

Tipsy Girl gave a firm nod, tapped Layla on the

knee with her hand, then slid off her stool and marched over to Cute Guy with a smile and said something to him that made him grin back at her.

"That was a nice thing you did."

Layla turned to Aria, who had been serving drinks at the other end of the bar a second ago. "She seemed lonely and a little lost." Layla could relate.

Most people probably felt that way at one time or another in their life.

Tipsy Girl seemed to be stuck in that rut. Layla encouraged her to climb out of it.

Aria wiped her hands on a clean white towel. "She comes in, sits at the bar, drinks, and never gets hit on because she's too busy drowning her sorrows and not looking at the guys. Most of them need a little sign of encouragement. A smile is usually enough for most of them to make a move."

Layla got that. No one wanted to face rejection. "She's got just enough liquid courage in her to be bold."

"And look what that got her." Aria raised her chin toward the dance floor.

Layla turned and found Tipsy Girl pressed up close to the cute guy with her head on his shoulder and him grinning like he'd won the lottery. Layla turned back to Aria and chuckled. "I hope it works out for them and they are very happy together."

"I haven't seen Jax smile the way he smiles at you in a long time."

Layla caught on quick to the change in subject. "I haven't felt this way about someone in a long time, too."

"Jax is a good guy."

"You don't need to tell me that. It's easy to see. I haven't known him long, but I know that with him, what you see is what you get. It's probably what I like most about him. I'm trying to trust in that because I once thought I knew someone. And when they did something I never saw coming, it messed with my head."

Aria frowned. "I'm sorry that happened to you. But Jax doesn't play games. He's up-front about everything, including what he wants from women."

"I imagine with three sisters and a loving mother, Jax knows exactly how to treat a woman with respect. He's shown me that."

"That kiss he laid on you . . . that says something." Aria ignored the dozens of customers packed along the bar trying to get her attention and focused on Layla. "He saw every guy in this place checking out the new lady in town. And he staked his claim. Never seen that before." Aria grabbed a bottle of tequila and poured four shots for the guy leaning over the bar holding up four fingers.

She took a breath and tried not to read too much into Aria's statement. She tried to sort out her feelings about it, too. Did she want the kiss to be nothing but a message to other interested men? It hadn't felt like that to her. Jax didn't seem like he needed to pull some macho bullshit like that anyway. He was too direct. So maybe the kiss was exactly that, his declaration that he was interested in her.

She'd already known that from the first time he'd looked at her.

He didn't hide it.

"Hey." Jax set a laptop and a stuffed folder on the bar and put his hand on her back. "Do you want another glass of wine?"

"No, thank you. I'm good." She stared at the thick folder. "That's a lot of work."

"Yeah. It's not really fair to make you sit here while I plow through it, so I thought I'd drive you back to the ranch and do this at home."

She looked up into those gorgeous blue eyes and caught the dark smudges below them. "How long have you been up?"

He narrowed his gaze, then rubbed his hand along his stubbled jaw. "Since four thirty."

"Jax, you need some sleep." She waved goodbye to Aria, who was pulling a beer at the tap a few feet away, slid off the stool, and took his hand. "Come on, let's go."

He followed her out of the bar with a nod to John at the door and a "Watch the girls" that she took to mean for the bouncer to watch over Jax's sisters.

At the truck, she took his computer and the paperwork and set them on the seat before climbing in and pulling on her seat belt, while Jax closed her door for her and circled the truck to get behind the wheel.

He put his hand over hers. "Sorry to cut the night short. Sometimes, I get so tired, I just hit a wall."

"Do you want me to drive us home?"

Something flared in his eyes at her words, but then he just shook his head and pulled out of the packed lot. "I'm fine. I often stay at the bar way later than this. I just didn't want to end our date boring you to death watching me input expenses and do the payroll."

"I don't know, you're sexy just sitting there. I could stare at you for hours and not get bored."

Jax chuckled, took her hand, and kissed the back of it. "Thanks. I think you're the most beautiful woman I've ever seen. Like ever."

"That's nice to hear, but there were some seriously hot women in that bar and most of them were wearing a lot less clothes than I have on."

"Were there?" He didn't even grin and sounded so absolutely sincere, until he gazed at her again, and then burst out laughing. "I bet you're stunning in nothing at all. And it's a lot of fun to imagine you naked."

She agreed. Because she had a whole lot of thoughts about what all those strong muscles looked like beneath the well-fitted thermal stretching across his chest and arms.

But there was something else on her mind, too. "About that kiss."

He glanced at her. "What about it?"

"Was that for me, or to let the other guys in the bar know I was with you?"

He raised a brow. "Can it be both?"

She squeezed his hand. "At least you're honest."

"Always with you." He pressed the back of her hand to his thigh and rubbed his palm and fingers over hers, then entwined their fingers. "And if I'm telling the truth . . . the kiss . . . I just couldn't wait any longer."

That was sweet. "Well, maybe I'll let you kiss me good night, then."

"Maybe?" He eyed her with a mock frown. "I got

you your favorite wine. I even had the case over-
nighted from the winery."

She turned in the seat to face him. "Why would you
do that?" She couldn't imagine why he'd go out of his
way and pay extra like that for her.

"Why do you think? To make you happy. You're in
a new place. You don't know anyone here. I thought it
might be nice for you to have something you like, so I
made a call. No big deal." Such kindness and generosity.

"It means a lot to me." She loosened her seat belt
so she could scoot closer to him and kissed him on
the cheek. "I already knew it, but your sister is right,
you're a good man, Jax Wilde."

His bright smile at her words dimmed. "What else
did my sister say to you?"

"Not much. She thought it was nice that I encouraged a tipsy girl looking for love to hit on a cute cowboy. When we left, they were still in each other's arms
on the dance floor, even though Lyric was rocking a
classic Heart song."

"Why did you do that?"

"Because she was sad about you kissing me and
not her."

"I don't even know who you're talking about."

"Exactly. Because in a bar full of hot, scantily clad,
tipsy women, you never took your eyes off me, and
that was seriously hot, Jax. You are definitely getting
your kiss good night."

Jax adjusted his position, letting her know she'd
made one part of him uncomfortable, but the seriously
intent look he gave her said he didn't care if his pants
were now too tight, he wanted her.

She wasn't one to sexually frustrate a guy, then leave him hanging. And as much as she liked Jax and wanted that good-night kiss, she remained nervous about how fast things were going.

She really needed to stop thinking everything was going to end badly. It insulted Jax, even if she didn't mean to do it.

Before she could make her mind up one way or another about inviting him in and giving them a real shot at changing the relationship into something much more intimate, Jax pulled up behind the cabin and climbed out of the truck. He came around to her side to help her out, and walked her around the cabin to the front door. The second she turned to him, he nudged her up against the door and kissed her with unbridled passion. It was all demanding with tongues, gasps and moans, and his hands in her hair holding her head at just the right angle he wanted until he shifted and took the kiss deeper, his thick erection pressed to her belly.

She slid her hands beneath his shirt and up his back. She held on, her nails biting into his skin. He didn't seem to care. He just kissed her more, branding her with his lips, scalding her with that wicked tongue, and ensuring she never forgot him. Ever.

From one pounding heartbeat to the next, he ended the kiss, pressed his forehead to hers, and with his eyes closed and his breath heaving in and out and mingling with hers, he said, "Damn. I am never getting you out of my system." Those blue, blue eyes opened and stared into hers. "There is no other woman like you."

She didn't know what to say. She thought she forgot

her name. All she could feel was Jax's body oh so snug against her. His thighs against hers, his hard length something she wanted to wrap her hand around and stroke, his chest pressed to her aching breasts, and those gorgeous eyes locked on hers.

With gentle fingers, he brushed her hair back behind both her ears, kissed her softly, then ever so slowly rolled his body off hers. She nearly cried out at the loss of contact and all his warmth.

He grabbed the little purse she'd worn crosswise over her chest for the night and pulled out her cabin key. He unlocked the door and pushed it open at her back, then put the key in her palm, brought her hand up to his lips, and kissed the back of it. "Good night, Layla. I'll see you tomorrow."

"You will?" Was that her breathy voice?

"April signed you up for a fishing trip. I can't wait to teach you how to cast a line."

It only took a second for her to imagine him behind her, the heat of him, his hands on her, helping her hold the rod and send the baited hook soaring until it plunked into the water. She gulped and felt the blush rise on her cheeks.

Jax brushed featherlight fingertips over her face. "So beautiful."

"Thank you." She didn't mean for the compliment. Well, yes, she did. But . . . "For the date. The dance. The wine. Everything."

"My pleasure. All of it. Especially that seriously sexy good-night kiss. I don't know how I'm going to get any work done tonight when all I can do is think about you." And with that, he turned and faded into the night as he walked away and left her seriously considering calling him back.

Head spinning, she walked into the cabin, shut the door, and fell back against it, her shaky legs making her sink to her butt. She stared into the dark, her heart pounding, a giddy grin on her face and a flicker of fear in her gut because she wasn't sure she was ready for Jax Wilde. Because a man who could kiss like that, make her feel this way, he just might be able to mend her broken heart and make her believe that some men kept their promises and he was worth the risk.

# Chapter Eleven

Jax walked into the house through the mudroom, the scent of cinnamon and sugar enticing him into the kitchen. His stomach grumbled and his steps were slow after another short night and long early morning work schedule. He'd barely slept because he was thinking about Layla and that kiss they'd shared, then he'd dreamed about her naked in his arms and woke up wanting, hard, and alone.

Cody Johnson's "On My Way to You" filled the room with the classic country sound and Cody's rich voice and, for the first time, the song spoke to him. Because it made him think that maybe all the losses in his life, what happened with Helen, only left him with one place to end up. Free to be with Layla.

"I like her," his mom said, giving him a knowing look when she caught him standing there lost in his thoughts.

He didn't want to get ahead of himself. "Don't get all excited, it was one date."

She gave him another look. "No it wasn't. And she's not just another woman. You look at her differently."

Layla wasn't just someone he could let walk away. Not without doing everything he could to make her want to stay and see if this thing between them could last.

"And Aria told me that you practically branded her yours in front of everyone in the bar last night." His mom seemed to be holding back a laugh.

"Can't a guy kiss a girl and not have his sister tell the world?"

"She's happy for you. I am, too."

He tried to play it off. "It's not like I haven't been dating."

She rolled her eyes this time. "What you were doing was not dating. Not when you spend so little time talking and getting to know her and instead you're—"

"Enough." He so did not want to have this conversation. "I got the sex-and-respecting-women talk a long time ago. I'm a grown man. And I am not talking about my sex life with my mother." He cringed.

She frowned. "All I'm saying is this one matters to you."

"She does," he admitted, giving her that much, hoping she'd take the tidbit and give him some space. "So let's leave it at that. Let me have some time to figure out what that means and where this is going before you all scare her off."

She held out a plastic wrap–covered plate of cinnamon crumble muffins. His favorite. "I thought you might like to go have coffee and breakfast with her."

He took the paper plate and kissed his mom's cheek. "Thank you."

A serious look came into her eyes. "You work really

hard for this family. Take some time for yourself. You deserve it. You've earned it."

He sighed, feeling the weight of his responsibilities and too little sleep. "There just never seems to be enough time."

"If it's important, make time. It's the one thing we waste the most of and can never get back."

He headed out to the cabins, hoping Layla was awake and not lost in her painting. He didn't want to disturb her while she worked. He also didn't want to wear out his welcome by showing up uninvited.

He waved hello to the honeymoon couple in cabin three, who were sitting out on their porch drinking coffee. The family in cabin five sounded like the three little ones were fighting over which show to watch. The cabins had Wi-Fi but no TVs, so the parents had probably brought a laptop or tablet and were regretting not having one for each child.

When he got to cabin ten, his nerves kicked in. It wasn't like this was the first morning after and he didn't know what to say. In the past, he'd always been trying to figure out a way to leave without making any promises for a repeat. Not so in this case.

He and Layla had only kissed and already he wanted more.

He just wasn't sure how she felt about it.

He hoped he didn't look desperate, even if he was to kiss her again.

About to knock on her door, he hesitated and dropped his hand.

"Whatcha doin'?"

He startled, surprised to hear her behind him. He

turned and found her grinning at him, paint on her fingers. "Lookin' for you."

She frowned. "Except you didn't knock." She raised a brow.

"I was about to chicken out," he confessed.

Her head tilted to the side. "Do I scare you?"

"A little bit." The admission made her chuckle and the nerves in his belly flutter even more.

She narrowed her curiosity-filled eyes. "Why?"

"Because I couldn't wait to see you." *And you matter.* And if she was this important now, what would happen later, when he was all wrapped up in her and it fell apart and left him bloody? And alone again.

She took a step closer. "I couldn't wait to see you today, too." And out came the pretty blush he loved.

"I've been up since before dawn. I waited as long as I could." The confession made her smile.

"I barely slept last night and ended up in the studio painting." She held her hands out wide. "I have no idea what time it is, but it feels like you're late, and I've been waiting a long time."

He felt the same way, like he'd been waiting all this time for her to find him. "This is . . . wildly unbelievable to feel this way so fast."

"Is it though? Because at one time, everything I thought I knew about my life turned out to be true and a lie at the same time. It disoriented me. I thought I was losing it for a while. Because how could I have been happy while at the same time, without me knowing it, my world was falling apart? This . . . I don't know, Jax. It feels new, but also familiar, but with the bad stuff left out and all the good stuff making me feel buzzed with excitement. As much as I've thought the last few months that I wanted to move on and find someone new, I didn't actually think it would happen. I guess that's what surprised me last night. This isn't like before. It's different. Because it's you and the me I am now."

While a lot of that didn't wholly make sense to him because he didn't know all the details about her past and about how her relationship with her husband fell apart, he understood that he'd been another version of himself with Helen, and what he felt for Helen was nothing like what he felt for Layla.

He wasn't that man anymore. He was this one. The one he wanted to be for Layla.

"Can I come in?" It felt like he was asking for a lot more than an early morning breakfast at her place.

The look in her eyes told him she got it, too. "Yes."

She walked up the stairs and stood next to him. "Good morning."

He leaned down and kissed her softly, intimately, like he had a right to do it and could do it anytime he wanted to. "Morning, Layla."

She took his hand and pulled him inside. "The coffee's been on for a while. Want me to make a fresh pot? Or do we need to meet the fishing group soon?"

He set the plate of muffins on the small table and took a seat, not making any assumptions about her letting him into her very private cabin. "Whatever you want to do. We've got time."

She made a fresh pot and left it to sit with him at the table.

"Seems like work got a little messy today?" He nodded toward the paint splatters on her hands.

She did that thing she did with her lips when she was uncomfortable or nervous. "Hazard of the job." She looked down at her plain canvas shoes.

He followed her gaze and saw the paint there, too. Her clothes had avoided the same splatters because she wore a smock when she painted.

"Since I couldn't sleep, because that kiss you laid on me last night really packed a punch, and I couldn't stop thinking about you, I started painting the pools."

He loved that spot along the creek. He'd forever tie that place to her now. Holding hands. Kissing her on the forehead. Telling her he wanted to start something with her, even knowing she was probably bound to leave. He wanted her to stay. More than that, he wanted her to stick. Because he was stuck on her.

"I can't wait to see it."

"I don't know what to do with you," she blurted out.

It somehow made it easier for him to feel the way he felt knowing she was feeling it, too. So he leaned forward, took her hand, linked his fingers with hers, and looked her in the eye. "Whatever you want to do is fine by me." He kissed the back of her hand and grinned at the blush that spread up her neck and across her cheeks. He could just eat her up. "You are so beautiful."

"I think we should—"

Someone pounded on the door. "Jax."

He froze with the need to know what she was going to say, but knowing he wasn't going to get a chance to hear it because duty called. "What?" he shouted, hoping it was nothing, and knowing Zac wouldn't have come looking for him if it wasn't important.

"One of the guests broke an ankle on the sunrise hike, we need to go out and haul him down the trail and get him to the hospital."

Jax swore under his breath, leaned in, and kissed Layla, not like he wanted to, but with enough softness and finesse that promised much more later. "Hold that thought. Please. Because if you were going to say what I'm hoping you were going to say, I'm in. But I have to go. Also, this means fishing has been postponed."

She looked up as he rose to his feet, understanding in her eyes, because she was awesome and sweet. "I'll see you soon."

He kissed her again. "I'm sorry." More than he could express. And disappointed.

"It's okay. Someone needs you."

*I need you.*

"I'll be here when you get back. I'm not going anywhere."

He wished that were true. And wondered if he could ask her to stay when her life wasn't here.

The fact he wanted to ask her right now only highlighted how fast and deep he'd fallen.

# Chapter Twelve

APRIL: We have a buyer for Sedona Sunset. Full price!

LAYLA: I think I fell for the hot cowboy who kisses like I'm his sex dream come true.

It felt like Layla's whole body blushed after she texted that to her best friend.

No surprise, her phone rang immediately.

She answered with, "How are things at Donte's parents' house?"

Of course April did not want to talk about that. "Tell me you got naked with that gorgeous man."

"Layla," April snapped. "Don't hold out on me."

Layla laughed as she sat in her studio staring at the gorgeous man's face staring back at her from the sketch she'd finished of him. Those eyes. The way he looked at her. She needed to capture that in the painting. She'd started a few minutes ago on the background. That was easy. Yesterday after the fishing trip got postponed to the evening, she'd spent the rest of the day working on the creek and pools painting. It wasn't finished, but it was coming along and might be not just her best work yet, but her favorite piece ever.

"The other night Jax took me to his bar. We danced. We talked. He kissed me. I mean, really kissed me. Like he could just do that all night and be a happy man about it. Then he brought me back to the cabin and I thought we were going to . . . you know . . . because he kissed me again. There was all this fire and heat to it." She was getting a little breathless even now just thinking about it.

"And?"

"He said good night and went home, then he showed up yesterday morning with muffins. It's like every time I see him my whole body catches fire and I just wanted to jump him. But I was nervous, he was, too, and I was talking about making coffee and he's this massive man sitting in this little bistro chair at the table looking good enough to lick and staring at me like he can't wait to get his hands on me. And all I see in my head is us naked in bed."

"You are so gone for him."

"What the hell am I doing? I'm a widow, not some sex-crazed teen. But that's how he makes me feel. He's in front of me and I just can't help but want him." Except last night after fishing he'd had to work at the bar, so they hadn't ended up in bed together. Pity. For both of them.

"Yay! Finally!" April's infectious joy made Layla grin and blush at the same time.

"Finally? What is that supposed to mean?" Except she knew.

"You've spent all this time wallowing in losing

Christopher. I get that you needed to process all that, but he didn't deserve your mourning him the way you did, cutting yourself off from everyone. He tore your world apart. He stole all the joy out of you. It showed on your face, in your eyes, and in your work. And I know that last one bothers you the most."

"I don't want people to see pain and sorrow in what I create. I want them to feel like they want to be wherever I painted."

"I know. But some people understand sadness and loss and hurt. And those paintings sold because there's beauty in that, too. But it's no way for you to live your life. So I am thrilled that Jax brought joy back into your life and the young, vibrant woman you are woke up again. I don't want you to be alone because of what he did to you. Not all men are like him. It doesn't mean Jax is like Christopher."

"I know. I see that. It's just sometimes I wonder what's real and what's not. But Jax, he's so straightforward about everything. I don't have to guess with him because he straight up says everything he means."

"Sounds like he's perfect for you and what you need right now to get over Christopher."

"I am over him. I have been for a long time." She'd grieved. She'd let her anger go. She'd turned her focus back on herself and healing. "Now I'm trying to find my way to who I am after him."

"You're brilliant and beautiful, kind, caring, and have the biggest heart. None of that has changed. I couldn't have a better friend or business partner. You are always there for the ones you love. Now I'm ordering you to go after Jax with everything you are because you deserve to be happy. And I can't think of anything that would make you happier than having a hot, naked cowboy in your bed."

"I mean, it couldn't hurt." Layla laughed with April and it felt really good to feel this light and carefree again. "Thank you."

"For what?"

"Reminding me of who I used to be. Fearless."

"And a bit flighty, but that's why you have me to make sure you don't get lost in painting and spend too much time alone with your art."

She couldn't deny that truth, or another. "All I want to do is spend time with him now."

"Good. But also, don't forget the commission."

"We're still set for tomorrow, right?" Collin O'Brian had moved their original meeting because of business in LA that kept him from coming to his Wyoming ranch.

"Actually . . ." April hedged.

"He moved it again."

"I sent you an email with all the details. He's really sorry."

Layla wasn't upset. It gave her more time to work on her other paintings. "Until then, I'll just keep painting what I've fallen in love with here at Wilde Wind Ranch. I've finished this beautiful creek scene and started the amazing cascade of pools that are hidden in the woods where the light shines through in beams. It's gorgeous. I'm keeping that one. But I have plans for one of the orchard, too. And the river where we fished."

"You actually went on the fishing trip yesterday."

A second later April answered her own question. "Jax was there. Of course you went."

"I can't wait to see more. We'll put together a huge showing. I've been listening to the other guests talk about where they've gone. I'm hoping to check out some of the spots away from the ranch that piqued my interest soon."

"Ask Jax to take you out scouting."

"He's so busy."

"Ask him," April ordered. "Don't assume he doesn't have time for you. If he feels what you feel, he'll want to be with you, too. And if he can't make time for whatever reason, then at least you let him know you wanted to be with him."

"I'm a little bit scared."

"That's because it matters. Just don't let fear keep you from something that could turn out to be really good, Layla. Enjoy the flirting and kissing and everything else while getting to know him. The beginning is always the best part."

Yes, it was. "I really liked the settling-in part, knowing the relationship was on solid ground, too."

"I have that with Donte all these years after we met. And it's the best. Christopher built that foundation with you, but then what he did put a huge crack in it that you never saw. If this thing with Jax starts going the distance, you'll be sure that foundation is set in granite this time. But the only way that's going to happen is if you go for it. Don't hold back. Especially if he's giving you all of him."

Layla didn't know until that moment that was what she wanted. She wanted Jax to be exactly the man she saw him to be. She didn't want to be blindsided by secrets again.

Her phone chimed with an incoming text.

"Hold on. Someone texted me." She checked her message.

**MICHAEL:** I want what I'm owed. What doesn't belong to you.
**MICHAEL:** Answer your phone!!!

She'd ignored the incoming call, but couldn't do the same with the texts.

She put the phone back to her ear. "Sorry. Michael is . . ."

When she didn't finish the sentence, April chimed in. "An asshole. The few times we were all together, it was clear he was jealous of Christopher. He probably wished he had someone like you. I get that Christopher looked out for him their whole lives, but at some point, Michael has to take responsibility for his life and fix his own messes."

"He sabotaged himself with the inheritance and now he wants me to pay it out. But the old Michael, the one who was intense but nice, has turned into an angry, demanding, spoiled brat."

"Aren't you supposed to ignore toddlers when they have tantrums?"

"He's hard to dismiss when he won't give up."

Another text came in.

**MICHAEL:** Stop being such a bitch!

"What is it?" April either heard the chime of her phone, or sensed Layla's upset.

"Nothing. I'm just going to ignore it. He doesn't know where I am, so he can just stew in California."

"What else?"

"Christopher's death was just one loss of many. I lost Michael, too. I considered him a brother. Family. I never expected him to turn on me like this."

"He can't separate you as his brother's wife from you as a person. He's hurting and needs someone to blame. You're the only one here he can take it out on, even though you didn't do anything. He probably knows you don't deserve it, but he just can't help himself."

Grief. Everyone handled it differently.

"I'm tired of paying for what Christopher did. I just want to move on."

"If he doesn't stop, I'll ask your lawyer to send him a letter stating that his harassment is unwelcome and if it doesn't stop, there will be consequences. Christopher isn't here to make everything right for him anymore. Maybe a warning will be the wake-up call he needs."

Layla stared at Jax's image in front of her. "Michael will get tired of me ignoring him and he'll find some-one who will fill the void Christopher left in his life." He'd use them the way he used his brother. There had been a lot of love there, but the give-and-take had not been equal by any measure.

She dipped her brush in the blue she'd mixed for Jax's eyes and started to paint them in, feeling his gaze on her like she was staring at the man right now. "I'm going to focus on what I've found here and what I'm creating."

# Chapter Thirteen

Jax missed Layla like crazy and it was making him surly. Every time he turned around to go back to her, someone dragged him in the opposite direction. After the incident with the hiker, he'd gotten to spend an hour with her fishing. He taught her how to bait a hook and cast her line. And while they stood in the river waiting, they spoke softly, sharing details about how they grew up, her in suburbia, playing soccer, then discovering art, Girl Scout summer camps, and high school firsts like kissing, dating, and breaking up. She pretty much knew his life on the ranch but he filled her in on the cattle business they ran, how terrible he'd been at football, but that he could slug a baseball out of the park without really trying. He told her about his firsts, too, though he hated to admit that he'd played the field, thinking he was hot shit back in those days.

And then she'd yelped when her rod tugged nearly out of her hands. Luckily she'd hung on, and he'd stepped right behind her, held her steady, and coached her on how to reel it in. Man, her smile lit up like she'd won the lottery when that trout came out of the water, dangling from her line. She was so proud. He felt that way about her.

But her enthusiasm for fishing died when he tried to coach her through gutting the fish. She backed away with her hands up, shaking her head. He chuckled and handled the chore for her, then helped her fry her fish in a cast-iron skillet for dinner over the fire.

They shared it and a whole lot more, said and unsaid, by that fire.

One of the best days he'd had since the other days he'd had with her.

Her smile, laugh, the joy she expressed that day, all of it made him enjoy the simple pleasure of being with someone he liked and cared about, doing something fun and relaxing.

It had been the first time in a long time he set everything else aside and got caught up in the pleasure of being with someone.

But that happiness was short-lived because his days were packed with work and responsibilities. Any spare few minutes he could find to spend with Layla disappeared with new demands on his time that came up unexpectedly.

He'd had to check on a cow that had an injured foot. The cow had been ornery about getting the bandage off and him cleaning the wound and rewrapping it. Jax nearly got kicked twice. The more the cow fought, the longer it took. But he couldn't blame the cow. She was in pain. Didn't mean Jax wasn't frustrated that it took extra time when he'd rather be with Layla.

The ranch took up his days and the bar stole the nights. With the warmer temps, the bar was packed with people looking to unwind and have a good time.

Before he knew it three days had passed without him catching even a glimpse of Layla.

By the time he stopped by her cabin last night, it was late and the cabin was as dark as her studio. One look out back and he'd discovered her car missing, too. He had no idea where she'd gone, but he didn't have time to wait because he had to go to the bar. He didn't get out of there until after eleven. Tired to the bone, it was all he could do to drive home, shower, and fall into bed.

This morning he planned to go to her cabin and cook her breakfast but he just left her muffins on her porch when he saw she wasn't home.

Instead of doing what he wanted to do, he was stuck on a remote part of the ranch with two other guys fixing a fence line after a dead tree fell on it. He'd already spent the better part of an hour using a chain saw to cut it into logs and move it out of the way. He was tired, sweaty, and done. But he still had hours of work ahead of him, because once he finished this, he needed to get to the bar and cover for one of the bartenders, so she could attend some business function with her husband.

Everyone had a life but him, it seemed.

"Someone's coming," Wes called out as Jax forced the barbed wire into position so Ray could secure it.

Jax glanced over as the sound of the vehicle drew closer. At first, he thought he was seeing things. But no.

She was here.

Layla parked the Jeep, climbed out of the driver's

seat, and closed the door. She looked like temptation in a pretty red sundress that she'd paired with black hiking boots for the terrain, which still somehow worked with the dress. At least on her, because the bulky shoes didn't detract from her gorgeous legs.

She walked toward him with her hand up at her forehead, blocking the sun from her eyes. "I came to confess."

He didn't really care what she'd done. He'd forgive everything for just one kiss and started toward her. He didn't stop until he scooped her up with his arms around her waist and held her close.

At eye level with him, she looked him dead in the eye and whispered, "I ate all the muffins."

He burst out laughing, then kissed her with a lot of tongue and a bite on her full bottom lip.

Wes and Ray whistled and catcalled from behind him.

Jax didn't care. He took what he'd been missing for nearly four days, then let her up for air long enough to say, "I'm sorry I disappeared on you." He dove in for another kiss, then abruptly broke it and glared at her. "Why don't I have your number?" It dawned on him that her number was most likely in her registration profile. His brain was obviously not firing on all cylinders on so little sleep.

She cupped his face, not seeming to care one bit that he was still holding her off the ground and very snug to his body with his thick erection pressed to her belly. "You never asked. And I don't have yours either, that's why I had to ask your dad how to find you today. You have his eyes."

"It's a Wilde thing, the blue eyes. Did you just

come out here to cop to eating the treats I brought you?"

"No." She brushed his hat off his head, pressed her forehead to his, looked him in the eye, and confessed to the truth he saw in her eyes. "I got lonely and missed you. I couldn't wait anymore." She bit her bottom lip. "I was really hoping you'd be happy to see me."

He heard what she didn't say, that she feared he didn't want to see her.

If she couldn't tell how bad he wanted her by the thick rod pressing against her, then he'd just have to tell her. "I missed you, too. The last three nights I've come by the cabin but the lights are always off, so I turn around and go home, even though I just want to pound on the door, wake you up, and get you naked and under me."

Her green eyes lit with surprise and a desire that matched his. "Then you should do that the next time the urge strikes instead of leaving me alone."

"If we didn't have an audience, I'd have you on the ground in a heartbeat. I'm not just stupid for missing three days with you, I'm the luckiest man alive that you tracked my ass down all the way out here just to see me."

She rubbed her nose against his and hugged him close. "Worth it."

He finally set her on her feet, but pulled her in close and held her with his cheek pressed to her hair. When she looked up at him, he cupped her face and confessed, "I haven't felt like I was worth it to someone in a long time."

"I really appreciated the muffins." She tried to tease him out of the dark mood.

"You also like the way I kiss you. You melt and demand more all at the same time and it is sexy as hell."

"You two going to get a room or what?" Ray called out.

They were too far away for their conversation to be overheard. He had at least that many brain cells to keep some things private.

"Keep your eyes on the fencing," he called back over his shoulder.

The two knuckleheads laughed.

Jax didn't mind that he'd get razzed for this later. He didn't even want to think about what his parents would say when his dad told his mom Layla had come looking for him.

He really needed his own place.

Or to listen to the bright, gorgeous woman in his arms and knock on her door tonight.

She stepped back, looking a little uncomfortable, but she didn't go far. "Are you hungry? You always seem like you've missed a meal, and you're starving."

"That's because I never stop working."

She moved her hands from his arms and placed them on his chest. "Can you give me ten minutes?"

He frowned at her. "You ask so little." He wanted to give her more. Everything.

"I know what it's like to get lost in work because you love it. You love this place, the bar, your family. You don't want to let them down. And you never do, because it's important."

So kind. So understanding.

So out of his league.

He seriously didn't deserve her.

He needed to do better and started with pulling out his phone so he could stay in touch with her. "You should at least expect me to call or text you when I can't make it to see you." He pulled up his contacts. "Put your number in there for me."

She took the phone and quickly typed in her name and number. "Why didn't you call April to get it?"

"And tell your best friend that I'm such an ass that I didn't get your number and haven't spoken to you in days." He thought about that and groaned. "She already knows because you two probably talk about everything."

Layla shook her head. "Since you weren't around, I consoled myself with work. I did some exploring outside the ranch. I finished the pools painting and started another one. Though it's not quite right. I'm still figuring it out. So I haven't had time to talk to April. Besides, she's driving home from her in-laws'. That visit was probably stressful enough for her, even though they love her and she loves them. But inevitably they ask when April and Donte are having kids. That can be a lot of pressure."

Having kids usually made him pause for his own reasons, but something sad came and went in Layla's eyes that made him pay attention to her and not his own thoughts. "Did your husband want kids?" Maybe she was sad because her husband died before they had the chance to make it a reality.

"Yes. We both did. It just . . . didn't work out." She turned toward the car. "Let me get what I brought."

He liked that she wanted kids, but hated that he'd made her sad thinking about it.

When she returned with a paper bag in hand, he grinned, hoping to ease her mind. "What did you bring?"

"Roast beef and cheddar with chips and root beer." She glanced past him at Wes and Ray. "I didn't know you were working with them. But the sandwiches are huge. I'm sure there's plenty for us to share."

He hooked his arm around her shoulders and kissed her on the side of the head. "You're a good woman. We don't deserve you."

"It's a sandwich and a soda. Looks like you guys have been working hard. You need to eat."

Jax steered her toward the back of his truck, put his hands on her hips, and lifted her onto the tailgate. "I've got some making up to do with you."

She shook her head. "It's not about that, Jax. I don't want a scorecard between us."

He slid his fingers into her soft, thick hair and touched his forehead to hers. "Never. I just want to show you I appreciate you."

"You just did." She made him a little desperate being so . . . wonderful. So *her*.

Jax turned to the guys. "Hey, you hungry? Layla brought enough to share."

She was already breaking the thick sandwiches in half. "I didn't know what you liked. This is my favorite."

Jax took a half. Wes and Ray sat on the tailgate and split the other sandwich.

Layla held up the soda cans. "Sorry. I only brought two."

"No worries. We've got plenty of water," Jax assured her.

She handed a can to him, then held the full bag of barbecue potato chips out to the guys, who each grabbed a big handful.

"Thank you, Layla. I'm Wes."

Everyone had their hands full, so Layla simply nodded instead of shaking hands.

"I'm Ray. Mighty nice of you to share." Ray ran his forearm over his sweaty brow. "We ate earlier, but I know Jax probably missed lunch."

"Probably breakfast, too," Wes added.

"I ate both," he grumbled.

Layla raised a brow at him.

"What? I had a granola bar for breakfast and two apples during the hayride out to the hot spring that you didn't show for."

"Was that today?" She bit her lip and tried to hide her guilt. "Sorry. I was painting. If I thought you'd be there, I would have gone. I bet it's really beautiful."

He put his hand on her thigh. "I'll take you for a private tour."

Wes gave him a knowing look, but said, "He wasn't supposed to be there but there were so many little ones running around, we thought it best to have extra hands to keep them safe."

Layla let out a wistful sigh. "I'm sorry I missed it."

Jax didn't like the regret in her eyes, so he suggested something else she'd like to see. "You should check out the orchard in the morning. When the sun's just coming up, it's all misty. You'd like the colors. The grays against the green and red as the light filters through all of it." He'd be happy and lucky to be the one to roll over in the morning and wake her. He'd make love to her, then take her to the orchard. He got hard just thinking about it.

She smiled up at him as much with her full lips as her eyes. "It sounds really pretty."

"Not as pretty as you," Wes said under his breath.

Jax smacked the bill of Wes's ball cap. "Keep your eyes off her."

Wes gave her a wicked grin, then stuffed a potato chip in his mouth. "He's so easy to rile when it comes to you."

He wasn't usually possessive like that. It didn't faze him if someone checked out the woman he was with. It made him feel good that she was on his arm and not someone else's. At least for the time they were together.

But with Layla, he wanted to keep her close, keep her all to himself.

They finished the simple meal. Wes and Ray stuffed the wrappers in the bag, then went to the cab to grab a couple bottles of water before they went back to repairing the fence.

Jax helped Layla off the tailgate. "I've got another half hour here before I'll be back to the stables to set up for the bonfire tonight. Do you want to come with me?"

"I can't. I'm meeting my client at his home for an early dinner. He wants to show me his view."

"That sounds like a line." He tried not to let his jealousy show, but it leaked out in his words and the glare he couldn't help leveling on her.

"Probably. But with the amount of money he's paying me to paint for him, I can't say no." She took a step closer. "Don't worry. The only cowboy I'm interested in kissing is you."

He gave her a soft, sweet kiss. "Good. Because I will see you later tonight, even if I have to burn the bar down to get out of there at a decent time."

Her eyes went wide. "Don't do that."

"No promises," he teased again.

She smacked his arm. "I enjoyed this picnic but I should go. I'm still distracting you." She tried to walk away.

He snagged her wrist and gently tugged her to a stop. "Damn it, Layla, I'm busy, yes, but that doesn't mean you're bothering me or keeping me from something else. It's just . . ."

"What?" She eyed him. "Your life. I get that, Jax. I was just trying to do something nice. Not make you feel guilty because you have obligations. I understand that. I'm having dinner with a man I hardly know because of it."

He hated that. "Don't go. I'll take you out instead."

She pressed her lips tight. "That's not the answer and you know it." She put her hand on his cheek and brushed her thumb just under his eye. "Every time I see you, you look exhausted."

"I know. I haven't had the time to hire anyone new."

"If you made the time for that, you'd have time for yourself. Better yet, delegate it to someone in your family who is less busy. Do it for yourself before you burn out completely."

"It's not that bad."

"Are you happy, Jax, being everything to everyone while you put your wants and desires on hold to cover for everyone else while you work yourself into an early grave? Because that's what it seems like you're doing. I mean, I'll take the ten minutes here, twenty minutes there because I want to spend time with you. But is that enough for you? Because I sure would like another night of dinner and dancing and kissing if you can find the time."

"Just not tonight." He frowned because she was right.

She narrowed her gaze. "That's not fair."

No it wasn't. He shouldn't take out his frustration on her.

"I've had this planned since before I came to Wyoming. The meeting has been moved twice. I can't move it again. This commission is the reason I'm here."

Jax hung his head. "You're right. I'm sorry. I am tired and now I'm angry that everything you're saying is true. I haven't done what needs to be done to free up my time. It used to be that I worked so much so I didn't have to think about all the parts of my life that aren't what I want them to be. I didn't have time to think about what's missing."

"And now?"

"Now there's a beautiful woman who wants me and I can't seem to find more than twenty minutes to spend with her today or the next three days because I'm drowning in work."

"Then ask for a lifeline. Your family loves you. They don't want to see you sink but swim and enjoy it while you're doing it." She was right. It didn't make it any easier to hear.

And it felt like one more task to add to his list of things to do.

He cupped her face and pulled her into a kiss. He poured everything he wanted to say into it, until they broke apart panting and holding on to each other with desperate grips. "I'll fix this."

"I know you will. I also know it will take some time. But it will be worth it in the long run to see you rested and happy and not carrying the Wilde world on your impressive shoulders."

He couldn't help but grin at her appreciative gaze. "You're so good for me."

"I want to be."

He kissed her again, this time with all the tenderness she pulled out of him with those simple words. "Don't be too nice to the guy tonight. Eat and run."

She slipped out of his hands with a breathy laugh. "I'll see what I can do."

"You'll see me later tonight. That's a promise."

"I think there's a lot of promise here, Jax. We just need to make room for each other in our lives." She climbed into the Jeep and drove away, leaving him with those words and hope that they could make this work and both be happy.

# Chapter Fourteen

Layla enjoyed the drive to her client's massive log cabin home on a huge sprawling spread. She could see why he'd chosen the gorgeous spot. From the top of the hill the house perched on, there was nothing but three-hundred-and-sixty-degree views of the mountains, fields, and forests.

The massive wooden front door opened the second she stepped out of her Jeep. She'd met Collin at a couple of different art gallery showings of her work over the last few years. He was a nice man. Kind of pretentious, but he earned it as one of the biggest movie and TV producers in the industry. The Wyoming ranch was just one of his many homes between LA and New York. He had wealth, power, and all that came with them, including some dirt slung at him for being a womanizer.

"You made it." He stepped close, took her by the shoulders, leaned in, and kissed her cheek. He didn't release her when he stared down at her. "April said you've been in the state awhile. Do you love it?"

She took a step to the side and his hands fell away, giving her space to move. She turned to stare at the view off the driveway that led to a small pond, daisies, and thick trees as the backdrop. "It's beautiful here. I've already finished several paintings and started painting a couple new ones." She turned to him, not realizing he'd moved so close again. Nervous, she tried to keep the conversation going. "I'd love to hear your thoughts on what you want."

His gaze swept her with pure lust, even though he maintained an easy grin.

She'd dressed in a simple navy dress that hugged her breasts and torso, then flared out in a wider skirt. She liked that it had short sleeves with pretty lace trim that matched the edging at the bottom of the skirt. Her tan wedge heels made her only about two inches shorter than him.

She much preferred Jax's towering height and brawn. It made her feel feminine and safe next to him. Jax just seemed so big and strong, his looks arresting, whereas Collin's LA polish seemed like he was trying too hard to get everyone to look at him and see his success.

"Dinner won't be ready for about an hour. I thought we'd walk the property, so you could see the gorgeous views. I know you'll like it as much as I do."

She held up her camera bag. "I'll take some pictures and you can choose one for the painting."

"Sounds great." He held one hand out for her to go to the right and put his other hand on her back.

She walked with him around the house to the sprawling deck, grass, and flowering gardens that gave way to the natural landscape some distance away.

He watched her looking out at the land. "You like it."

It took effort for her to turn away from all that stunning beauty and look at him. "It's breathtaking."

"This view . . . I love it in the evening when the sun's going down and you know you've got, like, an hour of light left and it seems like it changes every five minutes. It goes from bright golds that flash against the blue, then it's like the sky turns to fire. When there are clouds . . . they turn to dark red right before night creeps in. I don't know how that happens."

"The blue light scatters further in the atmosphere, and at a greater distance, making it appear yellow and red."

"Really?"

"The greater the distance light has to travel through the atmosphere, the deeper the red. On the California coast, you mostly get light to medium shades of pink. Particles in the atmosphere play a big role, too. Makes you wonder what color the sky would be without all the pollution."

"Out here, it's stunning. Which is why I commissioned you to do the painting. I want to take *this* back to my LA home. Or maybe my office. I spend more time there, even though I'd rather be here. I bought this house and the land specifically for this untamed view. It speaks to me on a deep level."

She appreciated his connection to this place. "What does it say to you? Perhaps I can capture that in the painting."

He waved his hand out in front of him. "It's pristine. Nature at its most glorious. Acres and acres where no person has tainted any of it with roads and buildings and billboards and electricity poles and wires. It just gets to be like this under the sun."

She looked up at his rapt gaze. "And *you* get to just *be*, here under the sun."

His gaze turned to hers. "Artists. They have a way of seeing things differently than others. Sometimes with more clarity than the rest of us. Your art speaks to me. There's always a sense of serenity, realism, and depth. That's what I want you to put into this scene."

"I will. And thank you for the compliment. I appreciate it."

"Let's go inside. I've got some nice pieces you might like to see. We'll eat dinner, then watch the sun set on the terrace. You can see it with your artist's eye so you can paint me the perfect moment in time."

They walked up to the house and Layla felt his attraction and interest in her but she didn't feel the same.

Collin was nice. He had a great eye for art. The floral paintings in his home gave the masculine log cabin bright colors and softness. The big, bold blooms in cool, deep blues, pinks, and purples against pristine white backgrounds stood out against the wood walls.

The huge painting of a deer head with massive antlers and a bold green background made you stop and stare. "I swear he's looking right at me."

Collin grinned. "I prefer a picture to the real thing stuffed and hung on a wall."

"The artist did a phenomenal job."

After the home and art tour, he ushered her into the dining room. A personal chef served them a decadent four-course dinner. Crab cake appetizers. A spinach salad with strawberries, pecans, and goat cheese. For the main course, filet mignon, steamed broccoli with garlic butter, and wild rice pilaf with mushrooms and peas. And dessert . . . chocolate soufflé. Perfection.

She had a single glass of crisp white wine, not her favorite Moscato but a lovely Riesling.

The conversation was light. They talked about art, a festival he'd attended in Italy while on a movie shoot. He'd shown her pictures on his phone of the Italian coast. She wanted to go. He offered to take her anytime if he got a painting out of it.

She didn't even entertain the idea and politely asked him to go on about his trip and the other places he'd been. She shared with him a few of her favorite destinations, too. "Though I don't know if I've ever been anywhere like Wyoming. There's something about this place." She thought of Jax, like she had often while in Collin's company, because she couldn't help comparing the two very different men. She loved the exquisite meal, but the company she wanted was Jax, not her client. And that's all she saw in Collin.

She glanced out the massive windows that overlooked the back of the property and noted how the sky and colors had changed while they ate.

"Dinner was amazing. Thank you. I will definitely need to thank your chef and see if he'll give me that rice pilaf recipe. Not that I could make it as well as him, but it was amazing."

Collin chuckled. "I'm sure he'd be happy to give it to you."

"If you don't mind, I'll get my camera. We'll go out and see if the view gives you that sense of just being that you love so much."

"I felt that way with you tonight. You're so easy to be around. You don't seem to expect me to be charming."

"I thought you were charming. You tell great stories. Which is probably why you're such a great producer."

His eyes went wide and filled with gratitude. "Thank you. It's been a while since someone saw that in what I do and didn't look at me like they wanted something."

Her phone rang and she used the opportunity to pull it out of her pocket and check it. "Sorry." She declined the call and put it away.

"Boyfriend?"

"No. That was my brother-in-law. My boyfriend's working tonight." She didn't even think about it before that came out of her mouth and had to catch herself. Is that what she wanted? Of course it was, why else would she ask Jax to her cabin tonight? Except for the fact he was probably the most gorgeous man she'd ever laid eyes on. But it was more than that. She liked him. And there was something drawing the two of them together.

"I see. And what does the lucky guy do at night?"

"He runs the Wilde Wind Ranch and owns the Dark Horse Dive Bar in Blackrock Falls."

"Really? I've heard of that place. They say it's a party every night."

"Seems that way. His sister Lyric took the stage the other night with a local band. They were fantastic. The crowd loved it. She has an amazing voice. So much strength and vulnerability in it. If I could sing like that . . ."

"You'd still be a painter," he teased. "It's in your blood." The boyfriend thing had thrown him, but he seemed at ease again with her now that he'd set aside the subtle flirting and lust-filled looks.

"Like making movies is in yours."

Collin set his napkin on the table. "Come. You don't want to miss the window for the best sunset you're ever going to see."

She'd seen some spectacular ones at Wilde Wind Ranch.

The hour they spent together at the back of the house was quieter, casual, and easy. Like two friends hanging out watching the sun go down. Every ten minutes or so, she snapped a bunch of photographs from different angles and vantage points. When the sun was just the merest sliver on the horizon and the colors went from gold to the black night sky lit with a million stars, she snapped the final photograph, thinking it would make an amazing painting in a bedroom. And that thought made her think of lying in bed with Jax, tangled up in the sheets and each other.

She pulled the memory card from the camera, put it in her tablet, and handed it over to Collin to scroll through the photographs to pick the one he liked best.

"This one. It's the perfect balance between the light of day and the coming darkness. All the colors are bright and sharp."

She tucked that description into her mind to make sure that's what the painting held for him when she was finished. She was already thinking of how she'd mix the colors to get just that shade of deep red and the soft oranges that would set off the pale yellow that brightened all of it.

Collin touched her shoulder. "You're already painting it in your head, aren't you?"

"I wish I had my stuff here with me now."

"I wish you were staying to see the sunrise with me."

Neither of them was getting what they wanted.

She didn't want to hurt his feelings. "Thank you for the invitation, but—"

"Some cowboy stole your heart."

"He's definitely roped it," she confessed. "We'll see what happens next."

Collin bumped his shoulder to hers. "Like I said. Lucky guy."

"I think I'm the lucky one. I never thought I'd feel this way again after I lost my husband."

His eyes softened with sympathy. "I was very sorry to hear about that."

"Thank you."

"All the good women who have come into my life have walked away disappointed. The business and LA eat people up. That's why I stopped dating people in the business, doesn't matter what position they hold. I like the people in the art world. They're pretentious like me, but in a different way." The self-deprecating grin made him all the more charming.

"Maybe what you need is someone who loves a great story and knows how to just be."

He stared at her with an *It's you* look in his eyes.

She tried to bow out gracefully. "I had a really lovely time. Thank you again for everything."

He rolled his eyes. "You're just so nice. Come on. I'll get that recipe and walk you out."

"Really?"

"It galls me that you're that excited about rice pilaf and wanting to paint rather than about me."

She laughed because she knew he was teasing. "Sorry. I promise not to try to steal your chef on my way out."

"Don't even think about it," he warned.

She really did like him.

While she packed up her tablet and camera gear, Collin got her the recipe and a container of leftover rice pilaf to take home. "You sure you can part with this?"

He smirked and shook his head. "I know you consider it as precious as gold, but I want you to enjoy it."

She hugged him. "Thank you. I can't really say how long it will take to finish the painting. It's a large piece." It would be the largest canvas she'd ever done, but he had a space in mind for it.

He walked her out to the car. "Take your time. If for whatever reason it doesn't feel right and you need to start over or whatever to get it just right, I understand."

She stowed her bag and the container on the passenger seat and turned to Collin. "I just want you to know it's really flattering that you asked me to paint this place for you. And I want to thank you for bringing me here. After I lost my husband, painting wasn't the same for me. My grief stole the joy in it. The colors just never seemed right. When I accepted the commission, I felt like the worst had passed and I was back to my old self. And then I arrived here and it was like everything was brighter, more complex, and the last remnants of what had been obscuring my true vision of the world were gone. I found my inspiration and excitement again."

"That have something to do with the guy you met here?"

"Maybe a little, but it was you who brought me to this wonderful place and showed me what inspired you so much that you want to take a piece of it back with you to LA." She pursed her mouth and gave him another truth. "I was also flattered by your offer to stay the night even if I didn't accept. You're not what I expected."

"My reputation is inflated, both lies and truth with a lot of in-between, so I understand that."

She knew all about thinking one thing was true because someone said it or made you believe it, but then you found out they were something else entirely. "You should stay here more and there less."

"Maybe I will. Thank you for coming. It was a really good night. I haven't had one of those in a long time."

"You're welcome. Good night, Collin."

"I hope I see you soon, Layla."

She slipped into the car, started the engine, and waved to him before she pulled out down the long driveway. At the bottom, just outside the gate, she stopped to text Jax.

**LAYLA:** On my way home.
**JAX:** Bar is busy but I'm going to try to get out early.

LAYLA: I'll be back in about an hour. See you at the cabin WHENEVER you can make it.

JAX: How did it go tonight?

LAYLA: Great. Beautiful view, lovely dinner, we talked about traveling.

JAX: Sounds nice.

She didn't want to hide anything from him and sent another text.

LAYLA: He asked me to stay and watch the sunrise with him.

JAX: WTF

JAX: If you're trying to make me jealous, it's working.

She grinned and her heart felt lighter just knowing he cared.

LAYLA: He's jealous of YOU because you're the only one I want to see tonight and at sunrise.

JAX: Hurry up and get here!!!

LAYLA: On my way.

# Chapter Fifteen

Jax couldn't stop thinking about Layla's words about how he put everyone first and himself last. He never really felt that way because he was doing what he wanted to do, working the ranch and the bar with his family.

But something had to give.

Helen still haunted him, even though they hadn't been together for three years. Since their breakup he'd never wanted to be with a woman for anything more than a mutually beneficial good time, no strings attached. A few even tried to change his mind about it. Until Layla, he'd never even considered something more.

With her, he couldn't seem to help himself.

So he asked one of the other bartenders to cover for him, and Aria and Melody gave him matching knowing smirks when he grabbed a bottle of Layla's favorite wine and beat it out of the bar in a rush right after Layla's texts. He stopped at the drugstore for a box of condoms and randomly grabbed her a gerbera daisy plant with deep pink blooms because he thought she'd like it.

He arrived at the cabin before Layla and took a seat

on the steps, taking a long moment to consider what this meant to him. For them.

What did he really want?

His thoughts were circling when he heard her car pull in behind the cabin. He was still sitting on the step when she walked around and stood in front of him, a sweet smile on her face and a plastic container in her hands, along with her camera case.

That smile lit up his world and he knew exactly what he wanted with her.

"Hi." She smiled down at him. "I hope you haven't been waiting long."

He tilted his head and just looked at her beautiful face. "I don't think there's a man alive who wouldn't wait an eternity for you."

She sucked in a breath and held it.

"I feel like I've been waiting forever. And finally, here you are, all mine." He didn't know if she understood that he meant, not just for tonight like they'd planned, but for . . . everything.

"I tried so hard to do the whole dinner-with-a-client thing. And I have to admit, he was a handsome, nice, smart man, who made me feel pretty, smart, and talented, everything he liked." She shrugged one shoulder. "And all I thought about was the way you look at me. The way you're looking at me right now. I feel like I'm everything you like, but the wanting, the need, the connection I feel to you . . . No one compares. So thanks for bringing my favorite wine and the sweet little plant. I appreciate them. But all I want, all I need, is you." She leaned down and kissed him like she'd never get to do it again.

He wanted to put his hands on her. He wanted to slide his hands up her legs and under her dress and feel her soft skin against his rough hands. He wanted to strip her bare and just stare at all her pretty perfection. Then he wanted to find all the spots on her lithe body with his fingertips and tongue that made her moan his name.

Hell, he'd settle for dragging her into his lap and kissing her all night.

She broke the kiss, set down her bag and the plastic bin, and was about to straddle his lap when her phone rang. She groaned, took it out of her bag, glared at the thing, swiped the screen, barked, "Stop calling me," hung up, took his hand, grabbed the rest of her stuff in the other, and pulled him into the cabin.

He didn't know what just happened. "Who was that?"

"The only thing that is important right now is you." She dropped her camera bag on the bistro table, put the container in the fridge, then turned to him with a look of intent on her face.

He left the plant and wine on the table. With the drugstore bag in his hand, he walked her backward into the bedroom. She had his thermal off and on the floor before they cleared the door. Her lips left a trail of kisses over his chest as her hands went to the buckle on his belt. The leather slid out of the loops on his jeans with a whoosh and the metal clanked on the floor when she dropped it. She undid the button and zipper on his jeans, her hand sliding into them and clamping onto his hard cock. He groaned.

"It's been a while for me, so I'm a little impatient,"

she warned. "Catch up," she ordered on her next breath and rubbed her hand up and down his shaft, making his eyes roll back in his head.

He knew how to follow directions and didn't waste time. He reached down just enough to drag his hands up her legs, gathering the material of her dress at his wrists. He swept his hands up over her hips and torso and took the dress right up over her head and let it fly so he could cup her breasts in his hands. "I'm impatient, too, but that doesn't mean I'm going to finish this before I really get a taste of you."

She shoved his jeans and boxer briefs down over his ass as far as she could reach. "We have all night."

He cupped her face and made her look at him. "I want more than that."

"You can have whatever you want."

Both of them stared at each other in the soft light filtering in from the security lights outside the cabins. He didn't think she'd grasped the depth of meaning in what she'd said, just like he hadn't, until the words had left their lips and they looked at each other realizing they meant it.

He did want more.

He backed her to the bed and guided her down, taking her bra off as she lay back, then reaching for the scrap of matching black lace at her hips. He removed that as she scooted back on the bed, her gaze locked on him. Appreciation and lust filled her eyes as they traveled over his shoulder, chest, and abdomen until she stared at his thick length standing proud and oh so ready to be buried inside her.

It only took a few seconds to pull off his boots,

shuck the rest of his clothes, grab the condoms from the bag he'd dropped at his feet, and crawl up over her. He handed her the box. "You open that, while I"—he swept his gaze down her body, then back up—"indulge." He closed his mouth over one pink-tipped nipple and sucked it into his mouth.

She arched up and moaned his name.

"You like that." He did it again to her other nipple while pinching the one he'd just left between his thumb and finger. One hand slid over his head, her nails scraping his scalp as she held him to her. He swirled the tip of his tongue around the tight bud. Her hips rose up against his, her slick folds meeting his hard length. All he wanted to do was bury himself in her.

"You want me inside you . . . condom." He licked and laved her breast again and she abandoned her quest to open the condom box so she could slide her hands over his shoulders and through his hair, urging him on.

As much as he liked her plump breasts, there was somewhere else he wanted to touch and taste, so he headed south, kissing his way down her chest, sneaking a dip of his tongue into her navel, then pressing one open-mouthed kiss after another down her lower belly, over her mound, until he licked her soft folds from bottom to top. He clamped his hands on her legs, then pushed her thighs wide to make room for his shoulders and splay her legs so she was open and bare to him. He looked up over her and caught her staring down at him.

"You look like heaven and taste like sin." He dipped his head and thrust his tongue inside her. Her hips rose off the bed to meet his exploring tongue. He slipped his hand under her ass and held her in place and used his other hand to slide one finger deep while he licked her clit with the flat of his tongue.

She moaned and raked her fingers through his hair as he settled in. He didn't want to be anywhere but here. He wasn't kidding about her addictive taste. All her little moans and mewling sounds went straight to his cock. He could get off on just the sounds she made and the bite of her nails raking over his shoulders.

He stroked her again, then added a second finger, stretching her as he slid both in and barely grazed his teeth over her sensitive clit, making the ripple of tension in her core tighten as he sucked her clit and sent her over the edge. She pushed against his mouth and he licked his tongue over her clit again, sending a wave of aftershocks through her. She was so responsive and wet for him.

He kissed the inside of her thigh and reached up to her shoulder where she'd left the unopened box. He took care of the condom, while she fell limp and came back to herself. He couldn't help the satisfied grin that he'd done that to her, then he pushed her thighs wide and nudged the tip of his aching cock an inch inside her and waited for her to look at him before he thrust balls deep into her.

He savored the moment of pure ecstasy and the feel of her tight around him, holding him inside her like they were one. He leaned down and kissed her. She put both hands on his face and kissed him back, her tongue tangling with his, her teeth nipping his lower lip, right before she rolled her hips against him. He didn't think he could get any deeper, but somehow that move made him sink in and she moaned into his mouth. He lost it and pulled out, then sank deep again in long, sure glides that had both of them breathing hard.

One of her hands landed on his ass, squeezed tight, and pulled him in as he thrust deep again. Her other hand slipped between them and she touched herself, making her inner muscles clench. She went over the edge and he chased her with a few more quick, hard thrusts until his balls clenched and he spilled himself inside her.

He didn't want to crush her, but she'd wrung him out. He fell on top of her, his face in her neck as his hot breath fanned over their damp skin. He managed to brace his forearms under him and take some of his weight off her and realized she was holding him so close, he could barely move. If that's what she liked, he'd stay right where he was and enjoy the feel of her fingers brushing over his sweaty skin.

It took a second for him to realize the moisture that fell across his cheek wasn't from him. He shifted just enough to see her face and spot the trail of tears leaking out the sides of her closed eyes.

He pressed up and tried to move off her, but she held him in place. "Did I hurt you? Layla, I'm sorry." He tried to move again, but she shook her head, her grip so tight on his sides her nails dug into his skin, and she wouldn't let go.

He pressed his forehead to hers. "Layla, sweetheart, look at me."

She didn't open her eyes. "It's never been like that."

He stared down at her, his head pounding and his mind reeling. "Just tell me what hurt, what you didn't like, I'll fix it. I can be soft and slow and anything you want. I just want you to feel as good as you make me feel. Let me make this right."

She shook her head and continued to hold on to him for dear life instead of pushing him away like he expected, making him completely confused and feel like shit that he'd made her cry.

Finally she opened those gorgeous green eyes. He expected to see all kinds of recriminations, but all he saw was an apology. "I'm sorry. You're wonderful and amazing and such a good guy for putting up with this."

He went utterly still. "I don't understand. Are you hurt?" At this point, he'd slipped out of her as gently as possible, but she still wouldn't let him roll off her.

"I'm fucking fantastic and I don't know what to do with that. Sex has always been . . ." She made a bland face. "It was nice. But that . . . you . . . us . . ."

He grinned. "You're about to start stuttering."

She cupped his face and looked him in the eyes. "I know this is going to go straight to your head, but I don't care. You showed me everything I've been missing." Her gaze went soft, her eyes filled with tears again. "I didn't know it could be like that. I could really feel how much you wanted me, how much you liked touching me and being inside me, that it was me that made you lose yourself and just let go."

He didn't know how to process what she was telling him, but he knew it was important and ran deep. He gently brushed his thumb along her soft cheek. "What you do to me is make me want you so bad, I'd do just about anything to keep you happy and in this bed with me forever. Yes, I'm attracted to you, but it's so much more than that. Maybe that's what you're feeling, too.

"I think you're gorgeous and sexy and the way your body moves against me, the way I feel locked inside you . . . Yes, it makes sex amazing because we feel something more for each other. And I'm sorry if your husband didn't make you feel that way. But I'm not sorry I'm the one who gets to do that now, because you deserve a lover who cares that you *love* it, not just like it. Because if you love it with me, then I am going to be a very happy man reminding you over and over again why you love being naked with me so you don't want to be naked with anyone else. Ever. Not even that asshole who asked you to stay with him tonight."

"I didn't stay with him. I came home to you, the only man who's ever made me feel like this. The only one I want to do it again with." She smiled wolfishly. "Or maybe I'll have my way with you this time."

He groaned and kissed her softly. "Let me clean up, then you can have your wicked way with me." And he'd enjoy every minute of it, and then return the favor because he would never get enough of his Layla.

# Chapter Sixteen

Layla sat on the end corner of the bed. It wasn't often she sketched, but something about having a gorgeous, naked man in her bed, who looked absolutely well used and satisfied, made her want to capture the moment. A picture wouldn't do. Jax would probably make her delete it. Maybe he'd even burn the sketch, but she simply had to draw him.

The dim light in the room only made him look more ruggedly handsome. She wanted to capture the shadows and light, the planes and dips of his sculpted muscles, the softness of his lips, the hard line of his jaw, the texture of all that dark hair that she loved to slide her fingers through and hold while he did all kinds of erotic things to her body.

She knew just how to finish the painting she'd started of Jax, now that she knew him in a deeper, intimate way.

She couldn't believe she'd cried after what they shared together last night. Just a few hours ago really. And then, like, twenty minutes after that. And another couple of hours after that.

She should be asleep, snuggled up close to him.

She was until about a half hour ago.

Now she traced the line of the sheet that barely covered one leg and that very delicious private part of him that she enjoyed to the fullest. His other leg was bent at the knee and lightly dusted with dark hair. He had big feet, toned calves, and thick thighs. Ranch work did a body good. All of him was built strong and lean. She'd already finished her study of his chest and abs and had them replicated on the page to perfection. She could still feel his strong arms holding her close. That face. She could look at it forever.

But it was what was on the inside that really made her heart beat faster and melt all at the same time. He'd been so concerned about her last night, then he'd said those wonderful things about wanting to be the man who made her feel everything he made her feel during sex. It wasn't just that the caresses and kisses made her want. It was that he made her burn with desperation for more. She didn't just go through the motions to get to the climax. She wanted to bring him to that point, and then do it again, because pleasing him made her feel so good. When he made her come, she saw it on his face and in his eyes, he'd been just as turned on by that as he was when his turn came.

It had all been so . . . she didn't know how to describe it, except that it had been about them finding that special place together.

She thought it was exceptional the first time. And then they shared that same magic the second time and the third. She had no doubt they'd feel that way when they made love again. They made each other burn every time they touched, it just felt so right and passionate; like an extension of the huge feelings building inside each of them. Because she didn't doubt that Jax felt about her the way she felt about him.

She stared at the finished drawing and then at the man lying in front of her and sighed out her contentment. She'd come here to paint and maybe get a fresh start on her life after Christopher. She got so much more than she expected.

Jax wasn't just any man. He was one who took care of the people he loved, the places that belonged to him, and the things that mattered.

He reached out the hand that had been resting on his rock-hard abs to her empty side of the bed. When he didn't find her, his eyes opened and filled with concern when he spotted her at the end of the bed staring at him. "What are you doing, sweetheart?" That sexy, sleepy, rumbly voice made her insides quicken with need.

She turned the large sketch pad toward him. "You are the sexiest view I've ever seen."

His eyes went wide as he studied the picture she'd drawn of him. "Every time I think I know how talented you are, you blow my mind again. That's . . . impressive."

"*You* really are," she teasingly agreed.

He laughed under his breath. "I think you made me look better than I do."

She turned the pad toward her and looked at it, then at him again. "It's exactly right. Every line and curve. All your strength and softness. The confidence you exude even in your sleep. All the rumpled goodness that you are is right here."

"Exactly. You made me look like that." He rose up, took the pad, tossed it onto the floor, took her hand, and pulled her over him. "Now do it again." And then he kissed her and she lost herself in his arms.

# Chapter Seventeen

For the last two weeks, Jax woke up every morning happy because Layla was sleeping next to him.

After Helen, he'd infrequently spent the night with other women at their places. But it never felt comfortable. He was always up and out the door by dawn.

With Layla, he wanted to linger. He liked holding her. He liked seeing her sleepy eyes open and a smile bloom on her lips when she woke up.

He liked staying with her in the cabin. It felt like their private little getaway. He didn't want to go back to his bed in the main house. He liked that at any given time during the day he could go down to the cabin and find Layla relaxing, drawing, or painting.

They'd gotten into a routine of getting up early and having their coffee together. He was late out the door a lot because he liked making love to her before he left and seeing her all rumpled in their bed. Which always reminded him of that detailed drawing she'd done of him before she'd hidden it so he couldn't destroy it. He didn't think he could actually do that though, because he loved that that was how she saw him.

Lyric popped up in the bar's office doorway and put

her hands on the frame and stared at him. "There's something strange on your face."

He brushed his hand over his mouth and cheek. "Did I get it?"

"No, it's still there. I think they call it a smile, though it's hard to tell when you do it, since I haven't seen it in forever."

He shook his head. "Ha. Ha. Very funny. What's up?"

"You tell me. How are things with Layla?"

"Fucking amazing." He didn't have to lie or pretty it up. That was the God's honest truth.

"Then what I have to ask you probably won't be a big deal."

He raised a brow. "What is it?"

"Helen scheduled a catering appointment for later today. I just saw it on the calendar and thought I'd better ask you first if I should go through with it."

"Really?" After the breakup, they'd silently agreed to steer clear of each other. She didn't come to the bar. He avoided her in town. And maybe that was stupid. The bar was really the only place around where everyone came to socialize, have fun, listen to live music, and eat the best food in town, thanks to his sister.

Lyric stepped up to the desk. "I'm all for sticking with the Wildes-back-Wildes code. But I thought since I've heard rumors through the family grapevine that you prefer sleeping with a certain blonde than in your own bed, you might not care what your ex does anymore."

Living at home sucked. He had no privacy.

He did have a bunch of money saved up and thought now might be the time to really start thinking about getting his own place like Lyric and Mason had done a couple months back.

He thought about Helen's request and waited to see if he felt anything.

Nope. Nothing.

"I don't care what Helen does anymore. That's all in the past. I think it's time we both moved on and let it go."

Lyric eyed him, curiosity written on her face. "What exactly are you letting go of? Because you never said what ultimately made you end things."

"She wanted things to be on her terms and didn't think about my feelings. And then she did something I couldn't forget or forgive because she never gave me the chance to be on the same page with her in the first place."

"That doesn't make a hell of a lot of sense, but I feel like it sucks."

"It really did. And that's why I like Layla so much. She's not afraid to say what's on her mind, or tell me how she feels. And if you're going to be with some-one, shouldn't they be able to tell you anything?"

"Absolutely. Mason and I have no secrets. I saw the painting that she did of Moon up at the ranch house the other day when I went to take care of the horses. I swung by her studio afterward to say hi and ended up begging her to do one of Bruin for me."

Jax gaped at her. "Are you serious? Her paintings sell for hundreds of thousands of dollars. You can't just ask her to paint something for you."

"I don't actually expect her to do it. I just blurted it out."

"Knowing her, how kind and generous she is, she will. And you can sell it and put three or four kids through college with it."

Lyric plopped into the seat in front of him. "Does it bother you that she makes that kind of money?"

He shrugged like it didn't matter, but of course it did. "I don't know how I feel about it, except that I'm proud of her. She's amazing and so talented. Painting seems effortless when I watch her, but I know it's not. She's so meticulous about the perfect color, the right shade, the play of light and dark, the feeling she wants to evoke. I walked in the other night and she said the yellow was too dark. I stared at the painting for a full minute, trying to see what she saw. But I only saw a pretty yellow. She saw that it made the painting feel like the wrong season." He held up his hands and dropped them. "How would anyone know what season she painted without snow or spring flowers or dead leaves? The yellow in the sunset didn't say that to me."

Lyric laughed under her breath. "Maybe it's like music. A note was off. Flat. Sharp. Too high-pitched. Whatever it was, it messed up the composition of the whole."

"That actually makes a hell of a lot more sense to me now. No wonder you two seem to get along so well. You understand the same concepts."

"She seems to relate to you really well."

"I don't know how I got so fucking lucky. Seriously, what did I ever do that brought me her?"

Lyric stood, came around the desk, and put her hand on his shoulder. "From the moment she arrived, you saw her. She saw you. Whatever it was in the universe that brought you together . . . kismet . . . fate . . . you should thank your lucky stars and hold on to her. I've never seen you this happy. You've never spent this much time with a woman since Helen. I know what it feels like to want to be with someone that much, so much so, you'll do anything for just another minute with them." Lyric's cell pinged with a text message. She turned it to him. "Speak of the devil."

**MASON:** I'm yours and I love that you're mine
**MASON:** I miss you
**MASON:** Can't wait to see you tonight

Jax stared up at his sister. "You should definitely marry that guy."

Lyric grinned, her eyes glassed over with emotion. "I already said yes." The wedding was coming up quick. "But the ceremony is just a formality when there's love like this. I know you and Layla just started seeing each other, but does it feel like this with her?"

"Yes. I think it does. I just want to be with her. I don't want to think about her ever going home. I just want, like I've never wanted before. The thought of waking up without her . . . it terrifies me. Because I know the fallout would be a million times worse than my breakup with Helen, and I didn't think anything could be worse than her tearing my heart to shreds."

He thought about that and found his answer was wrong. "Actually it wasn't even Helen, really, but the possibility of what could have been that devastated me the most. I know what I have with Layla is different and special and worth whatever we might have to face together. Right now, I'm just holding on while we settle into it."

"Maybe when it's something this big, Jax, you don't settle into it, you live it out loud." She kissed him on the head, then went back around the desk. "Mason's working at home today. I've got the kitchen covered, so I'm going home. Be back in an hour." The mischievous grin made him shake his head.

"I hate that I know why you're going home and what you'll be doing." He cringed, thinking of his sister grabbing a quickie with Mason, and wiped that out of his head.

"Maybe you should text Layla and see what she's doing. Who knows? Maybe you'll get lucky, too."

He threw a pencil at her. It hit the wall because he wasn't really aiming for her, anyway. He had a lot of work to catch up on, but he did text Layla, because if it made her as happy as Mason's words made Lyric, totally worth it.

JAX: I'm thinking about you
JAX: I'm ALWAYS thinking about you
JAX: You're brilliant and you're mine
JAX: I wish you were here with me right now
JAX: Whatever you're looking at right now I hope it's as beautiful as you
JAX: If you were here I'd have the perfect view

He waited to see if he got a response, knowing she was probably working and too focused to check her phone. She often got lost in her art. And that was okay. When she saw the messages later, he knew she'd appreciate them. That's all he wanted, to make her day a little brighter and better, the way she always made his that way.

# Chapter Eighteen

Layla walked into the Dark Horse Dive Bar about an hour after Jax had texted her, with a small canvas in her hand and him on her mind. She couldn't get to him fast enough, but first she'd had to do something to show him how much those sweet messages meant to her. And she did that with her art.

Aria was behind the bar checking bottles. "Hey, Layla. He's in the office. Whatcha got there?"

She held up the painting. "My heart. It's for him."

Aria grinned, her eyes bright with delight. "Well, okay, then."

Layla pointed down the hall. "That way?"

Aria nodded. "Go get him."

"Thank you." She headed down the hall and found the door with the OFFICE sign on it. She tried the handle, found it locked, and knocked.

He opened the door and stared at the canvas she held up in front of her.

"This is what you do to me. You light up my heart and make it melt all at the same time." And that's what she'd painted, a big red heart melting with a background of blazing light coming out of it.

For a few seconds all he did was look at the painting, then her, then back at the painting. "You painted that and then came here to see me because of the texts I sent? You painted that in, what? Like, less than a half hour?"

She looked down at the painting. "I mean, it's not my best work, but I just . . . sometimes I don't know what to say, so I paint."

"All the rays of light are tiny little hearts. The entire heart is made up of tiny little hearts."

"I did it with the brushstrokes because a heart is like that. A whole. But it can break. You lose pieces of it sometimes. You give pieces of it away." She met his gaze. "*You* stole the whole damn thing."

"You signed it."

She held it out. "Because it's yours."

He carefully took the painting, using his fingertips on the inside edge so he didn't smear any of the paint. He looked around the office, looking for somewhere to put it, she guessed, then he took one of the framed documents off the wall and hung the painting there. He stared at it again for a long moment, then turned to her.

She was still standing in the doorway, trying to read his mood and figure out what he was thinking, when he walked to her, pulled her into the room, slammed the door, then backed her into it, taking her mouth in a searing kiss.

She was wearing a simple pair of loose-fitting olive-green linen overalls and a white T-shirt with sandals. Jax undid the straps and the overalls fell to the floor in a puddle at her feet. Jax was kissing her and undoing his jeans at the same time. While he kept her occupied with his mouth, tangling his tongue with hers, he somehow pulled out his wallet and a condom and sheathed himself. She managed to shimmy out of her panties and kick her clothes to the side just in time for Jax to grab her by the backs of her thighs and haul her up so she could wrap her legs around his waist.

"I need to be inside you."

She had no objection.

Jax did manage to slow down enough to slide his fingers between them to make sure she was ready. She was dying for him.

"Fuck. You're so wet." He slammed into her, hard and deep.

Her back pressed against the door. Jax kept his hands clamped on her hips and drove into her again and again. She mostly held on and went along for the ride. He thrust deep and rubbed against her. She went over the crest, trying not to be loud, but at this point, she had no control. Her body was still contracting around Jax's thick cock when he slid out and back in. The long strokes kept up until her inner muscles were holding on to him and letting go with each thrust.

Jax picked up speed again, but kept that even push and pull, then he slipped his hand between them. "Look at me."

She found those blue, blue eyes had gone deep blue with desire.

Jax brushed his thumb over her clit and she felt the rush of completion coming on for both of them. Then he pressed on the nub and sent her over the edge again. His eyes filled with satisfaction and something so warm and intense she wanted to believe it was love. Then he slammed into her once, then twice, and groaned out his pleasure as he pinned her hard to the door and buried his face in her neck, biting her pulse point and sending a wave of aftershocks through her. Nothing sounded better than Jax's "So fucking fantastic."

Her strong man held her close and walked the couple of steps to the small sofa and sat with her straddling his lap. She cuddled up to his chest, his arms wrapped around her. She didn't mind that she was half naked and he still had all his clothes on, though his jeans were down around his thighs. "Someone could come in and see us."

"Trust me. If anyone saw you come back here, they aren't interrupting us." He nuzzled her hair and tightened his hold on her. "I fell for you the second I saw you. I thought that was it. I was in. But somehow you make me fall deeper and deeper, until I'm drowning in you and all the sweet perfection of this thing we have together. I don't ever want to come up for air. I just want to be here, like this, with you."

Amazed by his words and feeling everything he was feeling, she leaned back and saw the love so clear in his eyes.

He put his hands on each side of her head, their gazes locked. "How do you do it? How do you make me want and need you so much?"

"You do the same to me. What you said in those texts . . . it was so honest and raw and open. I appreciate that you can be that way with me."

"I miss you all the time. And I know that's mostly my fault because I'm working so much. But Lyric was here earlier and she got a text from Mason. She showed it to me. He just wanted her to know he was thinking about her. He couldn't wait to see her. So he told her, not expecting that she'd do anything about it because she was at work. He just wanted her to know it. Do you know how often I think about you?"

She brushed her fingers over his jaw. "I hope it's as much as I think about you."

"But isn't it better when I tell you? Then there's no guessing or wondering. This is the most honest relationship I think I've ever had and I want it to be just like today. Where you know how I feel, and it makes you create something beautiful and come to me to tell me that it matters."

She touched her forehead to his. "You matter, Jax. And you've made it very clear that you care deeply for me, too. So if you've harbored any doubts about us, I hope those have faded now."

"Is it hard for you to be in a new relationship?"

"I was ready long before I came here, I just hadn't thought I'd find someone I could trust to move on with. But what I think you really want to ask me is, am I still in love with him? I will always love the Christopher I married and cherish the memories I have of that time I had with him. I didn't love the man he turned out to be, which is why I'd asked him for a divorce, though he died before I filed."

Jax's gaze narrowed. "He killed himself. Because you left him?"

"For a long time I thought so, but April made me

see that he did it because he was a weak man who couldn't live with *his* mistakes and how he hurt the people he loved the most."

"What really happened? You never really said."

She pressed up and looked down at them. "I can't talk about it when we've just shared something this . . . changing. Ask me again later. I'll tell you everything. I promise."

He rubbed his hands up and down her thighs, understanding in his warm eyes. "Okay. You're right. This isn't the time to talk about exes."

She raised a brow, catching a tone in his voice. "Something you want to share about someone you used to know?"

It took him a minute to respond. "It's a secret I've kept a long time. But yeah, I want to tell you. I think you'll understand. But you're right. Now isn't the time or place for revealing past pain."

"There's no rush, Jax. When you're ready."

"That's just it . . . I am ready to share everything with you."

"Okay. But we should at least be in the same state of dress when we reveal our hearts. It's only fair." She could feel the blush heating her cheeks.

"It's adorable that you're embarrassed to be half naked with me when you've been completely bare with my face between your legs more than once."

The heat turned to an inferno. "I'm more concerned about someone else finding us like this."

"Don't be. I'd never let that happen." He pointed his chin toward the bottom of the door, where he'd shoved the wedge under it to keep it closed rather than open.

"I don't want to share you, or what we have together, with anyone."

She kissed him softly. "Thank you. That's sweet."

He lightly smacked her bottom. "I love that you came, and we did this, but I have work to do."

She slid off his lap and grabbed her clothes off the floor. "Bathroom?" she asked, pulling the loose overalls up and stuffing her panties in one of the pockets. "I'll just clean up, then head back to the studio to finish what I was working on before you distracted me in the best way."

He tugged up his boxers and jeans. "Come on, I need to ditch the condom." He removed the wedge, kicked it to the side, then opened the door and let her go out first. "The ladies' room is just past the men's. Meet me out in the bar before you leave."

She took care of herself and got her panties back on, then went to find Jax in the bar. The office door was closed, so she headed out into the main room. The bar opened in another hour, so the place was bright and looked much bigger than when it was packed with people. The floors were clean, along with the tables and chairs. Aria was still behind the bar stocking the fridge with bottles of beer. "Have you seen Jax?"

"He ran into the kitchen to get something. I take it from that pretty flush on your cheeks that Jax liked his painting."

"I like *her* more," Jax said, coming out of the kitchen with a to-go bag in his hand. "So stop teasing her, or she'll never come back here."

Aria stuck her tongue out at her brother. "There's blue and red paint in your hair."

Layla pulled her blond hair over her shoulder to look at it.

"I meant in Jax's hair. I wonder how it got there."

Layla held up her paint-splattered hands, then bit her bottom lip and looked up at Jax's smiling face. "Sorry."

"I've already learned it washes out. And you can put your hands on me anytime you want." He held up the bag. "For you."

She took it. "What is it?"

"I'm guessing by the way your stomach was grumbling just a little while ago that you haven't eaten since I made you eggs and fried potatoes this morning, so this is apparently your lunch, even though we're closing in on dinnertime."

She scrunched her lips, feeling caught for losing track of time. "I got busy."

"You got lost in your art, which is fine, except you need to eat. Chicken and cheese flautas, two fried chicken drumsticks, a garden salad, and some really awesome potato skins. Not exactly healthy eating but it's all good."

She opened the bag and inhaled the scent. "Amazing. I don't deserve you. You're the best. Thank you."

He chuckled. "I'm pretty sure I'm the one not deserving, but I'm keeping you all the same."

"Hey," Aria called out. "Take that happiness and love outside. Some of us are alone. And men suck. Not you, but men."

Jax shook his head at his sister. "Seriously. I'm a man."

"You're my brother. That's different. You're yucky in a different way and I love you anyway."

"Thanks." Jax turned back to Layla and dropped his voice to a whisper. "Her ex cheated on her and she booted him to the curb."

"That kind of betrayal leaves a mark."

Jax stared intently at her. "Yeah. There are lots of ways to hurt someone." He brushed his hand down her long hair. "Listen, I'm off early tonight."

"Nice. You work too hard."

"Which is why I'm hiring a couple new people for the ranch and one for the bar. It's going to take some time to get them up to speed and working on their own, but soon I'll have more time for us. Okay?"

Her heart did that flutter thing he always made it do when he was like this. "I'd love that."

"And there's something else I want to talk to you about, too, but later when we're alone."

"Sure. Whenever you want."

He kissed her softly and she felt the promise of him wanting to be with her again soon. "Drive safely. Eat before you dive back into painting."

"The one I gave you needs time to dry, so just leave it until it does. At least several hours."

"I'm not leaving it in the office. What's that thing worth?"

"What's it worth to you?"

His gaze sharpened. "Everything. It's a piece of you."

She kissed him. "That's the right answer. That's everything." She turned and headed for the door, but glanced back and said, "I can't wait to see you tonight."

It was important to tell the person you cared about that they mattered.

And the look in Jax's eyes when she said it was worth so much more than the simple gesture she'd done for him.

This was the foundation they were building their relationship on. With each new thing they discovered about each other and the days they spent like this communicating in ways that strengthened the bond between them, they turned their connection into a lasting and thriving unbreakable love.

Her heart wanted that to be real and true so badly; she didn't let doubt creep in and steal this amazing feeling building inside her that they could make it happen. Together.

# Chapter Nineteen

Jax hurried through the bar payroll and paid the bills. But sitting in his office after Layla left only made him think about her and what they'd done up against the door. He should have used a little more finesse. Taking her somewhere more private and appropriate probably would have scored him some points. But Layla hadn't seemed to mind.

He glanced up at the painting on the wall, so out of place in here, but so perfectly right for him. He loved it. And every time he looked at it, he'd think of her.

He wasn't lying. All he thought about was her. Which was why he wanted to get out of here and meet her at the cabin. Maybe he could barbecue a couple of steaks and they could have dinner together. He'd grab a bottle of her favorite wine from the bar before he left.

He was so glad he'd ordered the case. According to Aria, it had become popular with the ladies, even at the elevated price from their usual fare, and she'd ordered a few more cases.

After he cleared his desk, he went out to make sure everything was running smoothly. The bar opened ten minutes ago and wouldn't get busy for a couple of hours. The early birds were perched at the bar, a few at the tables. His sister Melody was running orders out to everyone. Aria was chatting up someone at the bar.

Lyric came out of the kitchen with her catering binder tucked under her arm and headed to the woman Aria was handing a glass of water. The woman turned on the stool to greet Lyric and it finally dawned on him why she looked familiar, though she'd gained some weight and her hair was longer.

"Helen." He knew Lyric was going to help her with a party, but he didn't expect to see her here.

She turned to him fully. She'd more than just gained weight, she looked nearly ready to pop.

"You're pregnant." Shock blanked out everything but that in his mind as he reeled.

She rubbed her hand over the mound of her belly. "Jax. Lyric said you probably wouldn't be here."

"You're pregnant." He really couldn't get past that.

"Jax, what's wrong?" Lyric looked from him to Helen and back.

He zeroed in on Helen's hand over her protruding belly, like she was protecting the baby. "I haven't heard anything about you getting married. So who knocked you up?"

"Jax," Aria snapped. "Seriously?"

He was acting like an ass, but he'd earned it, even if his sisters knew nothing about why this affected him so much.

Helen's face flamed red.

He didn't know if he'd embarrassed her, or she was angry. He didn't care. Not after what she'd done to him.

Her lips fell into a frown, her eyes pleading with him to understand. "I've upset you. That wasn't my intention. I really hoped it wouldn't be like this if we saw each other again."

Was she serious after he'd found out what she did behind his back? "What? You thought with time I'd be okay with you aborting my baby without consulting me, or even telling me you were pregnant in the first place? It would have been nice to make the decision together, instead of me seeing you coming out of the clinic after it was all said and done. Did you really think we could just go on like nothing happened?"

His sisters both gasped and exchanged a look that said they were angry on his behalf.

"Fuck." His emotions got away from him and he'd outed their secret in front of his sisters. He hadn't meant to do that, but in the moment, in his state of shock, his mouth got away from him.

He couldn't take it back now. But he should walk away. Instead, he found himself repeating what he'd said to her three years ago. Because why the hell not. He hadn't gotten a say back then, but he could have it now. "If you'd told me, I probably would have understood your concerns about not being ready for a child. I probably would have assured you that we could figure it out together. And if you still didn't want to have the baby, I would have at least been there for you. We could have shared the loss together. But you shut me out of all of it. You weren't ever going to tell me."

"It was *my* choice," she replied, anger in her voice.

"Yes. Absolutely. But that baby was a piece of me, too. We were in a committed relationship. We talked about our future. I didn't think we kept secrets from each other."

"It wasn't yours," she snapped, under her breath.

"Bullshit." He shook his head. He didn't believe her.

She leaned in and stared hard at him. "You were working all the time. You never had time for me. I was lonely."

Aria cocked her head. "You'd come to the bar, drink, dance, catch a little time with Jax between him pouring drinks. You'd get tipsy and Jax would have one of the guys take you home. He wanted you to be safe."

He hadn't wanted anything to happen to her. Ever. But Jax remembered those days now with hindsight and perspective and his gut went tight. And those little red flags from the past came back to bite him in the ass. "Mike got off shift early. He took you home the most. He's been working your dad's spread now for the past, what, two-plus years?" He pointedly stared at her baby bump. "I guess this time it's easier to explain the baby than it was last time, right?"

She huffed out a frustrated breath, not liking one bit she'd blurted out the truth about their past. "I thought we could stay together if I got rid of it." That statement floored him. "I couldn't be sure if it was yours or his. And if it didn't have the Wilde blue eyes, you'd know and leave me. I didn't want to be a single mother."

"Congratulations, you ended up right where you didn't want to be. Because Mike isn't the kind of guy who takes care of what's his."

She gaped at him. "What's that supposed to mean?"

She eyed him, daring him to say what she obviously didn't want to see about her current relationship. She needed a reality check. At least then she could prepare for what was to come. He didn't owe her anything, and upsetting her wasn't his goal, but even though the news sucked, at least she'd know the truth. She hadn't given it to him in the past but he would do this for her now.

"He's still one of the bar's best customers. You figure it out."

She gasped as it dawned on her what her baby daddy was doing at the bar without her.

"He wouldn't do that to me."

"If it makes you feel better to believe he's an upstanding guy, the kind who'd take his buddy's girl home and keep his hands to himself, then by all means enjoy the delusion. As far as I'm concerned, it's none of my business anymore. We're over. Done. But I thought you should know the truth so you aren't blindsided by it later." He shook his head, dumbfounded by this woman he'd once thought wanted to be a wife and a mother to their kids and his partner in all of it. "I don't think I ever really knew you at all."

Her face fell into disbelief. "Don't say that. What we had was better than anything I've ever had."

"I'm sorry for that baby's sake and yours if that's true. But you and me, we were over the second you lied and cheated. Good luck. And I'm sorry about blurting out our business in front of my sisters."

"That's it?"

"Yeah. This ended for me a long time ago. I was just holding on to my grief and anger about a baby that maybe wasn't even mine. And now I have an amazing woman in my life. And right now, the only place I want to be is with her." He turned to his sisters. "I'm out of here."

Lyric rushed in and hugged him before he turned to leave. "I'm so sorry, Jax. I had no idea this is what's kept you so alone."

"Not anymore." He set his sister away from him. "I have to go. Layla's waiting for me."

Helen's statement about him working all the time and leaving her lonely hit home because he was doing the same thing to Layla. He wouldn't make the same mistake twice and lose her.

He walked away just as Lyric said to Helen, "I think it's best if you find someone else to cater your baby shower. Please leave."

Helen burst into tears and rushed past him right before he got to the door. He didn't like to see a woman cry. Normally, he'd try to help. But Helen had made this mess and she needed to own it.

He needed to finally let it go.

And maybe in sharing it with Layla, he could put it firmly in the past.

# Chapter Twenty

Layla had finished the painting of Jax, feeling like she'd gotten it just right with a mix of his strength, determination, caring, and the deep desire he felt for her in his eyes. She left it drying out of sight. She wasn't ready to show it to Jax.

As she waited for him to come home, she sat on the lounge chair in the studio sketching. She shaded in the tree she was drawing in her sketchbook as she looked out the window and re-created the view of the trees and dark night on paper. The lights were out. The moon full above her, giving her plenty of light and a gorgeous scene. She didn't draw much anymore, but since she'd sketched Jax in bed, she found herself picking up the sketchbook more and more.

She should thank him for the inspiration and bringing back something into her life that she used to love to do.

Painting had become the more important and lucrative enterprise. But she found drawing to be a relaxing hobby that allowed her to think. When she painted, it was all about the brushstrokes, the details, and getting the perfect colors and composition.

The second tree was taking shape just as she heard Jax's truck. It sounded like he'd hit the brakes hard and cut the engine quickly. The door slammed. She was about to get up when the studio door flew open and he stepped in looking intent with a sense of rawness about him.

"Are you okay?" She sat up from her reclining position on the lounge and faced him with the sketch pad still on her lap.

"No. Not even close." The intensity coming off him made her anxious.

"What's happened?"

"You."

She raised a brow, not understanding at all. "What did I do?" Whatever it was, she'd apologize. She never wanted to hurt or upset Jax.

"You made me feel again. And I don't want to disappoint you. I don't want you to be lonely and wanting me and I'm not around or too busy to show up."

She didn't expect any of that and needed a second to sort through it, because when she'd left him earlier, she thought everything was great between them.

She set the pad aside and dropped the pencil on top, then stood to face him. "I'm not disappointed or lonely. Yes, you're really busy, but I have my work, too. As for wanting you, well, that's your fault. You're handsome and kind and honest with me about everything. And don't even get me started on what you do to me in bed. Or up against a door." She grinned at him, letting him know she didn't understand what brought this on, but she was willing to give him whatever truths he needed to hear right now.

He raked his fingers through his hair and stared at her, the intensity draining from him. "You."

She still didn't get what he meant by that, but he seemed happy about her now. "Me. Tell me what happened to bring this on." She sat again and stared up at him, ready to listen.

Jax closed the door and paced the room for a few seconds. She gave him the time he needed to collect himself and his thoughts.

Finally he stopped in front of her. "She showed up at the bar to set up a catering order. I told Lyric I didn't care. I'm with you."

*She?* Obviously someone from his past. Someone who made him act out of sorts like this. "Okay. So why are you upset?"

He glared. "It was for a baby shower. A fucking baby shower!"

Her heart pounded as she asked the hard question. "Is the baby yours?"

He went still and stared at her like she'd grown a second head. "No."

She cocked her head, trying to understand. "Still don't see the problem?"

He went down on his knees in front of her and put his hands on her thighs. "Do you want to have kids?" The sincerity and desperation in his voice took her by surprise.

Tears welled in her eyes and the grief that always came with thinking about babies made her heart heavy. "Yes. I do."

He tilted his head. "Then why does it make you sad?" He didn't know. He couldn't know.

"Why are you asking me about this right now?"

He stood and paced some more. "Because Helen, my ex, the one who came into the bar to set up the catering for her baby shower, aborted my baby without even telling me she was pregnant." He stared down at her, waiting for a response.

Shocked, she didn't have one for him.

Jax raised his hands, then let them fall and slap the outside of his thighs. "I get that it's her choice. I believe every woman has the right to make that decision. But as the father, don't I get to even fucking know she's pregnant? Don't I get to at least say what I want, even if she ultimately decides to terminate it? Instead I find out by accident after the fact."

"In most circumstances, I agree, the father should know and be a part of the decision process. If you're in a relationship, it affects both of you. And you're a man who'd be reasonable and sympathetic to your partner, so I can't say why she'd keep it from you."

His shoulders went loose and he hung his head for a moment, then looked at her again. "We've been in this relationship together several weeks. She'd known me for years. And you know that very simple thing about me, but she still didn't come to me." His pain and hurt poured off him and filled the room. "What's worse, now she confesses she didn't know if the baby was mine or if it was the guy who got her pregnant again. A guy who is at the bar carousing all the time behind her back. That's who she chose over me."

Was he still hurt that they'd split? Did he want her back? "It sounds like you're better off without her."

"Damn right."

That eased her mind.

"Because now I have you."

Okay, that was very clear. She smiled up at him. "So why are you mad?"

"Because it didn't bother her at all to end that pregnancy. She thought ending it meant she'd get to keep me. I don't want to be the reason she did that." His pain made her angry at Helen for not handling the situation with some care for Jax's feelings.

"You're not the reason she terminated the pregnancy. That's her excuse. If she really wanted the baby, she'd have had it no matter what. And maybe in hindsight she's realized that she wasn't ready then."

He shrugged. "I don't know."

"That's right, Jax. You don't know because you've moved on. Let her do the same. Her life is none of your concern anymore. You weren't responsible for what she did then, or now."

"I just . . . grieved so hard for what was lost. I spent so much time thinking about what that baby would have been like, all the things we could have done together, a future I didn't get to have because she ended it before it ever really got started."

"I know exactly how you feel."

He stared down at her and his gaze followed the tear that trailed down her cheek. "You do?"

"I was five months pregnant when my son's heart stopped and he just died right inside me." The confession choked her up and opened that old wound.

Jax went down on his knees in front of her again. He wrapped his arms around her, scooped her right off the lounge and into his chest, and held her as she straddled his lap. "I'm so sorry that happened to you." He hugged her closer. "I can't even imagine how that felt and what you went through."

"It's the hardest thing. They tell you he's gone and then make you go through labor and delivery. After . . . you're left with nothing. There's no baby to bring home or nurse or hold. You're just . . ."

"Empty. The loss spinning out into memories you'll never make, all the things you'll never know about them." Jax's words touched her deeply.

"All the wondering of what could have been."

He brushed his hand down her hair, soothing her. "Do you know why it happened?"

She leaned back and brushed away her tears. "A defect in his heart. Something Christopher was born with, too, but was repaired. He never told me. He'd been healthy his whole life, no complications. It hadn't occurred to him that our child might inherit the same thing."

"Why the hell not?"

"Once he was healthy, no one in the family really talked about it. He thought it was fixed and done and just didn't think about it anymore."

Jax brushed the hair away from her face. "Is that what tore your marriage apart?"

"In some ways, yes. I grieved for a long time. Christopher couldn't understand what it felt like to have a life growing and moving inside me, how connected I was to the baby. One minute he's rolling around my belly and the next I wake up in the morning and I just knew. The stillness, it scared me like nothing I'd ever felt. I called the doctor and went in immediately. They did an ultrasound. No heartbeat. No movement. No life left in him. He was just gone. And then everything fell apart without me seeing it. I was too busy missing my son and trying not to blame myself."

He pressed his forehead to hers. "It wasn't your fault."

"I know. The doctors told me there was nothing that could have been done to save him even if they had found the defect sooner." She shrugged. "But still, I just felt like if I'd done something, or not done something. I wanted him here, with me, in my arms, and I would have done anything to make that happen."

Jax brushed the tears away for her this time. "You're so strong. To get through something like that . . . I don't know how you did it. You'll be an amazing mother."

"Thank you. Maybe one day, I'll try again."

"It'll be different," he assured her, and she believed him.

Because Christopher had carried the defect. Not her. So she had hope that one day she would have a healthy child. She still had plenty of time.

Jax kissed her forehead. "What was his name?"

She didn't often talk about her stillborn child. No one ever asked her the baby's name when she did. "Miles. After my grandpa. I told you he used to watch me when I was young and my parents worked. He taught me how to paint. He never cared that I made a mess of it."

Jax kissed her paint-splattered fingers and made her smile.

She sighed at the memories popping up in her mind of her granddad. "I adored him."

"Just like you did your son."

She nodded.

Jax touched his forehead to hers. "I'm sorry my shit night brought all this sadness back for you."

She squeezed his shoulders. "It's actually nice to talk to someone who understands."

"I never got the chance to get attached, not like you were to Miles."

"Still, I feel like you get it, because they mattered, even if they didn't make it into our arms."

Jax pulled her into a hug and just held her for a long moment, both of them needing to be close, so they could let the hurt fade back into the past.

"What are you drawing?" He looked from the sketch pad on the chaise up through the windows at the night sky, then tapped the drawing. "Can I have this when you're done? It's amazing."

She leaned back and stared at the sketch he held in his hand. "Sure. If you want it. I was just passing time, waiting for you."

"How long do you need to finish it?"

"Maybe a half hour. But if you want to do something . . ."

"It's late. Have you eaten?"

"Just what you gave me earlier. I thought I'd make something after I finished the drawing."

"I'll make us dinner." He kissed her, picked her up, and dropped her butt back on the lounge. "I need to run up to the main house to grab a couple of things, but I'll be back in a few minutes and cook dinner at your place."

She shifted and leaned back on the lounge with her sketch pad on her lap. "I'm happy to let you feed me and put me to bed tonight." She grinned to go with her teasing.

He stared down at her. "How about every night?"

She held his steady gaze. "That's not really realistic with your schedule, but I get where you're going with that."

"Do you want to go with me on that?"

"Yes." But he needed more honesty than that. "But you have to know that there's some logistics and schedules and other things that have to work out to make what you're proposing doable. I'm here now, but my job requires me to travel."

"We can figure it out. If it's what you want?"

"It's starting to be everything I want. I just don't want to rush it and have it all fall apart when I finish my commission and have to leave for a showing or to find a new view to paint."

He cocked his head. "After you do those things, will you be coming back?"

She held his intent gaze. "If you want me to."

"There's nothing I want more."

She felt the same way. "I don't want you to feel like my job and what it requires is more important than you."

He shook his head. "I understand that your art is a part of you. You love it. It makes you happy. I would never ask you to stop being you, or stop doing what makes you fulfilled and brings you such joy. I love seeing you excited when you find the perfect scene to paint. It lights you up. And I've seen the sense of accomplishment that comes over you when you finish something and it's everything you wanted it to be. I see the pride you feel when you know someone is going to love what you created. You really enjoyed the fact that I loved the painting of Moon and appreciated your hard work and amazing talent."

"Being an artist means everyone gets to be a critic. But when someone loves and appreciates what you do, then it's this amazing feeling to know you've touched them."

His gaze narrowed. "Why would you think I'd want to take that away from you?"

"I don't think that. I just wonder if you can accept that doing what I do means I will sometimes have to be away from you."

"I can deal with that, so long as I know you're coming home to me."

"Of course I am. You're a smokin' hot, cook-for-his-woman cowboy with a heart so big I don't know how there isn't a line of women banging on the door to kill me to get to you."

He chuckled under his breath and shook his head. "And I don't know how your husband managed to fuck up so badly with you that you were going to leave him, when he should have been doing everything he could to hold on to you."

His words stunned her. They touched a very deep place inside her, where she kept the secret of what Christopher had done, and awakened her sadness and regrets.

Jax's gaze narrowed. "What did I say that made you sad?"

"Another time. I can't . . . not after talking about Miles. It's too much." She blinked back tears.

Jax closed the distance and leaned down and kissed her softly. "Okay. Not tonight. But soon."

She nodded her agreement and let out a very undignified groan when her phone pinged with a text. Michael had called several times today. It seemed the past wanted a front-and-center seat in her life today.

Jax snagged the phone off the table to bring to her, but scowled at the screen when it lit up with another incoming text. "What the fuck? Who the hell does this guy think he is, threatening you like this?" He turned the phone to her, but the screen went to black.

She took the phone, entered her pin, unlocking it, then read the messages with Jax reading them beside her.

MICHAEL: Answer the fucking phone or I'll ruin you!
MICHAEL: You can't keep putting me off like this
MICHAEL: You didn't deserve a dime
MICHAEL: Where is all the money?
MICHAEL: Give it to me! He was my brother! My family! Tell me, or I'll make you!!!!!!!!!!!!!!!!!

"What's he talking about?" Jax's voice was sharp and inquisitive.

LAYLA: I was his WIFE! I said all I have to say in court. I won't explain it again. Leave me alone.

Her hand trembled. Without the safety net Christopher had always been for Michael, he was losing his damn mind. Anger and grief were pushing him over the edge.

"Layla?" Jax stared down at her, fury in his eyes. "No one should talk to you that way."

She brought her gaze back to Jax. "Michael contested Christopher's will, claiming that Christopher had told him that I asked for a divorce and that we were separated. Legally, he had no standing. California is a community property state, which meant everything went to me, except for what Christopher bequeathed in his will, which I signed off on when he had it executed because for me it wasn't about money or things. Michael didn't see it that way. He thought because my relationship with Christopher had deteriorated to the point that we weren't speaking, that meant Michael should get everything. What he didn't realize was that I made more money than my husband. The house was in my name only, even though Christopher and I bought it together."

"Why only in your name, then?"

"Because that's how Christopher wanted it. He said if we ever split or he died before me, then it gave him comfort to know the house was mine and I would be taken care of."

"That still makes no sense, legally it's yours. And if you split, because you bought it together while you were married, he'd have a claim on half its worth."

"He would have never taken my home from me. He wasn't that kind of man. He was the kind to take care of what mattered most to him. And there were circumstances that we haven't talked about and Michael doesn't know. I didn't know them until the very end. And when I learned it, it made even more sense why the house was in my name only. But before I knew everything else, I thought it was a sweet gesture that he wanted this kind of security for me if something should happen. The house was worth a lot of money, so I could sell it and not have to worry about my future if my career tanked and I didn't have Christopher's financial support for whatever reason."

"Okay. He sounds like a good guy."

"He was a very good man. He took care of me. He loved me. And because he did, what he did hurt even more."

"But you don't want to talk about it now."

"It's got nothing to do with Michael and how he feels about me. He lost his claim to what Christopher left him because he contested the will. Now he's desperate and greedy to get his hands on whatever he thinks I'll give him to make him shut up and leave me alone."

"Why not just give him in good faith what Christopher left him and let that be the end of it?"

"My lawyer advised against it because Michael is the type of guy who is never satisfied. So if I give in now, he'll keep coming back for more. And Christopher is the one who put the stipulation in the will to protect me from him."

"So what are you going to do?"

"Nothing. Ignore him like I've been doing. He doesn't know where I am, so at least he can't badger me in person. The phone calls and texts are a nuisance but easily dismissed."

"You could get a protection order for harassment."

She pressed her lips tight. "I try not to poke the bear, but if he keeps this up, I'll contact my lawyer."

Jax narrowed his gaze. "I don't like that he's being so aggressive about something that's been settled already."

"Some people just can't take no for an answer. I've tried to be nice. But it's getting harder to take the threats and accusations, especially when he knows nothing about what really happened between me and Christopher. It was private. It was ours. Good and bad. And while I've moved on, Michael can't. Michael is lost without Christopher. They were best friends. Michael relied on Christopher as a confidant, for advice on everything, and to bail him out when he was impulsive. Grief has turned him into someone I don't recognize. I feel his pain, but that doesn't mean he gets to keep coming at me like this and dredging it all up again and again. I'm done with the past."

Jax squatted beside her. "Do you mean that?"

She took his hand and squeezed it. "Yes. I'm here. With you. And I'm happy. I won't let him ruin it for me."

He threaded his fingers through hers. "Will what happened with Christopher come between us? Because if it will, I hope you'll tell me."

"No. It's not like that. What he did made me afraid to trust in others, but I don't feel that way with you. I hope you know that." She was trying hard to not let her past make her suspicious. That would only lead to their destruction. And she didn't want to lose Jax.

He used his free hand to brush her hair behind her

ear. "What Helen did made it hard to believe another woman wouldn't lie to me, too."

"You thought you knew her, that what you had together meant she'd always come to you. When she didn't, it hurt. That's how I felt, that everything was built on a lie, even if everything in the beginning was real."

Jax nodded. "I don't want that to happen to us."

"It won't. Not if we keep talking to each other the way we do now."

He kissed her like it was the start of something that would last all night, but pulled back when her stomach rumbled and the sketch pad fell off her lap. His warm, teasing grin made her smile back at him. "Let me make you something you can work off later."

He handed her the sketchbook, stood, and headed for the door to go make a late dinner for them.

She stared at the texts on her phone, wondering if Michael would ever give up and knowing at the same time that this wasn't going to be over until he got what he wanted.

## Chapter Twenty-One

Layla walked into the bar with a "Hey, John. How are you?" for the bouncer at the door as she stopped beside him and scanned the packed crowd.

"Doing well. Jax is behind the bar."

"Thank you." She headed that way, dodging the other patrons, most of them jumping up and down to the beat of the music as the crowd sang along to the chorus. She'd never been a country music fan, mostly because she never really made the choice to give it a listen. Now it was growing on her because it was always playing at the bar, except when Lyric declared it a theme night. Last night had been Women Who Rock. Didn't matter what was playing, or when there was a live band, everyone was here for the party. And the Wildes knew how to keep their customers happy, dancing, eating, and drinking.

Jax's sister Melody came up behind her. "Hey. You're back."

After their talk about Helen and Miles, she and Jax had made it a point to try to spend more time together. She didn't want to bother him at work, but he liked it when she stopped by even for an hour to have a drink and a dance. "Just couldn't stay away from my guy."

Melody raised a brow. "Well, now, that sounds like things are serious." Melody bumped her shoulder into Layla's without toppling the tray of empty glasses. "Good. He needs something besides work. And after that thing with Helen . . ." She shook her head, her eyes narrowing with anger. "She could have handled that better. Jax is a good guy. Understanding. It didn't have to go down that way."

"I agree. I feel terrible for Jax, but I think he sees now that the relationship wasn't going to last. They weren't a good fit."

"And isn't that what mistakes are for? Teaching us. We just have to learn the lesson. You are definitely nothing like Helen. At least, that's what Jax said to all of us this morning. I look forward to getting to know you better." She lifted up the tray. "But right now, duty calls. Have fun tonight." Melody dashed over to the far side of the bar where the waitresses' orders were filled.

It took Layla a second to process that Jax had been talking about her to his sisters. It must be nice to have siblings to count on. She barely spoke to her younger brother, who was always too busy to do more than send her a quick text after she left him a message. She was closer to April and her other friends than she was with her own sibling.

She didn't live and work with him, like Jax did with his family, so she got that time and distance had led to her and her brother living very separate lives.

A loud whistle pierced through the music and

caught her attention because she'd heard Jax do it on the ranch several times to get someone's attention. She looked up and found him waving her over.

She closed the distance to the bar, Jax's gaze on her the whole time.

"I don't know how you get lost in your head like that all the time, especially in a crowd like this." He set a glass of wine on the bar and looked at the guy sitting on the stool next to where she stood. "Mind giving the lady your seat? Your beer's on me."

The man slid off the stool. "No problem, man."

"Thank you," she said, taking his seat.

Jax leaned over the bar.

She met him halfway for a soft kiss that lasted only a few seconds. A couple of people catcalled and oohed over it.

She blushed.

Jax just shook his head and poured out three tequila shots. "How was the end of your day?" He'd stopped at her studio before he left for the bar.

"Good. I finished the view-from-the-studio-at-night drawing. I'll frame it and give it to you."

"At this rate, I'm going to need more than my four walls to display all the cool stuff you do."

She scrunched her lips. "If you don't want it—"

He put his hand over hers. "I want it. It's amazing. And I still want to see the painting you did a while back that you refused to show me. Don't think I forgot about it."

She pretended not to know what he was talking about and changed the subject. "Melody told me you were talking about me with your sisters."

He pulled two beers at the tap and rolled his eyes. "They're nosy and ask a lot of questions."

"They want you to be happy."

"That's why I told them I am. Because of you."

She sipped her wine while he handed the drinks over to a guy several customers down. "I spoke to April earlier today."

His gaze narrowed. "Do you have to go somewhere?"

"No. We were just catching up. She said I sounded like my old self, only better."

He grinned and his blue eyes went bright. "Yeah. What else did she say?"

"That you're good for me."

"Do you think so?"

"I'm here."

They shared a long look.

Someone called out, "Get a room. But first, I'll take an old-fashioned."

Jax shook his head and started pouring the guy's drink.

Her phone rang. She pulled it from the pocket of her pink sundress where she'd stashed it and her little wallet. "Hello." She tried not to shout into the phone because of all the noise in the bar.

"Finally you answer."

She should have checked caller ID. "Michael."

"We need to talk."

She put her finger in her ear. "It's kind of hard to hear you."

"Where are you? What's with all the noise?"

She didn't want to say. "What do you want?"

"The truth. But if you won't give me that, then at least pay out the money Christopher left me. I have an investment opportunity that's going to pay off big." This wasn't the first one he hoped would do so. The others never really panned out. Not like he wanted. Most of the time, he'd ended up losing everything he put in and Christopher ended up covering his ass.

"I can't talk about this right now," she shouted, reminding him she could barely hear. She didn't want to have another yelling match with him while she was out in public.

Jax must have sensed something and came closer, a question in his eyes.

The song ended. Instead of another starting right up, Lyric's voice rang out. "Hello Dark Horse Dive Bar!"

The crowd responded to Lyric.

"You're at a bar." Michael sounded incredulous.

"This isn't a good time."

"You're too busy partying to take care of your responsibilities."

"You are not my responsibility," she snapped. "Own your actions and the consequences. I told you to take what Christopher left you, that the legal battle would get you nothing. But you didn't listen."

"You're going to rent out the house. The yearly rent on that place is more than my annual salary. You can afford to give me what Christopher wanted me to have and then some."

Yeah, that last part is what made her leery.

Rentals in California went for top dollar. Especially for an oceanfront property. But that didn't mean she owed Michael anything. If he was in real trouble, maybe she'd help because he was Christopher's brother. But this wasn't a dire situation. This was Michael wanting something because he felt entitled. He thought bullying her into it would work. She hadn't allowed it when he contested the will. If she caved now, he'd just keep coming back.

"Michael, you and I have no connection anymore. I don't owe you anything. I'm not giving you anything. This has to stop. It's harassment."

"Are you threatening me?"

"I'm letting you know that you've crossed a line. I've moved on. You need to do the same. I do not want any further contact with you." She hung up and found Jax leaning over the bar, listening to everything.

Jax didn't look happy. "We need to talk about that."

"I handled it."

He grinned. "Yeah, you did." He sounded proud of her. "But people like that, they don't take no for an answer."

"Tell me about it."

"Remind me to tell you about the guy who stalked Lyric not that long ago and how that ended."

Her eyes went wide. She turned and stared at his sister singing up onstage, the crowd loving the pop country song. "Is she okay?"

"Yes. Because she asked for help. From Mason, my parents, all of us. We had her back. Let me have yours." The intensity in his eyes told her that if something happened to her, it mattered to him.

She nodded, letting him know she'd fill him in later.

Jax pushed off the bar and went back to pouring

drinks. She finished her wine in one gulp and thought about Michael. She didn't want to believe he'd pursue this further. Not after her warning.

But maybe Jax was right. She needed to be careful and not dismiss the threat Michael posed to her and her reputation. He wasn't in his right mind now.

She wasn't just thinking of herself. There were others involved. People who didn't deserve to have their lives turned upside down again because of Christopher and his lies. He should be the one protecting them, not her. But because of her past feelings for Christopher, it was hard not to want to do everything she could to keep the secrets buried.

# Chapter Twenty-Two

Jax headed down to Layla's studio. He made it a point now to find at least a few minutes to check in with Layla every afternoon. Even if it was only for a couple of minutes, he left happier. Today, he had something to ask her, somewhere he wanted to take her. He should have asked sooner, but he wasn't sure if she'd say yes. This was one of those things that meant a lot and defined a relationship, and he wasn't sure she was ready to take that step. But he hoped that after seven weeks and a few days together she was.

He found Layla sitting outside her studio on the grass with five kids. Two on one side of her, three on the other. They all had a sketch pad on their laps and a green-colored pencil in hand as they watched Layla, then tried to copy what she was doing on their paper.

Two sets of parents were sitting on the porch of the cabin nearby watching and drinking wine.

"So, you're going to lightly sweep the pencil out in long arching strokes to create the tree limbs." Layla put action to words.

The kids watched her intently, then tried to re-create it on their pages.

"Very good," Layla praised the little girl on her right, who looked to be no more than five years old. She glanced at each child's papers. "You're all doing wonderfully. Now, let's add some texture, so our trees look really full." Layla demonstrated, filling in the branches on her evergreen tree, making it look even more realistic as she went.

The children began to copy her.

Layla picked up a darker green and handed it to the little one next to her. "Add some additional color."

The girl pressed her lips ti_'.. and concentrated as she worked.

"What do you think?" the boy at the end on Layla's left asked, holding his up.

"Fantastic. I love the bold strokes you used to make the tree really big."

The boy beamed, like the compliment lit him up from the inside out.

Jax wanted the people who visited the ranch to leave with good memories. These kids were going to remember this day. Maybe someday in the future their parents would remind them that they'd had a master class in drawing from a world-famous artist.

He had no idea how she'd ended up out here with the kids, but she looked content. His mind went to a place he tried not to let it go too often, because he didn't want to get ahead of himself, but he could so easily see her in the future doing these short classes with their visitors, or sitting at the kitchen table with their kids doing art just for fun.

Layla glanced up at him. "Hey there, cowboy. Are you done for the day?"

"Yeah. Do you have plans tonight and this Sunday?" *For the rest of your life?* He didn't say that last part, but he thought it. A lot. Especially after all the time they'd been spending together. He didn't spend a single night alone anymore. She was always waiting for him to come back to the cabin every night. He hated that he woke her. But she never seemed to mind. He made sure she enjoyed every second of it before they fell asleep together, her in his arms.

Every morning he woke up beside her, he was happier than the day before.

She gave him a sweet smile. "I'm free if you need me."

*Every second of the day I need you, want you, think about you.* "Um, it's a family thing."

"Okay. So you'll be busy tonight?"

He didn't like the confusion in her voice or her eyes. He was blowing this. "No. I want you to come with me."

Her face lit up. "I'd love to."

"You don't even know what it is."

She set aside her sketch pad and pencil and stood. She walked right up to him and looked him in the eye. "Lyric called and invited me to the rehearsal dinner tonight and the wedding on Sunday. She wanted me to know that if I'm important to you, then she'd like me to be there."

He studied her. "So you already said you'd go."

She shook her head. "I told Lyric that if you asked me and wanted me there, I'd attend. But only if you asked, because I wasn't sure—"

He cupped her face and kissed her hard and quick. They had an audience of tiny people, so he kept it tame.

"Be sure that I want you with me. For everything." He brushed his thumbs over her soft skin. "I suck at this kind of thing. Obviously. I could have been smoother about asking you. But never doubt that you're . . . *everything*."

Her eyes went bright and filled with tears.

*Oh shit.* He panicked at the sight, but he was also damn happy to see what he felt reflected back at him. "Please don't cry."

"I'm just . . . so happy."

He let out the breath lodged in his chest. "You make me happy. So come to dinner, the wedding, hell, just be with me."

Her smile lit up his heart. "Okay."

He pressed his forehead to hers. "Good. Now can we clean this up and go inside so I can kiss you without a bunch of little ones gawking at us?"

She chuckled under her breath, then turned to their rapt audience. "Okay, my friends, it's time to show off your artwork to your parents." She helped them pull their pages from the sketch pads and gathered up the pencils.

Jax inspected each one and praised each of the kids before they dashed off to their parents, who waved and thanked Layla for taking the time with them.

"How did you end up with all of them?"

"They saw me painting through the windows and knocked on the door. They wanted to see the painting up close. But they're kids and they tried to touch everything, so I grabbed some supplies and distracted them from all the colors inside the studio and brought them out here." A wistful smile titled her lips.

He brushed his fingers over her cheek. "You loved it, being with the kids."

"They're so eager and ready to try. That one little girl has true talent. I hope her parents recognize it and nurture it."

"I bet Miles would have had your talent. Or at least he'd have loved painting with his mom."

She went very still and stared at him for a long moment.

He thought he'd put his foot in his mouth again.

But then she got this soft look in her eyes and said, "Thank you."

He slipped his hand across her neck and up under her silky hair. "For what?"

"Talking about him. No one ever talks about him with me. They're too afraid I'll be upset or sad."

"He was yours. You miss him. You think about him. Talking about him makes you sad, but I bet not talking about him makes you ache even more."

"Christopher didn't want to talk about it. And I just wanted to share it with someone who would understand."

He brushed his fingers over her skin at the back of her neck. "I do, sweetheart. Maybe the baby with Helen wasn't mine." He shrugged. "It felt like mine when I realized it was gone. I grieved for what could have been." He pulled her close. "Now, maybe, I have a chance to make that future I imagined a reality. Maybe we both do. Together."

"I really want to be a mother." The words sounded like a confession and a prayer.

"You're going to be a really great one."

She stepped back and checked the watch on his wrist. "If we're quick, we can make it on time." She took his hand and tugged him toward the cabin.

He went willingly because wherever she went, he wanted to be right there with her. "We've got plenty of time."

The second she stepped through the door, she dropped the pads and pencils on the table and kept tugging him through to the bedroom. The pretty lavender dress she was wearing came off over her head and landed on the floor somewhere. He didn't know because he only had eyes for the gorgeous woman in front of him wearing nothing but a scrap of white lace covering her sex and an even sexier lace confection cupping her breasts, dusky pink nipples barely hidden behind the sheer material. All that gorgeous golden skin. Those long toned legs.

"Too little time, too many clothes." With that, she reached for his sweater, slid her hands beneath it, and pulled it up his chest.

He took over getting it off. She attacked his belt, button, and zipper. Since her hands were busy on him, he reached for her, cupping her breasts and molding them in his palms. He leaned down and kissed the rounded top of each one, sliding his tongue along her skin from one breast to the other.

She unhooked the bra and pulled it off while he ditched his boots, black jeans, boxers, and socks.

She sat on the edge of the bed and scooted back. He took advantage, hooked his fingers in that scrap of lace, and dragged it down her legs as she moved. Then he practically dove on top of her, taking one tight nipple into his mouth as his hand brushed down her belly, over her mound, to her already wet folds. "Damn, baby, you really want me."

"Now," she ordered, her hand sliding between them, her fingers circling his thick cock. She stroked him from base to tip, then rubbed her thumb over the bead of precum with a hum of satisfaction and need.

He wanted her just as badly and slid one finger, then two, into her tight sheath, making sure she really was ready for him. He never wanted to hurt her in any way. Her inner muscles contracted on his fingers, trying to hold him inside her, but he wanted his cock buried in her all the way to the hilt.

He licked and laved her other pretty breast and nipple, then grabbed a condom, sheathed himself, planted his hands on either side of her, and nudged her entrance with just the round head of his penis. She moaned his name. He thrust deep and her eyes went wide. Both of them held perfectly still, savoring this moment, him filling her, their hearts beating as one, and then she pushed into him, taking him just that little bit deeper and unleashing all the passion between them.

It was wild and primitive. A claiming. A giving and taking in equal measure. A declaration that they were a perfect match and made for each other.

He didn't want it to end. He wanted them to stay like this, feel like this forever. But all too soon her inner muscles clamped around his thick arousal, his balls tightened, and their releases overtook them in wave upon wave of pleasure.

He collapsed on top of her, trying to take his weight

on his forearms as her aftershocks pulsed around his dick, keeping him hard. Just to extend her pleasure, he found the strength to rock in and out one more time, teasing out more aftershocks and her surprised gasp and moan before she hugged him close and begged him, "Stop. It's too much."

He grinned against her neck. "That was amazing."

"We're going to be late."

"Worth it." He meant it.

"Is it weird that I'd really like to draw this moment?"

"You just really love the view of my ass." Because if she drew them like this, that would be the view of him lying on top of her, his hips cradled by her thighs, his body covering her, his face in her neck, her hair a mass of gold splayed across the pillow, his arms at his sides, his hands hidden beneath them and holding her close.

"It's a great view. One I'll never tire of seeing. But this is more than that. This feels like a perfect moment."

He rose up on his forearms and stared down at her. "It is. You are. This is us. You're what's been missing from my life. We've led two very different lives until now, but I know we can figure this out so that we can stay together. Right?"

She slid her fingers into his hair. "Yes. I haven't made any plans beyond the couple of months I thought I'd be here. Unless I decided to stay longer, which obviously I have because I extended my stay another month."

Though she could extend it as long as she liked, he

wondered why only another month. "Because you're not sure if we're going to work out?"

"It's like the invitation to dinner and the wedding. I'm waiting for it to come from you. I need to know that it's what you want."

"You are *everything* I want. I meant it when I said it before. I mean it now. There is nothing and no one I want more. Stay. Make a life here with me. A house. Kids. Whatever you want, I'll give it to you."

"I want you."

"You had me the second you got here. I don't know exactly what happened in the past. You said you thought everything was one way, but it turned out to be another. All I can promise you is that I am exactly what you see. I will never lie to you. I will always take care of you. I love you. I knew it that day at the creek pools when I looked at you."

Tears welled in her eyes.

"Please don't cry, baby. It kills me to see tears in your eyes."

"Happy tears," she assured him. "Because I love you, too. I don't know how it happened. I didn't expect this. But there is something so big and wonderful and exciting and terrifying inside me."

"What scares you?"

"That this isn't real." She bit her bottom lip, then confessed, "Losing you."

He brushed away the tears that ran down the side of her eyes and into her hair. "This is very real. And you are never going to lose me. I swear it. I'm yours. Be mine."

"I am. We'll figure out the rest as we go."

He kissed her softly, then looked into her vibrant eyes. "No more doubts, Layla. I love you. If you can't believe in that, in us, this is never going to work."

"That's the thing. I do trust you. I do believe you and in us, because you've shown me that I can. I just needed to hear you say it."

"I'm happy to repeat it as often as you like."

She twisted her lips the way she did when she was unsure. "I know it sounds needy . . ."

"I don't care if you need it, want it, or just like to hear it. If it makes you happy, I'll say it over and over again while also showing you that I mean it." He kissed her again to let her know how much he cared and that giving her what she needed wasn't a chore. He wanted her to be happy. Always.

The kiss turned sultry. How could it not when he had the woman he loved naked and in his arms? She loved him. It seemed amazing and unreal and he was damn happy about it. He wanted to hoard it close and let everyone know at the same time.

She rolled her hips into his thickening erection, then pushed against his shoulders. "Nope. Not again."

He stared down at her. "Uh, yes again. Please. And thank you." He dove in for another kiss, sliding his tongue along hers.

She gave in for a moment, then started pushing on his chest again. "We are so late for your sister's dinner."

"Shit." He'd completely forgotten about that. He pressed up on his hands and stared down at the gorgeous view below him. "This is a damn shame leaving this bed when I have you right where I love having you."

She giggled and leaned up and kissed him on the jaw. "You're adorable and you can have me right back here in a few hours."

"And that's one reason why I love you."

"Because I want you naked and in this bed with me, too?"

"Yes. And because you always want to be with me. You never say no to spending time together, even when you've spent the whole day working and I ask you to come to the bar to hang out with me. I know that's not exactly fun for you, but you come anyway."

"Because I get to be with you. And stare at your ass while you're there."

He slid out of the bed, took her hand, and pulled her up with him. "I knew you liked my ass."

"I love it." She kissed him quick. "Now, get dressed."

He turned to grab his clothes and she smacked him on the ass as she headed into the bathroom to freshen up. He grinned like an idiot, so damn happy, he didn't even care that he was going to get a ribbing when they finally made it to dinner.

* * *

THE RESTAURANT WAS packed as they made their way to the table at the back where everyone was seated. His parents were on one side, Mason's parents on the other, with Lyric and Mason were at the far end. Nick, Mason's brother, sat next to Aria. They looked cozy. The attraction easy to see, though it seemed the two had been circling each other since they met, because

Nick didn't live here and his busy schedule with the FBI kept him away. Though every time he visited Mason, who also worked for the FBI, he showed up at the bar to flirt with Aria.

Melody was staring down at her phone across from Nick.

Mason was the first to notice them. "You finally made it." The grin said he knew exactly why they were late.

Lyric finished saying something to Mason's mom and looked at Jax. "I'm so happy you two came together."

"We *are* together," he assured Lyric, letting all of them know.

Mason looked at Layla. "So you got yourself a Wilde, too."

Melody stopped typing on her phone long enough to grin at Layla. "Jax is wild for you, that's for sure. We've needed to hire help at the bar and ranch forever. Finally, he's doing it after we've all begged him to stop working himself to death."

Mason jumped on that. "Wildes . . . they love big and hard." He kissed Lyric like no one was watching them.

Jax's mom and dad stared at him and Layla. He saw their happiness for him, for them.

He pulled out a chair for Layla to sit and he took the seat next to Melody, catching the selfie she'd taken and the message she'd just sent.

**MELODY:** One of these days you're going to have to show yourself.

"What's that all about?" he asked, concerned.

She tucked away her phone. "None of your business."

"Do you even know who you're talking to, or did some random guy slide into your DMs and he's playing you for some attention or scam?"

Melody frowned and wouldn't look at him.

Jax put his hand over the back of her chair and leaned in. "Mel? Talk to me."

She folded her arms over her chest. "He says he's seen me at the bar and wants to get to know me."

Jax frowned at her. "Then why doesn't he do that in person?"

"I don't know. Maybe he's shy. Maybe it's easier to talk on the phone than face-to-face."

"So you've spoken to him."

"No. Just the messages. Nothing creepy though. Just the kind of stuff you ask to get to know someone." She furrowed her brow. "It's strange though."

"What is?"

"It feels like I know him. The questions he asks, it's obvious we're the same age, so of course we'd like a lot of the same music and stuff because of that."

"That sounds promising," Layla said.

Melody looked across him to her. "Right. If we like the same things, then we'll probably get along when we do meet. It's just strange that the things he picks are exactly what I'd pick. Like he's been watching me and learning all that stuff."

"Or maybe this is someone you already know." Layla looked on the bright side. "Maybe he's unsure you'd be open to a date if he asked you in person and is using the messages as a way to show you that you do have a lot in common, so you'll say yes when he does ask."

Melody nodded. "Yeah. Okay. But I don't want someone who feels intimidated by me."

"Women are intimidating, especially when we really like one." Jax took Layla's hand, but kept his focus on his younger sister. "Rejection sucks for everyone. Maybe this guy is just trying to increase the odds that you'll say yes to a date by going about it this way. If he really wants to be with you, he's going to have to come out of the shadows to do it. Then you'll know and can judge his true character. Until then, maybe start asking your own questions about who he really is, what he believes in, the type of man he is. Unless this is just a flirtation."

"I won't know unless I give it a shot, right?"

Layla leaned over him. "And if he starts being creepy or asks you to send him money or nude pics, block his ass."

"Damn straight," Melody said, taking a sip of her wine.

Jax flagged the waiter down. "What do you want, sweetheart?"

"You," she whispered in his ear, then turned to the waiter and said, "A mojito, please."

Jax ordered a beer, then turned to her. "You look amazing in that dress." The sexy little black number she'd slipped into after they made love hugged her breasts, then flared out in a wide knee-length skirt, showing off her amazing legs.

"Does my hair look as wild and tumbled as I think it does?" She whispered that to him.

"Yes. You're welcome."

She laughed and his heart beat a little faster and felt a little bigger.

He glanced at all the faces at the table. His family. Old and new. Then he looked at her and knew she belonged right here with all of them. With him.

# Chapter Twenty-Three

Layla tried to roll over to grab her ringing phone off the bedside table, but Jax's arm and strong body had her pinned partway beneath him as he spooned the back of hers.

Jax had woken her up when he came in from a long Saturday night at the bar. They'd made love before falling asleep in each other's arms. That was, like, two hours ago.

"Jax. I can't reach the phone."

The second ring had him jolting awake. "What?" He leaned back, giving her room to move.

If someone was calling at nearly two a.m., it had to be important. She snagged the phone and swiped the screen before the fourth ring. "Hello."

"Ms. Brock?"

"Yes."

"This is Stan from Forrester Security. We have on record that you are out of town."

"That's correct."

"An alarm went off at your home approximately thirty minutes ago. We sent someone to check it out. Unfortunately, we found several broken windows, damage to other property, and someone spray-painted the walls inside your home."

Layla sat up. The sheet fell to her waist, leaving her upper half naked. She didn't care. "What the hell?"

"The damage sounds bad, I know. We notified the police. They've taken a report and will be contacting you soon as well. Until you're able to secure the broken windows, we'll keep a security guard at the house to make sure no one else goes in."

"Um, okay. I'll figure out what to do about the damage and let you know when the security guard can leave."

"Sounds good. Just so you know, when the guard arrived, he did spot a man dressed in dark clothing fleeing the scene. He gave the description to the officers who arrived shortly after him."

So not kids pulling a prank.

"Did it appear anything was taken? Were they looking to steal the appliances or something?" Because she'd packed up the house. There was nothing of value to steal besides the appliances and fixtures.

"No, ma'am. It seems they just made a mess."

"How did they get past the gate?"

"We suspect they were on foot. At least it seemed that way, since he ran from the house."

"Did he run down to the beach?"

"No, ma'am."

"Please, call me Layla."

"Of course, Layla. Um, the suspect ran across your property and into the neighbor's yard before the guard lost him. The description is vague, but many of the houses, including yours, have outdoor surveillance.

The police will be asking your neighbors to supply any footage they recorded."

"Thank you. If you find out anything more, please let me know at this phone number. I'll be contacting my agent, April, to go to the house and assess the damage so we can hire someone to fix it. I'll be sure that either I or April will inform you who will be allowed on the property until this is squared away."

"We'll also be running a check on the security system and will advise you if there is anything that needs repair, or possibly an upgrade." Of course they'd want a chance to improve the system and charge her for it. Right now, she didn't care that they were trying to use the incident to make more money. If the property needed more security, she'd do it, but it sounded like the system worked, alerting the company to the intruder. The person simply didn't care that it went off and trashed her place anyway.

She thanked the man again and hung up.

"Someone broke into your house?" Jax sat up next to her, having easily overheard the conversation since he was right beside her.

"Yeah." She stared across the dark room. "It doesn't make any sense. The place is empty. I don't have renters living there yet. There's nothing to steal."

"Where's all your stuff?"

"Some of it I sold off through an estate auction." She turned to him. "I was ready to let go of Christopher's things. Most of the items in the house were things we'd purchased together as we settled into our life. That life was gone. I kept what had meaning to me and got rid of the rest. The paintings that were in the house—some mine, several from other artists I like and admire—they're in a secure climate controlled storage facility the security company I use offers as a service to their clients who have expensive things they can't just put in the garage or that won't fit in a lockbox at the bank."

"So all your stuff is safe."

"Yes. And so was the house. It has a security system. It's a gated area. The beach side is exposed, but the security company said the man who broke in didn't leave that way." She put her chin on her shoulder and stared at him. "It doesn't feel right."

"Maybe it was just some punk messing up your place."

She wasn't so sure. "Or someone wanted to upset me." Like her brother-in-law. But she didn't want to believe he'd take things this far, that he'd actually vandalize his brother's home. It didn't feel like him.

Then again, he hadn't been the same since Christopher's death.

Jax put his arm around her and hugged her to his side. "I'm sorry this happened. Whatever I can do to help, just name it."

She kissed his cheek. "I'll call April."

"Do you want to fly back to California and check on the place yourself? I'll go with you."

She shook her head. "I appreciate the offer, but your sister's wedding is today. She's expecting us to be there. It's family. It's important."

"She'll understand."

"No. It's just a house. Whatever's messed up can be fixed."

Jax frowned. "The windows are going to cost a lot to fix."

She shrugged. "It's just money. Your sister only gets married once."

He bumped his shoulder to hers. "Let's hope."

"Mason is not letting her go. Ever."

He kissed her shoulder this time. "I feel the same way about you."

She sighed out his name. "Jax."

"I told you. I love you. You're it for me."

She leaned in and kissed him with everything she felt in her heart. "I love you, too. So much that I don't even really care about the house. I just want to be here with you." She bit her bottom lip. "And there's something I've been meaning to show you. And after what you said the other night about how you fell in love with me at the pools . . ."

Jax squeezed her shoulders. "What is it?"

"Do you remember the picture I took of you while we were there?"

"Yeah."

She slipped from the bed and reached under it, pulling out the two paintings she'd done. One of the pools. The other of him looking at her with all the love she saw now in his eyes.

His gaze went wide with awe and surprise. "Layla . . . that's . . . they're . . . Oh my God."

"I thought you'd like the creek and pools. It turned out better than I imagined." She looked down at the one she'd done of him. "I'm not that great at portraits, but—"

"It's fucking amazing. It's like looking in a mirror."

She tried to hide a smile, but his reaction just made her love him even more. He really liked them.

"You are so damn impressive. So out of my league. So amazing and talented and . . . I don't know how you do what you do."

"I just . . . wanted this view, this moment. You looking at me like that. No one has ever looked at me the way you do."

"They better not," he snarled.

It had taken her a while to get the portrait just right. But the more she got to know Jax, the easier it was to visualize the man he was and complete the painting.

She grinned again. "I knew how you felt in that moment. I knew I didn't want to ever let you go." She propped the two large paintings against the wall.

Jax took her hand as she stood beside the bed. "Why did you hide them under the bed?"

"Because if you saw the one of you, you'd know exactly how I felt. It's in every brushstroke. After I finished it, I knew for sure exactly how I felt about you. I couldn't hide from it. I couldn't pretend it wasn't real. It is so alive inside me."

"But you're still scared this isn't real."

"I know it is. It's just . . . I don't know how to explain it, except to say I'm afraid of losing it."

He scooted across the bed and was standing in front of her, all sculpted muscles and intensity radiating off him. "You shouldn't be afraid. Because you will never lose me." It sounded like an unbreakable promise. "Maybe this sounds possessive . . . Hell, where you're concerned I am. You're mine. I want you until I can't think straight. I love you like I've never loved anyone.

And if you feel that way about me . . . then I'm the luckiest man alive. But it also means you have nothing to worry about because if we love like that, nothing can tear us apart." His words undid her.

She didn't know what to do with all that honesty and passion, except hold on to it for all she was worth.

And then he unleashed all that unbridled desire on her. He took her mouth in a hard, deep kiss, their naked bodies pressing together so close not even a whisper of air separated them. One of his hands gripped her hair, holding her head at just the right angle for him to take the kiss deeper, his tongue caressing hers, as his other hand cupped one ass cheek and he hauled her up to her toes and held her like he'd never let her go.

He shifted and it was almost like they were dancing; they moved in unison as he spun her toward the bed, backed her up, and followed her down onto it. With his strength, it was easy enough for him to lift her up the bed so he could slide up on his knees, pushing her thighs wide to accommodate his hips. That hand on her ass slid around her side and delved between her legs. His fingers brushed over her wet folds and then her clit. She was so revved up, she crashed over the edge right as his thumb pressed to that swollen nub.

He never stopped kissing her.

One finger, then two stroked inside her, setting off a wave of aftershocks. His hand left her. She felt the loss of that most intimate touch, while he grabbed a condom and rolled it on. But then his big hand molded her breast to his palm, her tight nipple caught between two of his fingers as the head of his thick erection nudged her entrance. She pushed her hips into him, taking him deep.

He broke the kiss and bit out a curse at her ear, followed by a well-satisfied moan when she clamped both hands on his ass and pulled him to her tighter.

"Layla." Just her name in that deep, dark growl made her inner muscles clutch his cock. He pulled out and slammed into her again, unleashing a frenzied wildness that had him pumping in and out of her until he clamped his hand on her hip and pulled her up and into him as he sank deep again. The pleasure exploded through her whole body as his orgasm hit at the same time. His cock pumped as he spilled himself inside her, then collapsed on top of her, his heavy weight making her sink deep into the bed. She didn't mind. Not at all. She was boneless and so damn happy she smiled and hugged him close, brushing her fingers over his heated skin and back.

Jax tried to move.

She held him close.

"I'm crushing you," he said against her neck.

"I like it."

He lifted some of his weight onto his forearms. "You still need to breathe, baby."

They were both still panting.

"That was . . ."

"Fucking amazing," he finished for her. "It always is with you, but that . . ." He lifted his head. "Did I hurt you?"

She shook her head. "No. Not at all. I loved it."

The satisfied and wicked grin only made him even

more gorgeous. "Good. Because I'd like to do that again. Soon."

She brushed her hand over his stubbly jaw. "Anytime."

He turned his face into her palm and kissed it. "I'm so lucky."

"I think that's me." She stared up into his eyes. "I thought coming to Wyoming would help me find my inspiration again." She turned and looked at the painting of him staring back at her. "I found so much more."

"Does that mean you're thinking about making this your new home?"

"You're here. There's nowhere else I'd rather be."

This time she got the sweet, adoring smile from him. "Good answer."

"I know this place and your family are important to you. This is where you're happiest. It's important to me that you don't give that up to be with me. You don't have to, not when I can travel when I need to and paint here."

"So long as you call this home, I know I'll have to let you roam to find those inspiring views you love to paint. I'll come with you as much as I can."

"I'd like that."

He left her only for a moment to ditch the condom, then slid back into bed with her.

She wrapped her arms around him, held on tight, and never wanted to let him go.

\* \* \*

HOURS LATER, HE was kissing her and rubbing his nose against hers. "Wake up, baby. You should probably call April about your house while I start the coffee and shower. Big day today."

"Lyric and Mason's wedding."

He kissed her on each cheek, slid out of bed, and pulled on his black boxer briefs before heading out to the kitchen.

She called April, knowing she was going to wake up her best friend because of the time difference.

"It's too early in the morning for this to be about work. Tell me Jax didn't break your heart."

"He loves me," she announced, a bubbly feeling in her belly. "And I love him."

They hadn't spoken in a few days, so April was a bit behind on the Jax and Layla story.

"I knew there was something special there." April yawned. "So what's going on? Are you eloping? I thought today was his sister's wedding. Are you having a double wedding?" April's excitement made Layla giggle.

"No. We are not horning in on their wedding. We just did the whole I-love-you-confession thing the other night before the rehearsal dinner."

"I hope you were in bed together."

Layla didn't confirm or deny. "Anyway, we'll figure the rest out as we go. But first I need your help at my house."

"The renters aren't moving in for a couple more weeks." They'd had to delay their move due to a family emergency.

"I know. But first you have to go assess the damage. Some asshole broke in and trashed the place. We'll need to contact the insurance company."

"Hold on. What? Someone broke into your house?"

Donte grumbled something in the background.

"Go back to sleep. I've got this," April said to him, then addressed her again. "I assume security called you."

"Yes. The alarm went off late last night. When they got there, the guy ran. I'd come back and deal with it myself, but—"

"No. I've got this." April always had her back. "Don't worry. I'll take care of everything."

Layla felt bad asking. "I know this isn't part of your job."

"I'm your best friend. I'll take care of it. You stay there with Jax. Because it is so good to hear you sound like you're really happy again."

She sighed and melted into the bed. "This is the happiest I think I've ever been."

Jax appeared in the doorway. He stared at her, a grin on his face, as he folded his arms and leaned against the doorframe. "Me, too."

"Hey, April. Thanks for taking care of this for me. I have to go."

"He's there, isn't he?"

"Yeah. And he looks so good first thing in the morning. It's just not fair."

April squealed. "Go get him." She hung up.

Layla didn't have to go after Jax. He came to her with a smile and a wicked tongue.

# Chapter Twenty-Four

You may now kiss the bride."

Mason slipped his hand along Lyric's cheek, leaned in, and kissed her like his life depended on it. Or like she was his life. When he leaned back and brushed his thumb across her smiling lips, she grabbed his tie and pulled him back in for another steamy kiss that had the crowd cheering again.

Layla's cheeks hurt from smiling so much. She was so happy for the now married couple.

Jax slipped his arm around her waist and turned her toward him. He kissed her just like Mason had kissed his wife. The kiss ended as abruptly as it started. "I love you like that." He nodded his head toward the happy couple. "Just so you know."

It seemed he couldn't stop telling her and she didn't mind it one bit.

She pressed her hand to his tie. "Good. Because I love you, too. And I don't want any of your sisters' single friends thinking they can hit on you during the reception."

"I'm all yours, sweetheart."

"Good. They can have one of the Gunns." Jax had

introduced her to Mason's cousins, Lincoln, Hawk, and Damon Gunn. The guys took great pleasure in kissing Lyric on the forehead every chance they got just to rile Mason. Lyric didn't seem to mind; she just rolled her eyes and kissed Mason's socks off to get him to stop threatening to kill his brother and cousins.

Nick, Lincoln, and Hawk had stood up for Mason, while Aria stood as maid of honor and Melody and Lyric's songwriting partner, Faith, stood as her bridesmaids.

Wade had walked Lyric down the aisle, proud as any father could be on his daughter's wedding day.

And the bride . . . She glowed from within with so much happiness and love, her gaze locked on Mason, who couldn't take his eyes off her.

The gown was gorgeous. White. Lace sleeves, a plunging neckline, the dress hugged the curve of her hips, then flared out into a multilayered floor-length full skirt. Her dark hair was pulled back in a pretty twist, secured by blue clips that matched her Wilde eyes.

Mason and the guys wore black suits with blue ties. The groom's was the same blue as Lyric's eyes, while the groomsmen wore a darker shade that matched the bridal party's dresses.

The photos were going to look amazing.

"I give you, Mr. and Mrs. Gunn."

The crowd cheered again as Mason and Lyric walked down the aisle. The guests tossed pink rose petals for them, showering the couple in the heady scent.

The wedding was held on the ranch in a gorgeous

clearing in the trees. The florist had done a wonderful job adding beautiful bouquets along the ground, marking the aisle between the two sides of seating, and atop the raised platform where the ceremony took place.

Layla thought her studio would fit here perfectly as a wedding chapel nestled in the woods. A unique and quaint place for a small wedding.

"Come on. Let's follow everyone to the reception." Jax took her hand and they trailed his parents and Mason's down the aisle as each row of guests followed behind them.

The nearby converted barn had been set up with tables for dinner and a dance floor.

Jax and Layla found his and Mason's family standing by the gift table just inside the entrance.

Lyric and Mason were in front of all of them staring at the gift Layla had painted for them.

"It's Bruin," Lyric said, awe and wonder in her voice. "It's . . . perfect." She turned and stared at Layla.

"I'm so happy you like it."

"*Like.*" Mason shook his head. "We *love* it. Thank you."

Layla felt herself blush. "You're welcome. Thank you for including me in your special day."

The guests were starting to line up, so the bride and groom walked into the reception to Lee Brice's "Soul." Everyone followed, Jax and Layla right behind them.

He leaned down and said in Layla's ear, "Lyric and Mason send each other songs. She sent this one to him to let him know how she felt about him early in their relationship." Jax pulled her onto the dance floor where Mason and Lyric were already dancing. He held her hand and they danced to the upbeat song and he sang the lyrics to her, along with everyone else in the room, because Lyric started singing it to Mason.

Jax didn't let go of Layla practically the whole night.

They ate, drank, and celebrated. The whole room felt like it was filled to overflowing with joy. Her feet hurt from dancing in her heels, but she was amped on the happiness of seeing two people who so obviously adored each other celebrate their new life together.

And just before Lyric and Mason left for their wedding night and honeymoon, Layla found herself dragged onto the dance floor by Aria and Melody as Lyric threw the bouquet.

And it landed right in Layla's hands.

Lyric turned with a triumphant grin on her face. "Perfect shot." She looked past Layla, and Layla knew she was grinning at her brother, Jax.

Layla turned slowly and held up the bouquet.

Jax winked at her with the most devastatingly gorgeous it's-going-to-happen grin on his face.

She buried her nose in the blooms and smiled back at him.

Melody hooked her arm over Layla's shoulders. "So, is it going to be a big wedding, or a small one?"

"Doesn't matter, as long as I get to keep him." She pointed at Jax with the bouquet.

Melody hugged her tight. "That's all that matters, isn't it? It's not the wedding, it's the one you get to spend your life with that makes a marriage." Melody leaned back and held her by the shoulders. "I'm so happy Jax found that with you."

"I hope you find it soon." Layla meant it.

Jax's sisters were amazing. They loved him so much. They'd welcomed her into his life and theirs with open hearts, minds, and arms. She wanted all of them to be as happy as she was with Jax.

Lyric certainly had it with Mason.

He was currently carrying his bride out of the building to loud applause and people yelling their well-wishes.

"What a night!" Jax took her hand again and squeezed it. "You ready to head to the cabin?" The other nine were occupied by out-of-town guests for the wedding, mostly Mason's family.

She glanced up at him, still holding the bouquet. "Yeah. I think I'd like to kiss the brother of the bride all night."

"I'm all in." The look on his face said he meant it and it included a hell of a lot more than one night.

Jax pulled her out of the reception to her Jeep and helped her into the passenger seat. He climbed behind the wheel and drove them back to the cabin, where he took her inside and loved her like they were celebrating their wedding night.

# Chapter Twenty-Five

Jax walked into Layla's studio and glared at the man who had his arm over Layla's shoulders, his body brushing hers, as they stared at one of her paintings he couldn't see on the big easel.

The guy read his *Don't touch* look and slowly released Layla and took a step away from her.

*She's mine, asshole.*

Layla's eyes flashed with surprise. "Jax. I'd like you to meet Collin. He's the one who commissioned me to come here and paint for him."

He got the message. *Be nice.*

Jax held out his hand, understanding dawning. "Then I owe you a huge thank-you for bringing Layla into my life."

The guy took his hand. "I'd say, you're welcome, but I'm still disappointed she chose you." Though his tone was light, his words rang very true.

Jax settled down and grinned at Layla. "I'm the luckiest man on the planet."

"That you are," the guy agreed. "And though nothing compares to the artist herself, the painting is stunning and more than I expected it to be. As consolation prizes go, it's a masterpiece."

Layla sighed with relief. "I'm just happy you feel like you got your money's worth. I'm also happy you'll be taking it home to enjoy."

"Yeah. Sorry I couldn't get it earlier. I had to go to LA for a while. I'm only back to collect the painting, check on my place here, then I'm headed to LA again. I heard your place got hit by some vandal."

Jax raised a brow. "How did you hear that?"

"Famous local artist's house gets trashed . . . that ends up on local news outlets fast. Mostly because they wanted to talk about how the house was empty. No art got destroyed. Everyone is wondering where she is. The intrigue of her disappearance makes for a great story. Even if there really isn't anything mysterious about it."

"Why is anyone interested in her whereabouts?" Jax didn't like that people were so curious about her. Not after what happened at her place.

"If you haven't figured it out, in the art world, she's huge. Everyone wants her paintings." He looked around the room at all the paintings lined up in the storage holders against the walls. "She hasn't painted anything significant in a long time." He turned to Layla. "It looks like you found your inspiration again."

"And then some," she confirmed.

Jax had no idea she'd painted more here than she usually did. To him, it seemed like she loved it so much she couldn't stop herself from getting the paint onto the canvas, to capture one more beautiful scene.

"Well, I don't want to take up any more of your time. Looks like you were working on something when I came in. I'll just let you get back to it. And I will try to wait patiently for the second painting."

She stepped back as Collin took the painting from the easel. "I'll go through the photographs I took at your place, send them to you, and you can pick the one you want to add to your office." Layla helped Collin pack the painting into the long narrow crate near the door.

Collin leaned in and kissed ' _r cheek. "Thank you again."

"You're turning into my best customer."

"I know art. This piece is going to be worth a hell of a lot more than I paid for it in a few years." With that, Collin left.

Jax found himself staring at Layla.

"What?"

"You just amaze me."

Her eyes went wide. "Why?"

"You spend hours in here painting. I see the strain, the concentration, the attention to every tiny detail, and then the joy when you step back and look at what you've created. I see the pride you have in your work."

"When it comes out just the way I want it . . . yeah, I'm happy. It feels like a huge accomplishment. So? Shouldn't I feel that way?"

"Yes. Because you're brilliant. And it blows my mind that all that talent is inside you and you just seem so . . ."

"What?"

"Normal."

She raised a brow.

"The guy paid you half a million bucks for a painting, yet you gave one to my sister for a wedding gift like it was just something you wanted her to have because she'd love it."

"That's why I gave it to her."

"Yes, but she could probably sell the thing and put three kids through Ivy League college with it."

She held her hands up and let them drop. "So?"

"It just floors me that the money doesn't matter to you. It's the painting you love."

"Yes. And I'm lucky that I get to do what I love and get paid for it." She picked up a dirty brush and stared at the green paint on it. "You seem to be stuck on the fact that I make a lot of money."

"It occurred to me that I can't compete with what you make for a living. I can't afford to take you around the world, buy you expensive jewelry, stuff like that."

"I never asked you for any of that. I don't care that you don't make as much money as I do. If you give me a gift, I'll love it because it came from you. But I don't need it to make me happy."

He took a step closer. "You love me."

She moved closer to him. "Yes."

"That guy that was just here. He's rich, handsome, he could probably buy you anything you want."

She shrugged. "I don't care."

"I know. You love me."

She put her hand over his heart. "I already said I do."

He put his hand over hers on his chest. "I get it even more now. You wanted something real. Our love is exactly that. It's what matters most."

"It's not about things," she confirmed. "You make me feel special, like I matter. You see me. You want to understand me. You want to make me happy."

He wrapped his arm around her waist and held her close. "If you're not, I'm not."

"Isn't that kind of love everything? What does money have to do with that? You can't buy it. You can't hold it. You can only feel it. A house full of things can go up in flames and leave you with nothing. But you can still have that sense of home with the ones you love and none of that lost stuff matters as long as the ones you love are safe."

"So, I guess we'll never fight about money."

"I don't want to fight with you about anything. I don't like that this conversation feels weird."

Jax kissed her softly. "I'm sorry. I never meant to make you feel like something is wrong. It's not. It's just . . . for a second there, I thought maybe you needed more than I can give you."

"That's not true."

"I know. The second I saw you look at me, I knew that I was everything you want."

"You are."

"So I won't stress about the money thing. It's not important. The life we build together, the home we make, the love we share . . . that's everything. *You* are everything to me." This time, he kissed her with all the passion and love he had for her. He poured it all into the kiss, hoping to erase all trace of his dumbass remarks and stumbling through getting to the very core of what he wanted her to know. He loved her. Wholly. Unconditionally. Unbreakably so.

Nothing and no one would come between them.

# Chapter Twenty-Six

Layla knocked on the Wildes' front door. She'd been invited to Sunday dinner. She shouldn't be nervous. She'd seen Robin and Wade Wilde on the ranch dozens of times. They were always nice and polite and welcoming. They were becoming friends, not just acquaintances. She appreciated that they always asked about her and didn't bring up anything about her relationship with their son, even though they had to know he spent nearly every night with her now.

She hadn't seen Jax since this morning. He'd had another busy day. But before he left, he'd stood by the bed for a long moment staring down at her lying in the rumpled sheets, then simply asked, "Will you please come to dinner with my family tonight? If you're not there, all I'll be doing is missing you, because I want you there with me. Do you get what I'm saying?"

She did. So she'd said, "Yes."

He kissed her like it was a thank-you, then left her smiling.

The Wildes' door flew open. "Why didn't you just come in?" Jax stared at her, confused.

She glared at him. "Because it's not my house."

"We're all expecting you."

She held her arms out. "And here I am. Can I come in?"

He blocked the door. Instead of opening it wider, he leaned in and kissed her first. The kiss was long and deep and spun out as she wrapped her arms around his neck, pulling her body close to his.

Seriously, the man could kiss and make her forget her name.

She thought after two-plus months things would cool down. They hadn't. Jax wanted her just as desperately now as he did the first time he'd kissed her.

They just got better and better with each passing day.

"Let her in!" Robin shouted. "You can kiss her later."

Giggles rose from his sisters.

Jax brushed his nose against hers. He took her hand and pulled her into the house, pushing the door closed behind her.

"I love your dress." Melody's gaze swept over her.

Layla wanted to make a good impression, so she'd slipped into the bright blue eyelet sundress with spaghetti straps that crisscrossed in the back and had a V neckline. It cinched in just below her breasts and had a drop skirt that hit her midcalf. The nude wedge sandals gave her some added height. "Thank you. It's supercomfortable."

Jax hugged her to his side. "You're gorgeous." He kissed the side of her head. "Can I get you a drink? Wine? We have yours."

"Sounds great." She walked with him closer to the

kitchen where Aria, Lyric, Mason, and Wade sat at the breakfast bar. Robin stirred something on the stove, and Jax poured her wine, then put the bottle back in the fridge.

"You have such a beautiful home," she said to Robin.

"We're so happy you came tonight. I love having everyone I care about together."

Layla appreciated that she'd included her in that sweet sentiment. "I'm just glad I didn't have to drive over." She looked up at Jax. "Can you change my flat tire later? I planned to go into town to do some grocery shopping, but . . ." She raised her shoulders. "Tire is totally flat."

"Maybe you ran over a nail or something," Mason suggested.

Jax stared down at her, concern in his eyes. "Was there anything damaged on the car?"

"Not that I saw. Why?"

"Nothing." Jax's expression definitely conveyed something.

Layla let it go. They could talk about it later.

"I heard about what happened at your home in California." Wade winced. "Was your agent able to get the repairs done?"

"The painters finished up today. The windows cost a fortune. There are a few other minor repairs outstanding. But otherwise, everything is secure and ready for the new renters."

"Have they caught the guy?" Mason asked. Since he was FBI, he probably knew how these sorts of investigations went.

"No. While the neighbors' surveillance footage showed the guy leaving the scene, nothing captured anything identifiable about him. It's a mystery."

"Why target a house with nothing in it?" Aria asked.

"The windows are all privacy glass. You can see out, but no one can see in. So they might not have known the place was empty," she explained. "If they knew it was my house, they may have thought there was some expensive art on the walls."

Mason leaned toward her. "Could it have been a message to you?"

"The graffiti was just a bunch of squiggles. No words." She thought about it. "I mean, if you're going to mess up the walls, do it with some artistic intent."

Jax shook his head at her.

She returned to Mason's question. "If they intended to leave me a message, I didn't get it."

"Is anyone upset with you?" Mason asked.

"Don't interrogate her." Lyric frowned at her new husband.

"I'm not. I'm trying to help."

"You're scaring her." Lyric gave her an apologetic look.

Layla shook her head. "It's fine. I didn't really think of someone doing it to let me know they're angry with me. Why not just say so?"

"Michael has made it very clear he's angry with you," Jax pointed out.

"Who's Michael and why?" Mason asked.

"He's my brother-in-law. And it's simple. He wants money. I inherited what was left of my husband's estate. Michael was named in the will, but he contested it, lost, and got nothing."

"Then that's his fault." Robin patted her hand, then took out a huge casserole from the oven. The scent of melted cheese filled the air.

Perhaps Michael's anger had turned to destruction.

She didn't want to think so. "He wouldn't vandalize my house."

"People do strange things when it comes to family and money," Mason said.

Robin pulled a second tray out of the oven. The scent of garlic bread mixed with the cheese made Layla's stomach grumble. "Let's eat." Robin put a large spoon in the casserole pan.

Jax led the procession from one side of the huge island to the other as everyone grabbed a plate and spooned up the delicious-smelling manicotti, garlic bread, and salad before heading to the massive dining room table between the kitchen and family room.

Layla dug into the food while the family talked about Lyric's wedding, the Hawaiian honeymoon they'd just returned from just yesterday, the bar, and the ranch. Their lives were so intertwined.

Since she was sitting beside Melody, she asked, "How's it going with that guy who's been DMing you?"

Melody frowned. "At first, it seemed fun. Flirty. But it's been six weeks and he still won't tell me who he really is. Now I'm suspicious, but I did what Jax said and started asking questions about him." She bit her bottom lip. "I like him. A lot. But if the guy doesn't want to be seen with me . . . that's a real problem."

"I'm sure it's not that. Maybe he's just shy and wants to really get to know you before a meetup. You're beautiful. Any guy would be lucky to be with you."

She tilted her head. "And yet he avoids an actual date, or telling me his real name."

"Has he said anything more about seeing you in the bar?"

"Yep. He drops those little hints that he's been there, seen me, liked what I was wearing, or how I handled a rowdy customer."

Layla raised a brow.

"Exactly." Melody took a sip of her wine. "He's playing with me and I don't like it."

"Stop talking to him," she suggested. "Make him come to you, in person."

Melody's grin spread very slowly as her eyes gleamed. "That's a great idea."

"What do you have to lose?"

Melody's grin fell. "I'd miss our chats. I really do like talking to him."

"That's a good place to start. But if you want more, tell him."

Jax looked across her at his sister. "If he doesn't step up, cut him loose."

Melody picked up her phone, checked the screen for notifications, frowned, then set it down.

"Who wants dessert?" Robin asked the crowd. "Someone told me that Layla loves strawberry short-cake with Chantilly cream."

Layla glanced at Jax, who kept his face blank, then back to Robin. "It is my favorite. I had it several times at this little place outside of Paris where I was painting a couple of years ago. I went back night after night just for dessert."

"Where is the painting hanging now?" Aria asked.

"One of them is hanging in the restaurant. I gifted it to the pastry chef in exchange for the recipe and a lesson on how to make it because, while I get by in the kitchen, I'm not that great."

Robin handed her a plate piled high with strawberries and a huge dollop of cream on top. "Let's hope this satisfies."

Layla stabbed a bit of cake, strawberry, and cream and slid it into her mouth. The second the sweet cream touched her tongue, she moaned. "That's fantastic," she said around the mouthful. "Thank you for going to the trouble."

"I like to make my kids happy."

Layla held Robin's stare and grinned, knowing she meant those kids included her now. "Thank you." The words barely whispered from her lips, but Robin heard them.

It had been a long time since she'd felt this accepted and included and part of a family. She saw her parents a few times a year, but time and distance made the visits feel different. Her life wasn't entwined with her parents anymore. Not the way the Wilde family was because they lived and worked together on a daily basis. She missed her grandfather desperately and spoke to him more often than her parents.

Dessert was delectable. The conversation around the table never stopped. She loved the funny stories they told about Jax. The atmosphere was fun and relaxed, and Layla enjoyed all of it. Mostly, she loved sitting beside Jax and feeling like this was where she belonged.

Wade and Robin both hugged her goodbye at the front door.

"Don't be a stranger. You are expected and welcome at all the Sunday dinners, so please come," Robin implored. "Otherwise Jax will stop coming because he'd rather be with you."

"I'll be here." She squeezed Jax's hand, letting him know she wanted to be with him, wherever he was, too.

She and Jax walked down the porch steps, but turned back when Mason asked, "Do you need help with changing the tire?"

Jax shook his head. "Thanks, man, but I've got it."

Mason scooped Lyric into his arms just to make her laugh, then carried her to their car.

"Those two are so gone for each other," Layla said.

Jax pulled her close and kissed her softly. "Just like I am wild for you."

She stepped back, took his hand, and pulled him down the driveway and toward the cabin. "You know I love you desperately."

Jax stopped and tugged her hand, making her come around and right into his arms. "Yeah? Prove it." He leaned down and kissed her on the gravel road leading to the cabins, the moon big and bright overhead. The kiss was soft and tender and filled with love.

And something else.

She stared into his blue eyes. "What was that for?"

"I know you felt it tonight, sitting at the table with my family. You belong there with us. With me."

"It felt like home. It's been a long time since I visited my family."

"This was just the first of many, many family dinners to come. We'll see my sisters married and happy, new little Wildes come into our lives. That table will overflow to more tables as all of us build our lives with the ones we love. And through it all, I will be by your side and kissing you under the moonlight. And in the sunshine. Pretty much everywhere we are, because I like kissing you." He did it again, making her sigh and laugh all at once against his lips.

With her arms locked around his neck, their bodies close, she stared up at him. "I don't know how this happened."

"I told you. I'm the luckiest man alive."

She laughed again, took his hand, and pulled him toward their cabin. "You're mine. That's all that matters."

They rounded the cabin to where she'd parked the Jeep. She held out her hand to the flat front tire. "I know there's a spare. The guy at the rental company pointed it out to me, but I don't know how to change the flat."

Jax crouched beside the tire and ran his fingers over the rubber. "Do you know when this happened?"

She frowned, thinking about the last couple of days. "I haven't driven it since I went to Sheridan a few days ago to pick up the supplies I had the art gallery there order for me. Parked it here when I got back, unloaded, then left it sitting. Why?"

"Because this isn't just a flat. Someone slashed the tire with a knife." Jax stood and walked around the vehicle. "The back tire over here is also slashed."

Which meant she was stuck without a car until she could get both tires fixed. "Who would do this? Why?"

Jax walked past her and along the row of cabins checking all the other vehicles parked along the way, then came back to her. "It looks like only your car was vandalized."

A sense of unease came over her. "Huh."

"That's it? Just, huh. Did you see anyone around your cabin, or lurking back here?"

She raised a brow. "I was in my studio most of the time. And when you were here, I was with you inside the cabin. I didn't have anywhere to go until today when I wanted to pick up groceries, so I haven't come back here."

"And you didn't hear anything last night?"

"Did you?" Because he'd been sleeping right beside her.

"No. I'll check the camera feeds and see if they picked up anything."

She glanced around them. "There are cameras back here?"

"Yes." Jax pulled out his phone. "There have been some thefts in the cabins and other vehicles. Opportunistic shit. We don't want our guests hurt like that, so we have cameras. Some you can see to deter people." He pointed to the one on the light pole nearby. "Others that are more discreet."

"I see. Well, that's a good idea. They're not in the cabins though, right?" That kind of creeped her out.

"No." He looked disgruntled by the notion. "We give our guests their privacy inside the cabin. But public spaces have cameras just in case. Good thing, too, because a couple years ago a woman was being harassed by another guest. He couldn't seem to take no for an answer. When she reported it to us, we used the footage to show the cops she'd been fending off his advances for days. He got booted off the ranch. She filed charges, and he spent a little time in jail."

"I'm sorry that happened to her."

"Me, too. I wish she'd come to one of us sooner. I don't want anyone hurt or threatened on this property. Especially not you."

"This is probably just some jerk or a kid."

Jax turned his phone to her. "Or some guy wearing exactly what he was wearing when he trashed your house?"

Layla snatched the phone and stared at the man in black with the same ski mask on his head covered by a black hoody. Black jeans. Black work boots. "It's a coincidence. I mean, lots of guys have black hoodies and boots."

"I don't believe in coincidences like this. Someone is messing with you. And I don't like it." He took the phone back and made a call. "Officer Bowers. Hey, it's Jax. I'm out at the ranch. Someone slashed my girlfriend's tires out behind cabin ten. I've got video of a man who looks strikingly like the guy who vandalized her home in California." Jax listened to whatever response the officer had for him, then hung up. "He'll be here in about twenty minutes to take a report. Until then, tell me who you think is doing this. I think it's your brother-in-law, Michael, but if there's someone else you can think of, now's the time to tell me."

"I don't know anyone who'd want to do this. Yes, Michael is upset about what happened with the will. Yes, he wants the money. But I think his antagonism and anger are more about his grief than anything else." She threw up her hands and let them fall. "Besides, why would Michael do this? It just makes me even less inclined to give in to his demands."

"Maybe he did it to get you to come home."

"It doesn't matter where I am, I'm not going to give him the money he wants."

"Is there some provision in Christopher's will that states if you die, he gets everything?"

Well, that sounded ominous. "No. While Christopher made a better-than-decent living in the import business, most of his money was gone at the time he died."

"Was that why he killed himself?"

"No."

"So you were broke when he died?"

"No. Christopher never touched my money. In fact, he purposefully kept our accounts separate. In the beginning, he made more money than I did. He said that whatever I made painting, it was mine to do with as I pleased, but he'd always take care of me."

"What about that house? It's got to be worth a fortune. Half of that was part of Christopher's estate."

"No. We bought the house when we decided we needed a bigger place. I'd always dreamed of a house on the ocean. So we started looking and found the place I loved. When it came time to buy it, I told Christopher I'd pay for it, as a thank-you for all he'd done while I was building my career and so that I felt like

I'd contributed to our life together. Like I told you before, he insisted I put the house in my name only."

"Right. He wanted you to have the security of
knowing the house would always be your home."

"Yes."

"So he was broke and you were rich. That must
have been hard on him."

Anger flared. "It was his own damn fault."

"Why? It sounds like he had a very lucrative job.
Was it bad investments? Overspending?"

"He thought he could have everything he wanted,
me and someone else."

Anger flashed in his eyes. "He was cheating on
you."

"Oh, that would have been simpler, less soul crushing."

"How? Being cheated on is really shitty."

"Tell me about it. But he wasn't just fucking someone behind my back. He had a whole relationship with
her. He loved her. He took care of her. He—"

Headlights swept over them as the patrol car headed
in their direction.

"He what?"

She stared at the cop car.

"What, Layla?"

She turned back to him. "We'll finish this later."

"Yeah, we will." Jax passed her and went to meet
the cop.

Layla leaned back against the cabin wall and
watched as Officer Bowers and Jax went over her car,
the video, and the report the officer wrote up.

Then Bowers asked, "Tell me about Michael."

She sighed, barely glanced at Jax, and focused on the cop. "He's my brother-in-law, though I'm sure Jax has already told you that information. He lives in California. We are not on good terms after my husband's suicide. He fought the terms of the will." She explained how that had gone down in court and how Michael lost because he contested the will and went against Christopher's wishes. "He's upset his brother is dead and I got what he thinks I don't deserve. But I was Christopher's wife at the time of his death, even if I had been planning to leave him."

"Has he threatened you?"

"Not the way you're suggesting. Not bodily harm. Just that he could ruin my reputation. But he says he's not going to stop until he gets what he wants."

"Do you think paying him off would end things?"

She raised a brow at the cop. "You've probably seen this a lot with bullies, right? They're never satisfied. Especially when they think they're right and no amount of reasoning will change their mind. Not even the law being on my side will change his mind. If this is him, then he'll eventually be caught and I'll be out some money and neither of us will get what we want."

"What do you want?" the officer asked.

"For him to leave me alone so I can move on. Like he should do."

"Do you think your relationship with Jax set him off?"

"I don't know why it would. Last I spoke to Michael, he had a big investment opportunity. One that would score big. The trouble is, Michael is always looking for the get-rich-quick schemes that are bound to pay off. They never do. Christopher and Michael were quite opposites when it came to doing things. Christopher worked hard for everything he had and Michael wanted it to be handed to him."

"So you think this is just about money."

"Yes. And he doesn't like me in a complicated way."

Officer Bowers eyed her. "How's that?"

"Christopher was happy with me. He loved me. And I loved him. Michael looked at us together, our happy life, filled with friends, no money worries, our great jobs, and he wanted it."

"Sounds like a good life."

"It looked like one, too, until it wasn't."

"Did that have something to do with Michael?" he asked.

"No. My husband ruined it all on his own. And then he killed himself, leaving the people he cared about most behind without ever taking responsibility for what he'd done or making amends."

Officer Bowers read between the lines. "You're a little angry about that."

"Wouldn't you be if you never got to have your say, never got to get past the anger so you could remember the good times? Because maybe if you could remember those times without the bitterness and anger, you could forgive and have your friend back."

"I'm sorry for your loss." The officer's gentle voice made it hard to stop the tears gathering in her eyes from spilling over.

She swiped them away.

Jax put his arm around her shoulder and pulled her

in for a tight hug. "It's okay, sweetheart, to be sad that he broke your heart and you miss him."

"I didn't want to stay with him, not after everything that happened, but I wanted my say. I wanted him to still be here."

"I know. But right now, we need to focus on who is being a menace in your life."

She stepped back. "Maybe it is Michael. Maybe it's random. Maybe it's someone else who's upset with me for whatever reason. I don't know. I just want it to stop."

Jax cupped her face. "We'll find who's doing this and make them stop."

Officer Bowers headed back to his car. "I'll file the report and send you a copy for your insurance. I'll call local PD in California where Michael lives and have them pay him a visit, ask him some questions. If he's not there and he's here, I'll do a sweep of local hotels and motels, see if I can track him down. Maybe that will be enough to make him back off, even if we can't prove he's behind the vandalism." He opened his car door. "I'll be in touch." With that, the officer left.

Jax pulled her back into his arms. "I'll call a local garage in the morning and have them come out and tow the car to town. They can fix the tires and I'll either drive you there to pick it up if I can or have them deliver it when it's ready. Is there anything from the grocery store you need right away? I can have one of my sisters do a grocery run for you."

She shook her head. "No. It's fine. It can wait until I have my car back."

Jax walked with her back around the cabin and inside. He closed the door, locked it, then asked, "Are you going to tell me the rest?" He meant about Christopher.

"Can it wait until the morning? Because right now, I just want you to take me to bed and make me forget all this."

He advanced on her, his gaze intent. His hands clamped onto her hips and he walked her backward into the bedroom and right up to the bed. The backs of her knees hit the mattress. Jax leaned in and kissed her. It was all tongue and need and hot, greedy mouths. Then he abruptly broke the kiss. "I'm going to do everything I can, everything you like, to make you forget." His wicked smile made promises his body kept as he took her down to the bed and started stripping her. His mouth trailed kisses over every inch of skin he exposed, until he had her naked and writhing with his head between her thighs, her legs over his shoulders, and his tongue licking her to the height of pleasure, not a single thought in her head but wanting more.

He gave it to her, stripping off his clothes, rolling on a condom, and coming down on top of her between her thighs. He took her in one long, deep thrust that filled her, the pleasure so consuming she climaxed again, her inner muscles clamping onto his hard length. He rode out her orgasm with gritted teeth, then pulled out slowly and rocked back into her with languid pushes and pulls, like he had all night to love her. While that was all nice and good, what she really wanted was something unrestrained and untamed.

She grabbed his ass and pulled him in as she pushed her hips right into his.

He groaned and swore under his breath.

"Baby, let go." She gave him enough leeway to pull out, then slam back into her. "Yes."

That was all the permission he needed to unleash himself. The ride was hard and fast and dirty as he leaned down and took her nipple in his mouth and sucked hard.

A wave of heat shot down to her core as he slammed into her again, then swiveled his hips against her. She moaned, planted her heels in the bed, lifted her hips, taking him deep. He clamped his hand on her ass, holding her up against him as her orgasm hit hard and fast. Jax rose on his knees, fastened his hands on her hips, and thrust into her again and again, amplifying her orgasm as he bucked against her and spilled himself inside her.

They were both heaving and panting when he settled her back on the bed and fell over her, keeping most of his weight on his forearms, his face in her neck.

"Layla?"

"Is that my name? I don't remember." She felt his smile against her skin.

"I love you. I love us. Like this."

She tightened her arms around his back. "You really are wild for me."

He lifted his head and kissed her with just as much passion as he'd shown her moments ago, then abruptly broke it and looked her in the eyes, his filled with absolute conviction. "That will never change." He kissed her again, this time more tenderly and sensual, then he rolled onto his back, taking her with him so she settled on top of him with his arms locked around her. He held her close as the quiet night surrounded them.

Safe, protected, loved, she drifted off, barely noticing when Jax rose to take care of the condom cleanup in the bathroom before sliding into bed next to her again and pulling her into his arms.

Whatever happened tomorrow, the next day, the days after that, she'd have Jax by her side, his love always surrounding her. She couldn't ask for more.

Except for whoever was harassing her to leave her alone. So she could be happy and carefree with Jax, the man she was going to marry, even though she never thought she'd want to do that ever again.

Jax made her believe in a future where they had it all—and it lasted forever.

# Chapter Twenty-Seven

J ax put a bowl of strawberry shortcake with Chantilly cream in front of Layla, along with a cup of
coffee. He should have been at work an hour ago, but
he'd gone up to the main house to get this treat for
Layla, then came back to wait for her to wake up. After making love to her a second time last night when
she woke from a bad dream, he wanted to be sure she
got the rest she needed.

She stared at the dessert. "Did you get this just
for me?"

"It's your favorite. I thought it might sweeten your
day, even though we're going to have that talk now."

She sipped her coffee, then looked up at him. "Sit.
We'll talk."

He took the chair beside her, and scooted closer, so
they were face-to-face, their legs brushing. He put his
hand on her bare thigh, trying not to think about how
soft her skin was and get sidetracked by taking her
back to bed. "What did Christopher do besides cheat
on you that you don't want anyone to know?"

She forked up a bit of cream, put it in her mouth,
and slid the fork out of her still kiss-swollen lips. Sadness

filled her eyes as she sighed. "After I lost the baby, I pulled away from him, April, everyone. I didn't want to talk. I didn't want to paint." Tears gathered in her eyes. "I missed Miles so hard and deep I couldn't feel anything else but the loss of him. I felt empty."

He took her hand and squeezed it softly. "That's completely understandable."

She didn't look at him, just stared at the bowl in front of her. "After a while, Christopher suggested we try again. I told him I wasn't ready." She met his gaze. "I was so scared it would happen again." A tear slipped down her cheek.

He softly brushed it away with his thumb and didn't say anything, giving her the space and time she needed to tell the story. Her own way.

"Christopher kept asking. I kept saying no. He begged me to start living again, to look toward the future. We could be happy again." She met his gaze, hers still watery. "I just couldn't seem to get there. We had yet another argument about it, and he yelled at me that I wasn't the only one hurting. I wasn't the only one who lost someone. In that moment, I realized that I was so lost in my pain I forgot about his."

"You're compassionate. You care about others. I'm sure you tried to console him."

"I tried, but not enough."

"I imagine for a mother, the one who is carrying the child, the loss feels greater because of that intimate connection. I'm not saying he didn't grieve, but maybe he didn't understand your loss and the way you experienced it because he simply couldn't relate on that level."

"I couldn't do it again, knowing that the baby would more than likely have the same genetic disorder . . ." She shook her head and pressed a hand to her chest like her heart hurt.

"Did Christopher offer an alternative? Adoption? A sperm donor?"

"I wasn't ready to hear any of that. I was just trying to survive at that point."

Jax heard what she didn't say. "He turned away from you and to someone else."

"I probably would have taken some of the blame if it had just been sex. Someone he could find solace with."

"But he fell for the woman. They were close."

"I don't know how many there were. Maybe it was just her. And if he came to me and said he wanted her and not me, I'd have let him go without a fight, because I wanted him to be happy, and I knew I wasn't able to do that at the time. I would have been angry and hurt that he gave up on me. I'd have missed him and grieved for what could have been if only . . ." She sighed. "A divorce would have been better for both of us. But he loved me and didn't want to let me go. But he also wanted a family." Her somber gaze met his, and he knew.

Jax swore. "They had a baby together."

Another tear slid down her cheek. "A beautiful *healthy* little girl."

He cupped her cheek and stared into her sad eyes. "I'm so sorry, sweetheart. That had to hurt. It had to feel incredibly unfair."

She nodded. "It did. But there was more."

He cocked his head. "I mean, a cheating husband

who had a baby with his mistress had to be devastating enough."

"He bought her a house, then married her."

"What? No." That didn't make sense. "He couldn't do that if he was married to you."

"Exactly. It was all a lie she, and I, knew nothing about. They lived in a nearby town. He'd tell her he was going to visit his son with his ex or that he had a business trip. I was going to therapy and grief meetings, slowly trying to claw my way back to living again, trying to paint away the nights, exhausting myself so I could sleep. And all the while I didn't see that my husband was spending more nights away from home than in it. I didn't want to wake him when I came to bed at night, so I'd sleep in the guest room. It was so easy for him to lie and say he'd left for an early meeting before I woke up, when most of the time he wasn't even there. I mean, how stupid and blind could I be?"

"You can't blame yourself for what *he* did."

She dismissed that with a *Yeah, right* look. "It seemed the better I got, the more we got closer to being back to normal, the more our routine settled into something it had never been. He'd be there in the morning when I woke up, and then off to work, where he'd work late and I'd think he'd come home after I went to sleep. I was trying to keep a more normal schedule, eat better, all those things, so that I felt better during the day. We were both busy. He talked about all the deals he was making, the clients who were so happy with his furniture finds, and how great work was going, even though it meant lots of business trips. He made it up to me by always spending the weekend together."

"Because during the week he was with her."

"And on the weekends she thought he was visiting his son. He was being a good husband and father to her and her child. Providing for them, so she didn't mind the time apart. She was busy with a newborn and a part-time job at her family's business."

"How did you find all this out?"

"*She* figured it out. Christopher would tell her that he was staying at a motel when he went to see his son. I guess the baby got sick and she took her to the hospital for a very high fever. She tried to contact him, but he didn't answer his cell."

"Because he was with you and didn't want to get caught."

"There were a lot of weekend calls where he'd say, 'I'll call them back. This is our time.'"

Jax couldn't believe the audacity. "What a dick."

Layla nodded her agreement. "So she needed him, and he dismissed her call, so she contacted the motel."

"And he wasn't a guest there."

"Nope. She got suspicious. So the next weekend she followed him, figuring that he was sleeping with his son's mother, his ex."

He winced. "And she found you."

"She didn't confront him on the Friday he came home to me because she didn't want to make a scene in front of our son. She waited for him to leave for work on Monday, then rang the bell and told me that she knew I was sleeping with her husband and it needed to stop." Another tear slipped down her cheek.

"Fuck. That had to hurt when you found out."

"I imagine she was hurt to find out I was still his wife, and the son he was supposedly visiting was dead, and she and her daughter were the replacement family he wanted, even if he couldn't let me go."

Jax pulled her out of her chair and into his lap. He wrapped his arms around her. She pressed her head to his.

"She looked so much like me." The whispered words tore his heart to shreds and made him angrier than he'd ever been.

"That bastard."

"Yep. I called him at work and told him I was having a really bad day and I needed him to come home. When he arrived at our house, we both confronted him. He tried to make excuses and told us that he loved us both, that he didn't want to lose either one of us."

Again, the audacity. "Was he insane?"

"Maybe. I certainly felt that way after losing Miles, and then watching this all play out. I told him to get out and never come back. He had a child to raise and support and I wanted nothing to do with him ever again. I felt betrayed in so many ways."

He couldn't even imagine it. "How did the other woman take it?"

"She was devastated to find out their marriage wasn't legal. He'd faked the whole thing by hiring someone to do the ceremony and forging the marriage license. The house he'd bought her was in her name only, so she told him to go fuck himself, that she'd sue him for child support, he could have weekend visitations, but she was done."

"He lost both of you at the same time."

"And if it got out that he had a secret family, his reputation would have been ruined."

"So instead of taking responsibility and being there for his daughter, he took his own life to avoid facing the consequences of what he'd done."

"And left me to deal with the fallout, because his family didn't know, and Michael wanted to know what happened to all the money."

"He bought her the house and put it in her name, so no one could take it from her. The same thing he did for you."

"One moment you think you're special . . . then your whole world falls apart. And I wasn't the only one who felt that way, because he did it to both of us. I couldn't even be mad at her. She had no idea what he'd done to her either."

"What a clusterfuck."

"Tell me about it."

"Why not just tell Michael where the money went?"

"It's none of his damn business. I don't want him to know. Christopher killed himself because he didn't want *anyone* to know. *She* doesn't want anyone to know that she was the other woman. She doesn't want anyone in his family trying to insert themselves in her life."

"Did the child inherit from Christopher? Wouldn't that have given it away?"

"I spoke to her right before the lawyer was to read the will. Christopher had never updated it to include his daughter, but I felt like she deserved a portion of what was left, though it wasn't much."

"You were going to use your money for the child."

"I could have set up a trust fund, yes."

"And what did she say?"

"She didn't want it. She got the house free and clear and felt like that was enough. She wanted to move on with her daughter and not look back. She didn't want to be an unwelcome presence in my life. I didn't want anything to do with her. I wanted it done and over."

He thought of recent events. "Could she be behind the vandalism?"

She shook her head. "It's clearly a man in those videos."

"Maybe she hired someone. Maybe it's a boyfriend or friend doing her a favor."

"I don't think so. Like me, she wanted to move on and leave Christopher and what he did to us in the past. I doubt she'd want to open old wounds. We have nothing left to say to each other."

She brushed her cheek against his. "I hope this is the last time I'll have to talk about it. It's done. So let's let it be done. I'm here. With you. I love you now. I want us to be happy. I don't want what happened in my past to be any part of my life with you."

"You can't ignore that someone is trying to get your attention."

"Then they should knock on the door and tell me what they want."

"That's what worries me. The guy was here. He got

close to you. Instead of talking to you, he slashed your tires."

"Maybe he didn't realize I was in the studio when he came and he got mad."

"Yeah, maybe. But how many people actually know you're here?"

"April and her husband. Collin, who picked up the painting. Your family. That's it."

"You didn't tell Michael."

"No. I saw him the day I left California. All I said was that I had a commission and was leaving to paint."

"Would April have told him where?"

"No. Never. She knows Michael and my history."

"Does she know about Christopher and the other woman?"

"Yes. But she's a vault. She won't tell anyone."

"The vandalism happened at your house and here. It's got to be Michael. Somehow, he's found out where you are."

She pressed her forehead to his hair. "Shit."

"What?"

"He called me when I was at the bar. I answered without thinking. Lyric was about to sing . . ."

"And she called out 'Hello Dark Horse Dive Bar' like she always does."

"He heard it and asked if I was in fact at a bar. I dodged the question, but he probably looked up the bar, found it online, and tracked me here."

"Damn. Same thing happened with Lyric and her stalker, country-singer-wannabe."

"It is way too easy for people to stalk someone."

Layla kissed the side of his head, then picked up her coffee and sipped it. "Now you know everything."

He squeezed her tight. "I'm sorry, baby. You didn't deserve any of what happened to you. I seriously can't believe what that bastard did to you and that other woman. I want to be pissed at her for sleeping with your husband, but you have to sympathize with her, too." He shook his head.

"Yeah, it's kind of hard to be mad when she had no clue and will someday have to explain Christopher to her daughter."

"You think she'll tell her little girl the truth?"

"I don't know that I would. Probably some version of what happened. He loved them, but he was sad about losing another child, and took his own life. That's as much of the truth as she needs to know. Her mother and I will carry the rest of the truth for her."

"That's a heavy burden you've been carrying around."

She touched her finger to his scruffy chin and tilted his face up to hers. "I'm ready to set it down for a life with you."

"I understand now why you have a hard time trusting in what feels like a happy life and a good relationship. Because he loved you all the way to the end, didn't he?"

"Yes."

"Then that, at least, was real, even if he screwed it all up."

Her gaze sharpened. "How can you love someone and betray them like that?"

"I could never do that. You would never do that.

But maybe when he lost Miles, something broke inside him. Something was missing, and he tried to fill that hole up, while still holding on to you because you're amazing, sweetheart. I never want to let you go either."

"It's a twisted kind of love to hold on to me and create a whole other family."

"Yes, it is. But he loved you so much, he didn't want to be without you."

"I just want you to be mine. Only mine. And I'll be yours. Only yours."

"That's already true and nothing is going to change it."

She pressed her forehead to his and held him tight. "Promise?"

"I swear it." He crossed his heart, then hers, and held up his pinky.

She hooked hers around his, and held on. "If you ever want to be free, just tell me before you turn to someone else."

"Not going to happen. Ever. You're it for me. I promise." He sealed it with another of those hot, steamy, passionate kisses she liked so much.

She leaned back. "I'm going to call Michael and see if I can stop whatever he might do next."

"If you're not going to give him what he wants, and I don't think you should, then how are you going to get him to back off?"

"I don't know. But I have to try."

# Chapter Twenty-Eight

Layla tried to call Michael that morning, but got his voice mail. She left a simple message: "We need to talk. Call me back."

Jax kissed her goodbye and left for work, asking her to let him know if she left her studio.

She agreed that maybe it wasn't such a good idea for her to be alone. There were plenty of people on the ranch to look out for her. And she didn't have the means to leave on her own anyway. Jax had had her car towed to a shop in town.

She spent most of the day working on a portrait of Jax atop his horse for his mother. After their talk and sharing their heartache she understood him so much better. Their connection felt deeper. And she felt it when she stepped back from the painting and realized it was done when she saw all his strength and compassion, his fierce loyalty, his kind spirit, and love staring back at her.

Lost in the painting and what it invoked in her, she caught the tear that rolled down her cheek even as she smiled at his image.

*I love him so much.*

It felt so huge and special.

She didn't want anything from her past to taint it. So at lunch, she texted Michael, hoping to resolve their differences so they could both move on.

LAYLA: Did you have anything to do with the vandalism at my house? Or slashing my tires?
MICHAEL: I don't know anything about that.
MICHAEL: Are you ready to give me what's mine?

She didn't answer, because she'd already told him no. And the answer would remain no. Because she wasn't going to be the money train Christopher had been for Michael. She didn't owe him anything. As far as she was concerned, Christopher's daughter rightfully received the bulk of the benefit of Christopher's money. She had a free-and-clear roof over her head and a mother who could provide for her. Christopher spent all his money on them, and that was fine. Layla could provide for herself.

A few minutes later she got another text.

MICHAEL: Ignoring me won't make me go away. If I lose this opportunity because of you, you won't like what happens next.

Well, that deserved a response.

LAYLA: This is the last time I'll say it. You could have taken what Christopher left you.
LAYLA: I am not responsible for you wasting my time and money in court. Your refusal to

abide by your bother's wishes cost you enough already.

LAYLA: Let this go. I will not give you anything more.

LAYLA: We're done.

MICHAEL: You think you can just move on and leave your family behind. Christopher was the only person who always had my back.

MICHAEL: You never interfered in that. Now, you're cutting me out.

MICHAEL: He'd never do that to me. He'd want me to have what's mine!

MICHAEL: Give it to me, or you won't like what happens next!

Yeah, he wasn't her family. Not anymore. Especially when he acted like he was entitled to her money, but had no desire to fix their fractured relationship. At one time, they'd been friendly. They'd celebrated birthdays and holidays like family.

Now he was all about what he expected her to give him.

Jax was right. The only way to end this was for her to stop engaging with Michael. If he was the one who wrecked her house and slashed her tires, the cops would find the evidence and charge him.

She wasn't doing herself any favors by riling him up more.

The last thing she wanted was for him to come after her again.

It took her a while, but she found her calm and worked the rest of the day with only one interruption when the tow truck guy delivered her repaired Jeep with two new tires and handed her the keys.

She had just finished cleaning her brushes and organizing her supplies in the studio when Jax called.

"Hey, sweetheart, how was your day? Did you get the Jeep back?"

"It was delivered an hour ago."

"You don't sound like you had a good day."

"It was fine. I got some painting done."

"And?"

She wiped off the smudges of paint on her hand. "I missed you."

"I missed you, too. And I'm still waiting to hear what upset you? Is it about our talk this morning? I'm sorry I stirred up all those old memories and hurt."

"No, it's not that. I mean, yes, it does hurt to talk about it, but I wanted you to know everything. I don't want secrets between us."

"Me either. I'm glad you shared it with me. You can tell me anything."

"I texted with Michael today. He said he didn't know anything about the damage to the house or my tires. He just wants the money. I told him I was done. He didn't take it well. Let's hope the cops find some evidence to pin it on him."

"That's partially why I'm calling. I spoke to Officer Bowers. The cops who went to his house said he wasn't there. His car was missing. Did you know he lost his job a month or so ago?"

"No. I had no idea."

"So, he's in the wind. The Blackrock Falls PD is searching local motels and rentals for him, but it's slow going because they have other priorities and slashed tires doesn't exactly present as a major threat. Though I'm wondering what he's going to do next."

"Me, too."

"That's the other reason I'm calling. I don't like you at the cabin alone. Do you want to come down to the bar? Tyler Braden is doing a live concert tonight. Not sure how Lyric pulled that off, but we're lucky to have him. The place will be packed, but I'll save you a seat. You can have a drink, listen to some really great music, and I'll kiss you every chance I get."

"Now, that is an offer I can't refuse. Let me change clothes and I'll be there soon."

"I'll be waiting."

# Chapter Twenty-Nine

Layla arrived at the bar around seven. She shared a table with Mason near the stage. Jax brought them both drinks. Lyric made them a delicious dinner. And when Tyler Braden took the stage at eight, the place was packed, the music was loud, and Tyler rocked the house.

She enjoyed her time with Mason. He kept things light. They spent most of the time getting to know each other better. He told her about growing up with his brother and cousins back home in Montana and how he ended up in the FBI. Some of his undercover work sounded harrowing. She didn't know how he'd survived those dangerous cases without being exposed as a cop.

He grinned and simply said, "I'm a good liar."

"I'm not. I think everything shows on my face."

"It does." Mason grinned at her gasp. "And you've got no guile. The truth is in your eyes. And every time you look at Jax, it's so easy to see you love him. You're a goner. But I also see the way you keep scanning the crowd. You're worried *he's* here somewhere."

"Is that why you're here with me?" *To babysit me.* She'd thought so from the moment she sat down.

"Yes. Jax is distracted at the bar. He can't keep watch on you with this crowd. He wants you safe. And I love that gorgeous angel in the kitchen. So if there's a threat anywhere near her, or to someone in the family, I'm there."

Mason was right about the thick crowd. Tyler Braden was singing "Try Losing One" and everyone was swaying to the deeply emotional song. Most of the guys with dates were holding their lovers close. Others were lost in the heartbreak Tyler poured out.

Mason leaned in. "You hear this song . . . If something happened to you, if Jax lost you, it'd wreck him."

She leaned into Mason and held his gaze. "He is never going to lose me."

Mason gave her a firm nod, then focused on the stage.

Jax came up behind her and put his hand on her shoulder.

She jumped because Mason had amped her caution to paranoia that someone was waiting to get to her. And if that person was Michael, he would not like her next refusal to do what he wanted.

Jax brushed his lips against her temple. "Easy, sweetheart. It's just me."

She leaned into him. "I know. I'm sorry."

"What do you think of the band?"

"Tyler and his guys are awesome! I'm so glad you asked me to come tonight."

The band started playing "Neon Grave" and the crowd went wild and sang along.

She thought it fitting, since the walls were covered in neon signs and this bar was the Wildes' life. They loved this place, this town, the people who belonged to them, including all these rowdy customers having a great night because the Wildes threw one hell of a party.

Jax brushed his fingers through her hair. "Don't leave without letting me know. I'll walk you out to your car. When you get to the cabin, I want you to call me so I know you made it inside and you're behind a locked door."

"You're being overly cautious."

Mason leaned in. "No, he's not." He turned to Jax. "I can follow her home."

"That's not necessary. There's been no threat against me, just some nuisance crap. Obviously whoever is doing this just wants to rile me."

"Or he's just getting started," Jax pointed out.

She did not look at Mason for the confirmation he'd surely add to Jax's comment. "You're both killing my good-time vibes."

Jax kissed her like a starving man going after a steak, all greedy and hungry, but then it turned soft and tender, leaving Layla sighing with satisfaction. "I just want you safe."

"I love that you care."

"More than anything."

She put her hand on his chest over his heart. "Which is why I will be very careful."

"Promise me."

"Jax, I really think you're making this into more than it is."

"I'm not." He wasn't backing down.

She tried to ease his mind. "Better safe than sorry.

I get it. I feel that way, too. But I still need to live my life."

"You can do that, so long as you are aware there is a threat out there and you don't get lost in your head and painting or a view or whatever and not see it coming."

She narrowed her gaze. "Are you saying I'm flighty?"

"You're gorgeous and talented and sometimes unfocused on your surroundings."

*True. Damn it.*

He was right, and she couldn't deny it.

"I will be more . . . alert."

Mason grinned next to her and choked back a chuckle.

Jax looked mildly appeased. "I love every adorable thing about you, sweetheart."

"Uh-huh. Right."

"I know how it feels when pretty things distract you."

She slid off the stool and right into his arms and another steamy kiss.

A loud whistle pierced the quiet between songs.

Jax broke the kiss and looked over her head, back at the bar. "Gotta go, baby. Bar's busy. Aria and the other two bartenders need help."

She gave him a smacking kiss. "Go. I'm fine here with my federal agent bodyguard."

He touched his forehead to hers. "Don't be mad."

She put her hand on his jaw. "I'm not. Not even a little bit. I know you did it because you care."

He put his hands on each side of her head and stared

into her eyes. "So much." He kissed her quick, then dashed back through the crowd and behind the bar.

She watched him the whole time.

"I know how that feels," Mason said.

"What?"

"You know the person you love can take care of themselves and still you want to do everything in your power to make sure they don't have to do it alone."

"I feel that way about him. I know that's how he feels about me. Jax and I . . . we have no secrets."

"Good. Because if there's something you aren't telling him about whoever is messing with you—"

"He knows everything I know about it. I suspect Michael, but I can't say for sure it's him, because it seems ridiculous that he'd antagonize me and think I'll soften up and give him the money he wants."

"Maybe he thinks you'll go running back home where he can console you and gain your appreciation so you will give him the money."

"If you think that, you don't know Michael. He's too . . ." She didn't know exactly what to call him. "He just expects me to do what he says."

"People who can't reason or be persuaded to see the truth staring them in the face are the most difficult because you can't change their mind. They believe what they say or do is right and everyone else is wrong."

"That's exactly how he makes me feel."

"Then you're right to suspect he's the one doing this. Maybe your house was just him blowing off steam, since he couldn't get to you. Then he finds out you're in Wyoming and he comes here and slashes your tires. Another warning that something is coming."

"Like what?"

Mason's face turned grim. "A reckoning."

"That sounds ominous."

"Never underestimate someone who thinks they've been wronged."

"But he wasn't. His brother left him money in the will. It wasn't much, but it was something. I was the rightful, legal inheritor because I was Christopher's wife."

"Right. Legal. These things don't mean anything when someone talks themselves into believing you'd lost that claim."

"You make me as frustrated as Michael does."

Mason grinned and sipped his beer. "Just letting you know I understand the situation."

She held up her wineglass. "I thought my time in Wyoming would be peaceful. A new start. And it has been. I just wish my past would stay in the past."

"We'll figure this out."

She tried for a smile of agreement, but she didn't think she pulled it off, so she settled back into the music and enjoyed the last bit of the concert and the two encores Tyler did before exiting the stage to raucous cheers.

Within half an hour, most of the bar had emptied out and Jax came back to her just as she was pulling on her jacket and grabbing her purse. "Hey, you heading home?"

"It's late. I know you still have work to do cleaning up. I'll see you in a little while back at the cabin." She hugged Mason. "Thank you for hanging out with me. I really enjoyed our time together."

"Me, too. Let me grab Lyric, then we'll follow you home. You need anything . . . call. Anytime."

"I will." She took Jax's hand and they headed for the door. "Good night, John."

The bouncer nodded a goodbye.

Jax scoped out the parking lot as they walked to her Jeep. He checked out all her tires while she unlocked the door and climbed behind the wheel. "Everything looks okay, but if something happens on the way home, stay locked in the car—Mason will stop to help you—and call me."

She kissed him softly. "I'll call you as soon as I'm home safe and sound."

"You better, or I'm coming after you."

She kissed him again, spotted Mason and Lyric in the car pulling forward, and shooed Jax back. "Go."

He closed the car door for her, then waved her off, watching as she exited the parking lot. The drive home was quiet. After the loud bar, she kept the radio off and just enjoyed the night view. Stars overhead, the moon glowing above the trees. So pretty. So peaceful.

She parked in back of the cabin in her spot and called Jax before she got out of the car. "Hey, I'm home." She headed toward the cabin.

Mason and Lyric waited in the lot for her to give him the all clear that her cabin was secure before he left.

"Are you inside with the door locked?"

"I'm just walking around the cabin to the porch." She stepped up onto the porch, put her key in the door, opened it, checked out the small space, then went back around to wave at Mason that everything was fine.

He backed out of the lot and headed home.

She went back to the cabin and stopped short.

Something didn't seem right and her gaze landed on something glowing in the dark. She walked toward the studio and spotted the shattered glass on the ground, the moonlight reflecting off it.

The studio door stood wide-open.

"Jax."

"What's wrong?"

"I think someone broke into the studio."

"Is Mason still there?"

"No."

"Get back in your car and lock the door. I'll call the cops."

She couldn't help herself. She walked forward, her shoes crunching over the broken glass from the window beside the door. Whoever broke in must have smashed the pane, then reached in and unlocked the door. She stared into the small dark room. No movement. No one standing in the corners. With the glass ceiling and the moon out, there was plenty of light to make out most of the room. She walked up the step and inside and gasped.

"Baby, what is it?"

"They stole the paintings."

"I told you to get in your car, not walk into the studio where someone could be waiting."

"There's no one here." Her hand shook as she reached the table where all her paints were laid out. Nothing had been disturbed. Only the paintings were gone. "I need to call April."

"You need to get out of there, go to my parents' house, and wait for the cops. I'm on my way." His voice got muffled as he spoke to someone else. "Aria said the cops are on the way. Go up to the main house."

"There's no one here." Anger simmered. "He took all my work." The loss of it hit her like a sledgehammer to the chest. All those hours and hours of work. All those beautiful paintings. All the lost income.

"We'll get it back." Jax sounded so sure.

The reality hit her hard. "You don't understand. We're talking about millions of dollars' worth of paintings."

"I don't care about the paintings. I care about you being there alone."

"I'm fine. I'm just . . ." She didn't really know what she was feeling right now. Angry. Sad. Scared. Furious that this person, whoever it was, kept demolishing her sense of security.

*They came into my studio.*

The place where she felt safe to let everything go and create.

"Layla, honey, talk to me."

"There's not much to say. They're gone. But the asshole isn't going to get away with this. He won't be able to sell them. Not for what they're actually worth. I never signed them. April will spread the word that they're stolen. No one reputable will buy them." Her gut twisted with the sense of loss and sadness wrapped around her rage.

"Are you okay?"

She loved that she was what mattered to him. "No. Some of those paintings were the best ones I've ever done."

"I'm still twenty minutes out. But the cops should

be there in about ten. Sorry, baby, but this is the rural life."

"I like it out here."

"Good. Because I'm planning on you staying here."

"In that case, I'm going to need a real studio with better security."

"I can help with that." Mason walked in the studio door and flicked on the lights.

She thought she'd heard a four-wheeler, but gasped and jumped back. Her nerves were totally shot. "Jeez. How did you get here so fast?"

"Who are you talking to?" Jax asked.

"Mason is back."

"Good. I had Aria call him."

"Lyric and I don't live that far away." He took a sweeping glance around the room, and she noticed the gun at his waist. "No damage besides the busted window. Just the paintings were stolen?"

"Just?" She raised a brow at him. "Not just. A fortune in paintings."

The police showed up then, Officer Bowers in the lead coming in the door. "Both of you, clear out of my crime scene." He waved them outside.

She walked toward the door. "Jax, let me deal with this. I'll see you when you get here."

"Stay with Mason."

"I will," she promised, though she didn't think anyone was after her.

They'd gotten what they wanted.

# Chapter Thirty

Jax stood outside the cabin with Mason as the cops left. He'd had to apologize to a few of the other renters for the disturbance. The ones who were up and came out to check out the commotion gave their statements to the cops. No one had seen or heard anything, except the sound of a car pulling in, then leaving a short while later. They thought it was just Layla and dismissed it.

She was in the cabin on the phone speaking to April about the missing paintings.

He knew this was a huge deal, but all he really cared about was that she was okay. She was safe.

"She's right." Mason's voice intruded on his thoughts.

"About what?"

"Maybe this was all about getting the paintings."

He didn't think so. "Why trash her house?"

"To get her to come home."

"And when she doesn't, he comes here. Slashes her tires to make her feel even more unsafe."

"Or because he wanted to get the paintings, but she was here, too close to them for him to get to them."

Mason stared through the studio door, a grim look on his face.

Jax tried to follow along with Mason's theory. "So he thinks she'll go into town to get her car fixed and he can steal them?"

"Maybe. But you took care of her car. She stayed here and painted."

Okay, maybe this made sense. "Until she left for the bar."

"He was watching her."

"It's the same guy on the video. Dark clothes. Dark mask. Same height and build. But he's unrecognizable."

Mason shrugged. "How long do you think it will take him to figure out he can't sell the paintings?"

"If he's got a buyer set up, not long. If he took them hoping he can sell them later . . . It will be harder to do the longer he waits because April will let the art world know they've been stolen and are unsigned."

Approval lit Mason's eyes. "Genius on her part."

"She says they're not done until they're signed. Sometimes she goes back to them to touch up this or that. Change something. It's her process."

"The cops shouldn't have any trouble identifying the paintings if they find them, since she'd taken a picture of each one of them. If they don't get any leads soon, I can talk with my counterparts at the FBI, see if we can get them involved in tracking the paintings."

"I don't know if Layla wants that kind of attention."

Mason pinned him with his gaze. "This is a major art theft and she's being targeted."

Jax raked his hand over his head. Tired after a long

night, all he wanted to do was go inside and console Layla. "Why can't they find Michael?"

"He's in the wind. We don't know if it's him or not, but it doesn't look good for him disappearing like this. Especially after those texts he exchanged with her."

They had nothing, no evidence, no solid leads at this point. "It's late. Go home, Mason. There's nothing more to be done tonight."

"I'll follow up with the cops tomorrow. We'll go from there." Mason gave him a pat on the back, then headed behind the studio where he'd left the four-wheeler he and Lyric used to cross the property between their two houses.

Jax opened the cabin door and found Layla sitting on the sofa, staring at nothing, her phone beside her. "What did April say?"

"She'll take care of it." Her blank expression didn't change.

"You want the paintings back."

"I wasn't planning on selling all of them. A couple, I wanted to keep. One of them, I thought I'd give to your mother."

"I'm sorry, baby."

She shook her head. "I don't have it now to give."

He stood close, staring down at her. "We'll get them back."

"It's not about the paintings. Someone came into my studio and took them. He didn't care what they meant to me, what I had intended for them. He just took them because he wants the money he thinks they'll bring. And when he finds out that they aren't worth what he hoped, then what? Will he destroy them?" A tear slipped down her cheek. "All that work, just gone."

He squatted in front of her and put his hands on her thighs, offering comfort, though she didn't seem to want any right now. "You can re-create them."

She put her hands over his. Some of the tension drained out of her. "I can. But each piece . . . they're special. They're unique. Even if I paint the same scene again, it won't be exactly the same. And I don't know if I want to do it all over again. I already put that memory, that piece of my heart on the canvas."

Jax squeezed her thighs. "What can I do to make this better?"

She finally met his gaze. "You've done everything you can. You stood by my side tonight through all the chaos with the police." She leaned in closer. "You're perfect. It's everything else that sucks."

"I have a feeling we'll know tomorrow—well, later today given the time—who took the paintings."

She raised a brow. "Why do you think that?"

"Because whoever took them will want them signed."

Her head fell back on the sofa and she stared at the ceiling. "You think they'll come after me to get me to sign them."

"They're only worth something if you sign them. And I'm not taking any chances with you."

"How about you just take me to bed and make me forget all of this for a while?"

"I've said it before, I'll say it again. You're brilliant." He kissed the back of her hand, then stood, pulling her up with him. He knew this wasn't going to solve anything, but if she wanted a distraction, he was her man.

He was also the guy who would stand between her and danger.

No one would get away with hurting her.

# Chapter Thirty-One

Layla was in her studio, sitting on the lounge, staring across the room at a blank canvas, nothing in her head or heart that inspired her to paint. It had been like this the last two days. And, oh yeah, there was always someone around watching her do nothing. It made the anxiety worse, because it felt like everyone was waiting for her to do something. Paint. But she couldn't.

Why would someone do this to her?

If it was Michael—and surely it was—then the reason was stupid and childish and just . . . dumb.

The knock on the door didn't surprise her. Someone was always checking on her.

"Come in."

The last person she expected to see walked in the door.

She turned on the lounge to face him. "Michael." Anger roiled in her gut.

She bet someone was really close by, waiting to see what happened. After all, it was stupid for Michael to come in broad daylight if he intended to hurt her. But she didn't think he was that stupid, so she kept quiet and waited to hear what he had to say.

He held up a hand. "Just listen to me, okay? Give me five minutes to say what I want to say. Then you can tell me to fuck off again if that's how you feel, but I'm hoping you'll see my side of this and do the right thing because it's what Christopher would have wanted you to do."

She didn't say a word. She was so furious, she wanted to spit out all kinds of rage at him. But because of Christopher and the apologetic look on Michael's face, she stared him in the eye and waited.

"Thank you." He ran his fingers through his dark hair. "Okay. I didn't think it would be this easy to get you to listen. I mean, I hoped you'd be reasonable. You always are. Christopher loved you because you were this calm, lovely presence in his life. You always looked for beauty and good in everything and everyone."

"I'm not feeling real lovely or calm right now, so get to the point."

He sucked in a breath and let it out slowly. "I made a mistake. Lots of them actually."

"Tell me something I don't know."

"I have a real chance at something that could be not just financially amazing, but a career move that will give me stability and security for the future."

This sounded so familiar. But his tone was different. Pleading, yes. But also sure.

"I know those things are important now because I don't have Christopher to save my ass anymore. This isn't like in the past. I did my homework, like Christopher always told me I should do. I made sure that the proposal, the company, was exactly what they said. I had two other people I trust go over it." He put his hand behind his back.

She startled and leaned away from him.

He frowned and slowly pulled out a folded file from his back and held it up between them. "It's just the paperwork. I knew you wouldn't just take my word for it. I should have shown you this at the beginning. Please, all I'm asking is that you look it over. Have April and your business manager check it out. Show it to whomever you like for confirmation that this is a good investment. It will take time and effort to get it off the ground and making a profit, but the bones are there. I just need you to help me with this chance to be what Christopher always believed I could be." He held the file out to her.

She eyed it but didn't take it. "How much do you want?"

"It's more than Christopher left me. But I'll pay you back as the investment grows. It won't be right away, but I will pay it back. We can even sign an agreement." He lifted the folder closer to her. "Please. This is legit." He pressed his lips tight, his eyes filled with a plea. "Layla, please, just look at it."

She stood and took the folder. And then, because of Christopher, she gave Michael a shot. "How did you get involved with this company?"

Michael let out a sigh of relief, probably because she hadn't said no. Yet. "One of the founders is a friend from college. We recently reconnected. This is his third company he's started. The others sold for millions. This is what he does. And he's offered to bring me in on the ground floor. He's promised it's going to be a lot of work, but I'm okay with that. I think I'd like to build something and see it succeed for once, instead of crashing and burning because I cut corners and didn't put in the time and effort. I can't do that this time, because this is my friend. He's counting on me to deliver. And he's the kind of guy who won't let me get away with shit or stumble and fall on my ass. I trust him. I've seen what he can do. I think I can learn a lot from him."

That was something new, Michael wanting to work hard and learn from someone, instead of just expecting to be handed something.

He raked his hand through his hair again. "I need this. I think you know I do. After Christopher, yes, I handled things badly. I know, that's an understatement, and I'm sorry. Christopher and I . . . we were inseparable as kids and still very close as adults. You know I was so happy for him when he met you. I wanted him to be happy. He was. And I got to see what a great relationship you two had together. I wanted that for myself."

Michael's shoulders slumped. "He always showed me the way. And without him, I felt lost. I should have been there for you instead of fighting with you." The sincerity was there. So was the look of guilt in his eyes. "I just . . . didn't want to let him go. I was so angry he killed himself instead of coming to me if he needed help. I owed him. I'd have done anything to save him. But he didn't give me the chance. I had no idea he was in such a bad place. Was I truly that blind?"

"No. I didn't see it coming either." Everything had happened so fast.

"While you mourned, I raged."

"We all handle grief differently."

"I was an asshole. You were just trying to grieve for your husband."

*A lot more than that.*

"We used to be friends," he implored. "Please, forgive me for making things more difficult than they had to be. I'll be the guy you used to know, the one who looked out for you when Christopher traveled. He'd want me to do that now that he's gone. I want to make things up to you. Give me a chance to show you I can be a good friend again."

This was the Michael she used to know.

But . . . "Did you break into my house and vandalize it?"

He flinched. "What? No. Why the hell would I do that?"

"To get me to come home, so you could ask me to do this." She waved the folder in front of him.

"No." Anger filled his eyes. "Hell no. That's your house with Christopher. I'd never trash it."

"Did you slash the tires on my car three nights ago?"

Confusion drew lines across his forehead. "I just got here, like, an hour ago. I drove straight here from the airport."

She tried to trip him up. "How did you know I was here? At the ranch."

"I stopped at the Dark Horse Dive Bar. They said the owners own this ranch and the painter lady was staying at one of the cabins. I drove up, saw the easels in here and figured you'd set up a studio.

When I got closer, I saw you through the window and came in."

"You came all this way without knowing exactly where I was and got that lucky finding me."

"I actually thought I'd call you and invite you to the bar for a drink and talk. But one of the waitresses helped me out instead. I figured in a small town someone might have heard of the famous artist in town. Imagine my surprise when she said you were dating the bar owner." He looked at her uncertainly. "Is that true?"

"It is." Jax leaned against the open door. He'd been there, lurking behind Michael, for the last few minutes, listening, watching, making sure she was safe.

Layla saw him, but Michael had his back to the door and didn't notice until now.

Michael turned to Jax. "When did this happen?"

"The second I saw her." Jax stepped in and stood facing Michael, not looking happy at all. "So if you're here to harass her, shake her down for money, generally piss her off, or make her unhappy, you better think twice about that."

Michael turned to her. "You and him?"

"Jax is a good man. Kind. Honest. Protective."

"Yeah, I got that last one." Michael held her gaze. "Are you happy?"

She thought it a strange question coming from him. And though her instinct was to brush past it with a simple yes, she answered him with the honest truth. "Very. More than I've ever been."

Some kind of decision lit his eyes. "You know what?

I'm happy for you. I know you and Christopher had a good marriage. Until you lost the baby."

"Hey," Jax interjected. "Remember that part about not making her unhappy."

Michael's eyes went wide. "He knows about that?"

Layla nodded. "Jax and I have no secrets."

Michael's gaze narrowed. "But Christopher did, didn't he?"

She raised a brow, her gut knotted. "What do you mean?"

"After you both lost the baby, you weren't yourself for over a year. I mean . . . a loss like that, you don't just move on easily. Right?"

Her heart ached even now. "It was a very difficult time," she said carefully, trying not to be swept away by memories or the pain.

"Exactly. You were wrecked. I'd never seen anyone grieve so hard and be so sad." Sympathy filled his eyes.

"Michael, where are you going with this?" She didn't want to relive that terrible time in her life.

One side of his mouth kicked back into a half frown. "Christopher was suddenly happy again. You came out of it very slowly. But for him . . . It seemed like it was . . . fast."

*Christopher found someone to make him happy again.*

She couldn't tell him that. She'd promised Christopher she'd take it to her grave. "Yes, well, we all grieve differently and get through it in our own way."

"And how did he get through it so fast?" The look in his eyes said he had an idea. "It's nagged at me all this time. It wasn't anything big that hit me. It was the small things. Except for one thing that stood out, and I don't know if you noticed it in your devastated state."

She needed to tread very cautiously here. "What was that?"

"Christopher loved being by your side more than anything."

*Uh-oh.*

"And when you needed him the most, he spent more time away from you."

She couldn't deny it. "People need space sometimes."

"Not Christopher. He was the guy with all the friends." He held her gaze. "I've been obsessed with where all the money went."

"Michael, you don't want to—"

He pinned her in his gaze, leaned in. "Who was she?"

Jax was suddenly beside her, his arm over her shoulders. "Tell him, sweetheart. You don't have to carry the secret anymore. He knows."

"Fucking asshole." Michael raked his fingers through his hair and paced back and forth before meeting her gaze again. "He cheated on you. After you lost his baby, he—" Michael shook his head, anger in his eyes. "And people think I'm the asshole brother."

She put her hand on his arm to stop him from pacing again. "He wanted to be a father more than anything. When I refused to try again—"

He leaned into her. "Because you were devastated by the loss and he carried the gene. It could have happened all over again."

She choked back tears. She couldn't believe he understood so well. She squeezed his arm. "He wanted to be a father. So he found someone else and had a child with her."

"What?" Michael backed away, his eyes wide with shock. "What?"

"You have a niece. She's perfect and healthy."

"So you two were separated?" Confusion filled Michael's eyes. "How did I not know any of this?"

Jax hugged Layla to his side. "Because they were still together. Christopher had a whole other family and was still coming home to Layla like everything was fine. She had no clue. He made up a story to tell his other wife—because, yes, she thought they were married because your brother faked a wedding with her—so he could explain his time with Layla."

That shocked look came over him again. His breathing quickened. "What the fuck?"

Layla sighed. "It doesn't matter anymore. He's gone. But you have a niece. And if you'd like to get to know her, I'll give you Brandy's cell number. She probably doesn't know about you, because Christopher crafted a very specific story for her, so you'll want to introduce yourself."

Michael paced the room again.

She gave him some time to absorb everything.

He turned back to her. "How did you find out?"

"She showed up on my doorstep, thinking I was the one having an affair with her husband. She thought I was his *ex*-wife and he was spending weekends visiting his *son*."

"Oh, fuck no." Michael's expression turned furious.

"Please tell me he didn't use your dead son to carry on an affair." Michael's view of Christopher shattered right before her eyes. Michael's pain drew lines in his face and added sadness to his eyes.

She wrapped her arms around her middle. "Looks like we didn't know Christopher as well as we thought we did."

Michael put his hand on his head and stared at the floor. "And I made this all worse by coming at you for the money. Why didn't you just tell me all this? I would have understood your anger and hurt better. Hell, I would have understood why the money was gone."

"Because before he took his life, he begged me not to tell anyone. I thought for all the years we shared, I owed him that much. I expected a clean separation from him. And then . . ."

"He killed himself. In your home, so you'd find him, and take care of him like you always did."

She choked back tears and tried to block out the images. "He was ashamed of what he'd done."

"Of getting caught more likely," Michael spat out. "You don't owe him shit. Not a damn thing. I'm glad you've moved on." Michael pinned Jax in his hard gaze. "You better treat her right. Like a fucking princess."

Jax looked Michael in the eyes. "I already do."

Layla laced her fingers with Jax's. "He loves me. And I love him. Which is why I'm planning to stay here."

"You can paint anywhere," Michael pointed out, then pulled out his phone and handed it to her. "I'll take Brandy's number. Obviously, my brother played her, too. And I want to let her know I'm here to help with my niece if she needs me." He raked that hand over his head again and took a deep breath. "I want to meet her."

She entered the information into his phone.

"What's *her* name?" Michael asked, his voice soft and hesitant.

"Abby." The name brought back memories for her.

Michael's eyes went wide.

She guessed he remembered, too. "Don't say it."

But he did. "The name you picked out for a girl."

Jax swore.

Michael unexpectedly reached out and pulled her into his arms. He pressed his lips to her ear and whispered, "I'm so damn sorry. You didn't deserve any of that. You were always good to him, nice to me, to everyone around you. That wasn't right. Even an asshole like me knows that."

She hugged him close because they had shared many good memories, too, and she appreciated that he empathized with her. "Maybe you should stop being such an asshole."

He grinned. "I'm working on it. Hoping you'll help me do that." The self-deprecating humor in his voice reminded her of the old Michael.

She stepped back and found Jax ready to put his arms around her from behind and hold her close. Then she made up her mind about Michael. "I will have my people look over the stuff you gave me and I'll give you an answer in a few days."

"Thank you." Sincerity filled his eyes and voice. "It's more than I deserve, and I appreciate it."

"You're welcome."

"What about the paintings?" Jax asked.

Mason popped his head into the room. "It wasn't him."

Michael turned to their new guest. "Uh, who are you?"

"FBI Special Agent Mason Gunn. Jax's brother-in-law and Layla's new friend."

She grinned at him, happy to have a new friend like him. "What did you find out?"

"Michael hasn't been home recently because he, too, has a new love interest."

Layla raised a brow at Michael. "Share with the class."

Michael's cheeks went ruddy. "It's new. She's . . . awesome." The way he lit up with just those few words about her said a lot about how he felt. "She's another reason why I want to do this deal and provide a good future for us."

*"Us."* Layla understood why he'd changed his tune and came to see her for an amicable discussion instead of demanding what he wanted. He thought he'd have a better chance of getting what he wanted. More than that, he had a very good reason for wanting it. This wasn't just his greed talking. It mattered to him and his life.

Michael held her gaze, his grin open and honest. "You'd like her. She's got a lot of your qualities. Smart. Funny. Kind to everyone. Patient."

Layla laughed at the last one. "One needs to be with you."

"Yeah, well, what can I say? I'm working on not being such an asshole."

"Once you identify the problem, you can fix it," she teased.

"See, there's some of the spunk and sass Christopher and I loved so much about you."

Mason cleared his throat. "Michael did just arrive today. As far as the cops are concerned, he's in the clear for the art theft, but not necessarily for the vandalism at your house, because he had motive and opportunity."

Michael's brow furrowed. "When did it happen?"

Mason gave him the exact date and time.

Michael grinned. "Wasn't me. I was meeting with my friend at the new company space they rented, going over the plans for setting up the new office. We were there late, then I spent the night with Jessica. I was nowhere near your house. Not even in the same zip code. And I wouldn't do that shit to you." Michael, always so quick to be defensive.

Mason tucked his hands in his pockets. "So if not the brother-in-law, who is harassing you and stole the paintings?"

Layla held his steady gaze. "I have no idea."

# Chapter Thirty-Two

Layla and Jax walked into the Blackrock Falls Police Department the next day to go over her case and all the facts they had and questions they needed to answer. After her chat with Michael yesterday, he'd stayed to have dinner with her and Jax before he went to his hotel for the night. He was scheduled to fly home later today.

She was actually going to miss him.

She spotted Mason with Officer Bowers across the room.

"Layla, hi." Mason kissed her cheek. "Thanks for coming down. We have some information to share, and we'd like to ask some questions to see if we can come up with any new suspects."

"Anything I can do to help."

Jax shook Mason's hand in hello, then gave a nod to Officer Bowers. "Thanks for working so hard on this."

Bowers waved them to the conference room. "I want whoever did this as much as you do."

They all took seats at the table, Jax and Layla across from Officer Bowers and Mason, who led the questioning. "Since we've cleared Michael of any wrongdoing, who else in your life would like something from you?"

Before she could answer, Jax spoke. "I want her to stay, move in with me, marry me, have babies with me. You know, the whole happy-ever-after thing." Jax brought their joined hands to his lips and kissed her knuckles. "But I'm pretty sure she's okay with that."

Layla laughed. "I'm definitely in for all of that."

"Good." Jax squeezed her hand. "Now all we have to do is get your paintings back and take down whoever is harassing you and we can focus on the good stuff."

"Dude." Mason got Jax's attention. "I get that you're lovestruck—been there. Well, still there—but let's stick to the problem right now." He turned to Layla.

She answered his question. "No one has asked me for anything. I seriously thought Michael was behind this because of Christopher's will."

Mason tilted his head. "Anyone angry with you for something? Anything? Could be something small that they've blown out of proportion. You took their parking spot. You bumped into them. You criticized their work. You painted the same thing they did. Someone's husband looked at you a certain way and their wife is pissed. You turned someone down for a date."

Layla shook her head. "No to all of that. I mean, I did turn down spending the night with my client Collin, but he took it well. He was disappointed, but not mad."

"You sure?" Mason asked. "Because maybe he secretly wants you."

"It's not a secret," Jax put in. "I met him. He adores her. But I didn't get any kind of vibe he'd hurt her."

"Plus, he's been in LA. I'm sure you can confirm that." Layla dismissed Collin as a suspect and moved on. "I have a close group of friends. April is my agent and best friend. I spoke to her last night. I thought if I wasn't seeing things clearly, she'd know if someone was upset with me and I just didn't realize it."

"And?"

"Other than my friend Kara, who was upset I missed her baby shower because I'm here in Wyoming, there isn't anything. I called Kara this morning and spoke to her. She loved the baby present I sent, said she'd missed having me at the shower, we should get together as soon as I'm back, but that she wasn't angry with me. She understood that I had a job and that took priority. I didn't sense any animosity. I ended the call feeling like our relationship was still on solid ground and we were as close as we've always been."

"The commission you did for Collin." Mason leaned in, going back to him. "Tell me more."

"He liked the painting I did for him so much, he commissioned a second. He loves my art. Has a couple other pieces, too. He's a collector. He has the money to pay for it. He wouldn't steal it. And because he knows art and what it's worth, he'd make sure it was signed before he took it—if he was going to do something like that. Which he wouldn't." She didn't believe it for a second.

Mason's shoulders relaxed. "I'll look into him, see if he's got any money troubles."

She didn't think so. "He just wired half a million dollars to me. I don't think money is an issue."

Mason's and Officer Bowers's eyes went wide.

"Yeah. See. Not Collin. April would have heard through the grapevine if he was having money problems, anyway. People gossip in the art world. A lot."

"Have you had any unsatisfied customers?" Bowers asked.

"No. People don't buy art unless they really love it. I mean, pieces get sold from one buyer to another for lots of different reasons. I had one person who damaged a painting ask if I would repair it. I did. She was happy."

"What happens if you die? Who inherits?" Mason shifted in his seat, looking uncomfortable about asking the question that probably made the most sense. Who had the most motive?

She narrowed her gaze, concern amping her anxiety. "Do you think my life is in jeopardy?"

He shook his head. "No. We have no reason to suspect that yet. But if this is about money . . ."

She picked up where he left off. "I suppose at this point if I die my estate would go to my next of kin, which would be my parents and brother. I haven't updated my will since Christopher died." She caught her breath.

"What?" Mason asked.

Jax put his hand over hers. "If the will says it goes to Christopher, then maybe it would go to his next of kin since he's dead? Is that what you're thinking?"

"I'd have to check with my lawyer."

"You need to change the will ASAP," Jax encouraged.

"Fill me in," Mason ordered. "Are we back to Michael?"

"No. Christopher's daughter would inherit if that line of inheritance is true."

"Daughter?" Mason raised a brow. "He had a child with someone before he married you?"

"No." Her heart hurt again. This secret would not stay buried. "*While* he was married to me."

Mason sucked in a breath. "Oh, damn."

Layla scrunched her lips and gave him a *Yeah* look.

"So you inherited everything from Christopher and his daughter got nothing?" Officer Bowers tried to piece things together.

"Not exactly. Christopher bought her mother a home. After Christopher died, I spoke to her. I wanted to be fair for the child's sake. Brandy didn't want anything more than what she'd already gotten. The house. There was barely anything left of Christopher's estate when he passed. It cost him a lot to support two households."

Layla's phone rang. She checked the caller ID, then held the phone up to Jax.

"Why is Michael calling? I thought he was going home today?"

"Maybe he just wants to say goodbye. But let's find out." Layla shrugged then accepted the call. "Hi, Michael."

"Something weird is going on."

That spiked her attention and concern. "What do you mean?"

Jax, Mason, and Officer Bowers were all staring at her.

"Put it on speaker," Jax whispered.

She did.

"After we talked yesterday, I texted Brandy last night when I got to my hotel. I wanted to introduce myself like you said. I told her I was here with you and that you'd told me the truth about Christopher and I was interested in meeting her and Abby. I made it clear I'd like a relationship with my niece, but I understood if she needed some time to get to know me before we met in person. She didn't text me back until just now."

"And?"

"She's here."

Mason's eyes lit up and he pulled out his phone. "What's her name?" he mouthed.

"Here? Where?" she asked.

Officer Bowers handed her a pen and his notebook.

"In Wyoming. She said she wants to see you."

"What? Why?" She wrote down "Brandy Sinclair. Torrance, CA." She slid it toward Mason.

He typed on his phone.

"I don't know. I texted her back and asked why, but she hasn't answered me. I thought you should know."

Layla heard an announcement in the background.

"Listen, I'm supposed to board my flight in, like, twenty minutes, but maybe I should stay here and see this thing through with you."

She glanced up at Jax. He shook his head.

"No. I'll be fine. I've got Jax and Mason and the police working on this."

"You sure? Because that's one hell of a coincidence, her showing up here when you haven't spoken for, what, a year? More? And now, your paintings are stolen. How does she even know where you are? I only figured it out because I heard the bar name on our call."

Shit. She hadn't thought of that. *How did Brandy find me?*

"Go home, Michael. I'll keep you updated. But right now, I need to contact her—" Her phone pinged with an incoming text.

"Is that her?" Michael asked.

She looked at the notification.

BRANDY: I'm in town. Can you meet me at the Stardust Motel on Cedar Creek?
BRANDY: Room 111

Layla's gut tightened with dread. "Yes, it's her. I have to go. I need to call her."

"Be careful, Layla. Watch your back. This feels very off to me."

"You and me both. Don't worry. I've got help." She wasn't alone in this.

# Chapter Thirty-Three

"Call her," Jax prompted. "Find out what she's doing here."

Before she could do that, her phone rang. She held it up and showed all of them the screen. "Speak of the devil."

Mason leaned over the table. "Answer it. Put it on speaker. Act like you're surprised to hear from her."

She did as he asked. "Hello."

"Layla, it's Brandy. I'm so sorry to call you out of the blue like this. Especially since . . . well, you know."

Yeah, she did. "Is everything okay? How is Abby?" Just talking about the little girl pinched her heart.

"She's fine. Staying with my parents. But . . ." Brandy didn't say anything more.

"What's wrong?" There was no reason for Brandy to contact her unless she was desperate, otherwise the two of them really had nothing to say to each other.

"I'm so sorry, Layla. I know we'll never be friends. But you have to know I didn't know what Christopher did to us any more than you did."

"I do know that." It had been painfully obvious

when they'd first met on her doorstep. "And I thought that we had settled everything last we spoke. Has something changed?"

"Unfortunately, yes. Will you come to the motel? I need your help. You need to come now." The desperate words were spoken quickly, but also seemed forced.

"Why?"

"Just do it," she snapped. "If you don't come in the next half hour, things will get worse." The line went dead.

Layla frowned at the screen, then looked up at Jax. "Something isn't right. She didn't sound like herself."

Brandy sounded scared.

"Are you sure?"

"Yes. I mean, I don't know her well, but . . . that wasn't like her at all. Even when she found out about me and Christopher, even in her anger she tried to maintain being civil. 'Just do it.' She never tried to order me around. I never heard her speak to Christopher that way either. And she was plenty mad at him."

Mason looked thoughtful. "If you had to guess, what do you think is going on?"

Layla thought about Brandy's words. "She said, 'I need your help,' almost desperately."

"She needs you to sign the damn paintings," Jax pointed out.

Layla shook her head. "I don't think that's it. 'Things will get worse.'" She ruminated on that. "What did she mean? For me? If she has the paintings, there's not much worse she can do to me. I've lost time and the income." Layla didn't think Brandy would physically harm her. She didn't seem like that kind of person. "Maybe she's talking about herself. If I don't show, something will happen to her? What if someone is using her to get to me?" At this point, she could only speculate.

Mason handled the practical. "Let's find out when she got here." He turned to Officer Bowers. "Call the motel. Ask the clerk who booked room 111. How many people are staying there? When did they check in? I'll use my contacts to see when Brandy flew in. Maybe she's the one who slashed your tires and stole the paintings. Well, not her, but an accomplice, since we have someone who appears to be a very tall man on video."

Layla sucked in a breath. "That's true. It couldn't have been her. So maybe she's in trouble."

"Maybe she *is* trouble," Jax said.

Layla didn't want to think that Brandy would hurt her on purpose, not after the hurt they'd both suffered because of Christopher's selfishness. "We need to make this quick. She's expecting me to show soon."

Bowers came back in. "Joshua Dreger checked in four days ago. He's due to check out tomorrow. The front desk person hasn't seen anyone with him."

Mason had been typing on his phone and it pinged with several texts now. "Brandy Sinclair arrived in Wyoming only a few hours ago."

"So she definitely didn't steal the paintings." Layla breathed a sigh of relief on that one.

"Doesn't mean she's not involved." Jax squeezed her hand. "Want to bet Joshua is either her boyfriend or hired help?"

"She's not like that." At least, Layla didn't want to believe she'd do this.

"You don't know her," Jax reminded her gently. "You don't want her to be like that, because it's one more way that Christopher screwed you with her."

"He was the one doing the screwing."

"And maybe she wants what she thinks you owe her," Mason chimed in.

"We settled this long ago. And I don't owe her shit. *She* was sleeping with *my* husband."

Mason held up a hand. "We're just speculating here. We need to get to that motel and take them into custody so we can figure this out."

"And how do you plan on doing that?" Jax eyed Mason.

"With Layla's help."

Jax stood, planted his hands on the table, and got in Mason's face. "You are not sending her into a motel room alone without knowing what she's walking into."

The other man rolled his eyes. "Of course not. I just need her to draw Brandy out so we can take down Joshua."

Sounded easy enough. Layla didn't think it would be.

# Chapter Thirty-Four

Jax didn't like the setup one damn bit. The motel stood two stories tall and twelve units long, the rooms stacked on top of each other with a central staircase leading up to the upper balcony. Room 111 was near the end on the right with the office way on the left side of the building. Officers had surrounded the place, out of sight. Some were lurking on the side of the building by room 112, waiting for Layla to approach the door and knock. She wasn't alone though.

Jax had insisted on going with her, but that idea got squashed because he wasn't law enforcement. They didn't want one more civilian involved if things went to shit.

But he'd lay down his life for Layla in a second.

Mason had planned all along to be the lead on this and the cops hadn't balked because Mason had a ton of experience working undercover. He stood next to Layla now, pretending to be her new boyfriend. An armed and trained stand-in for Jax.

They didn't know if Michael had told Brandy about Jax. He was on a plane right now, so they couldn't confirm. But Brandy wouldn't know what Jax looked like, so she wouldn't know Mason wasn't him.

Mason and Officer Bowers dug up everything on Joshua they could in the short time they had to get to the motel. The last time he'd been arrested for breaking and entering, burglary, and possession of stolen property he'd been nineteen, his juvenile record sealed. But it probably had a few more similar crimes on it that led up to the last arrest. Joshua had seemingly turned his life around while he attended trade school. He'd spent the last many years working as a plumber.

And now, it seemed, he'd gone back to his old ways, trying to make a quick buck. Or a million of them.

Jax's heart double-timed in his chest as Layla and Mason approached room 111. Layla had protection. That's what mattered. Mason wouldn't let anything happen to her.

She knocked on the door and Mason pulled her back two steps, putting space between her and the room.

Jax felt too far away in a surveillance van tucked back by the office. An officer in an unmarked car in the parking lot was feeding them a live video, while he could hear everything Mason and Layla said on the open comm they'd hidden on Layla's purse strap.

The motel room door opened just enough for a woman who looked strikingly like Layla to poke her head out.

"You didn't come alone," Brandy said, her gaze darting back into the room, then returning to Layla and Mason.

"This is my boyfriend, Jax."

Brandy bit her bottom lip. "You were supposed to come alone."

"Jax and I were out to lunch when you called. You made it sound like you needed to see me right away, so we came right over."

Brandy's eyes filled with fear. "You shouldn't have brought him."

Mason put himself partially in front of Layla. "Look, there's been some trouble around Layla and I'm just looking out for her. She didn't have to come here to see you. Not after what happened. So if you have something you want to say to her, then say it. Otherwise we're out of here."

Brandy glanced back in the room, then quickly took a few steps out, looking back like someone might chase her, or something.

Mason had to back up to get out of the way and pushed Layla back, too.

"I'm sorry," Brandy rushed to say. "I just thought we could talk. About what happened."

"I have nothing more to say about it. It's in the past. We settled things, you and me, so I don't know what else we have to say."

"Brandy, why don't you invite your friends inside so we can have a private chat," someone, probably Joshua, called from inside the room.

Layla instinctively stepped back behind Mason like he'd told her to do if things got tense.

Brandy hesitated. "Um." Her gaze darted from Layla to the room and back.

The door to the room opened enough for the tall,

dark-haired man to fill the gap, a big smile on his face, even as he blocked the view into the room. He probably didn't want them to see the paintings. "You must be Layla. Brandy told me a lot about you." He glanced at Brandy. "She didn't mention you had a boyfriend."

"Why would she know that?" Layla asked. "We're not exactly friends. In fact, we barely know anything about each other."

He glared. "No. I guess not. Just two women who were fucking the same guy."

Mason took Layla's hand, but still blocked her with his body. "We're leaving."

Joshua took a step closer to Mason, trying to intimidate him. "No, you're not. Not until Brandy gets what's coming to her."

*Bad move*, Jax thought. After going up against bad-ass killers, thieves, anarchists, and biker gangs, no one scared Mason. "Back off," he warned.

Brandy rushed to Layla and held her arm in both hands, dragging her forward a step. "I don't want any of this."

Mason shifted and pulled the gun from his back, still hiding it at his side from Joshua.

Jax nearly jumped out of his seat and rushed out of the van, but the cop beside him anticipated his move and put a hand on his shoulder, and shoved him back into the seat. "Not yet."

"You're coming with me." Joshua stepped toward Layla.

The next thing Jax knew, Mason did some kick-ass move, grabbed Joshua's arm as he reached for Layla, and tripped him with his foot. Joshua went sprawling onto the pavement, his feet still up on the walkway in front of the rooms, and his arm yanked up behind his back as Mason cuffed him.

Joshua's face went red with rage. "What the fuck, man?"

Mason delivered the news with a grin. "FBI, asshole. You're under arrest."

"I didn't fucking do anything," Joshua bellowed.

"Yeah. We'll just see about that." Mason hauled Joshua back onto his knees, then to his feet.

The cops covering Mason came around the building and swarmed around Joshua as Officer Bowers pulled Layla and Brandy away. Then he took hold of Brandy's arms, pulled them behind her back, and cuffed her.

"He made me do this!" Tears glistened in her eyes.

"We'll sort that out soon." Bowers pulled her to the raised walkway in front of the open motel room door and instructed her to sit down.

Jax turned to the cop beside him in the van. "Don't try to stop me this time. I'm going to Layla." He jumped out of the vehicle and ran to her.

She rushed into his arms. "Oh my God, that was so fast. I didn't see that coming at all." She trembled in his arms.

Jax looked at Mason. "Thanks for keeping her safe."

"What are brothers for?" Mason smacked Jax on the back. "I'm going to check the room."

Joshua stood between two officers. "You can't go in there. Do you have a warrant? I have fucking rights." He turned his angry gaze on Layla, and then tried to charge her, headfirst.

Jax punched him in the jaw, sending him to the ground. "Not fucking happening, asshole. You don't touch her."

Joshua shook his head and blinked several times after Jax rang his bell.

Layla pulled Jax back as Joshua rolled to his side and tried to kick Jax.

The officers rushed forward; each grabbed one of Joshua's arms and hauled him up to his feet. "Be still," one ordered, "or we'll restrain your feet, too."

Mason stood on the walkway next to Brandy, staring back at Jax. "Nice shot." He disappeared for, like, five seconds into the room, then stood in the doorway again. "Guess what I found?"

Layla brushed her fingers over Jax's sore knuckles and breathed a huge sigh of relief.

"You got your paintings back." Jax hugged her close and kissed her on the forehead.

Brandy's eyes filled with tears that overflowed down her cheeks. "I have the worst fucking taste in men."

# Chapter Thirty-Five

Layla felt defensive about Brandy's declaration, though in this case, she was right. Joshua was bad news. She took a seat beside Brandy. "While Christopher deceived us, he was also very good to us." Those words hurt, but they were also true. Which made it so hard to resolve her feelings about him.

Maybe Brandy felt the same way.

She frowned. "That's just it, isn't it? You want to hate him, but . . ."

"He loved us." Layla finished the sentence because Brandy couldn't seem to say the words. "He loved his little girl."

Brandy sniffled. Her tears had stopped and were drying. "Yes. He did. And sometimes I wish things were still the way they were when I was blissfully ignorant and happy. I wish he could see his little girl growing up into such a wonderfully happy little angel."

Layla wiped away a tear of her own. This was so painful. "Then talk to me. Tell me what happened. How did we end up here?"

Officer Bowers stood next to them, listening, giving

Brandy a chance to confess to whatever she'd done and tell her side of the story.

Brandy sighed. "That's just it, I saw the red flags. I planned to end things. I just hadn't worked up the nerve to end them. He can be intense."

"I noticed." Layla tried to smile to ease some of the tension, but Brandy just looked sadder.

"We had yet another argument. He left, then he called me and said he was going to make everything right. We'd be set for life. I asked him what he meant, and he said he loved me and he was going to make sure I had the life I deserved. And then he disappeared. That was several days ago. And now I'm sitting here in handcuffs." Her eyes went glassy with tears again.

Jax stared down at her. "Did you know this is what he meant?"

Brandy shook her head, her gaze distant. "No. I'm not even sure how exactly he planned to get away with this."

Layla kept her focus on Brandy. "Who is this guy?"

Another deep sigh. This one filled with resignation. "I met him about six months ago in the grocery store. He seemed so nice. He made funny faces at Abby and got her to laugh. I thought it was sweet and cute." She looked at all the cops around them. "This is not."

Joshua was handcuffed, glaring daggers at them, and sitting about ten feet away in front of another motel room, a cop standing over him.

Brandy didn't spare him a glance. "Everything was fine, until I told him about Christopher. Joshua thought what he did to me was horrible. He thinks I got the short end of the stick because I wasn't really his wife when Christopher died. He said I should have gotten more. That Christopher owed me after what he did."

There hadn't been more. Christopher's life insurance policy hadn't paid out because he took his own life. Christopher hadn't been thinking about that, or the future for Brandy, Abby, or Layla.

She could take care of herself, but maybe Brandy was struggling and needed help. "Is that how you feel? That you should have gotten more?"

"No." Brandy's face scrunched up. "Absolutely not. And I told him that. I got to keep the house. I can take care of myself and Abby."

"But he's been pushing you to ask me for more," Layla guessed.

"Yes." Her gaze pleaded with Layla to understand. "I told him that what's yours is *not* mine. I didn't have any claim to the money you make on your paintings. But he kept insisting that half of what's yours belonged to Christopher, therefore . . ." She didn't finish that statement. "You were his legal wife. I was the unknowing other woman. I don't expect you to pay for his sins. I know that what Christopher gave me took away from you."

Layla didn't expect that kind of honesty or understanding. Not everyone would feel like Brandy did.

"I appreciate that you understand the big picture. And just so we're clear, I'm not angry with you for what happened. You didn't know. You weren't knowingly hurting me."

Brandy hung her head. "But yet again, something I did has hurt you. I don't know why Joshua thought

I would be okay with wrecking your house, slashing your tires, and stealing your paintings."

Mason had found the ski mask in the hotel room, along with the clothes Joshua wore that matched those in the video they had of him in Layla's neighborhood and at the cabin.

Brandy huffed out a frustrated breath. "What kind of person does that? I knew something was up when he asked me to fly here yesterday. He begged me to come. Said it would be worth it. We'd celebrate. I tried to find an excuse to get out of it, but he kept insisting." She turned to Layla. "Truthfully, I thought Joshua was setting up some elaborate getaway where he might propose and I'd have to say no and it would be this huge, awkward disaster." She looked at the scene around them. Cops everywhere, her boyfriend in handcuffs. "Disaster achieved." If possible, she looked even angrier now. "I told him I didn't want to come. He said he'd already bought the ticket. I felt bad about wasting the money and got on the plane against my better judgment. I thought if nothing else, this will decide whether or not we move forward." She glared over at Joshua. "Definitely not." She adjusted her shoulders and the handcuffs' chain clinked at her back. "Anyway, Michael contacted me last night, saying he was visiting *you* here. I got even more suspicious. I knew I needed to come and stop Joshua from doing whatever he was doing."

"When did you figure it out?" Jax asked.

"When I walked into the motel room and saw all the paintings. He told me everything he'd done and I immediately told him to give them back. He got mad.

Said he'd gone to a lot of trouble to get us what we needed for our future. I got scared and tried to leave. He blocked the door and made me call and tell Layla to come. He said if I didn't keep it vague and didn't get you here, he'd take all the paintings and leave."

She shifted her gaze from Jax to Layla. "I just wanted to get them back to you. I tried to talk him into just returning them, but he was so adamant and agitated. He wanted you to sign them. I guess they're not worth anything if they aren't signed. He said the guy he lined up to buy them laughed when he saw the pictures Joshua texted of the paintings, then got really angry on the phone thinking Joshua was playing him by trying to pass off just any old painting. Joshua was furious the guy wouldn't take him at his word and authenticate them some other way. The guy hung up on him." Brandy met Layla's gaze. "How did he even get them?"

"He broke into the studio I set up on Jax's ranch."

Brandy looked at Jax. "So you're her boyfriend, not the other guy who arrived with her and took down Joshua?"

"Mason is my brother-in-law. He's FBI. My sister would kill him if he let me play cop and take down Joshua myself, so he stood in as me."

Brandy grinned at Layla. "Looks like you got a good one."

Layla brushed her hand over the side of Jax's face. "Yeah. He's amazing."

Officer Bowers moved behind Brandy and undid her handcuffs. "You'll need to come to the station and give your statement. But from what I can tell, Joshua lured you here so you could get Layla's cooperation to sign the paintings."

Brandy rubbed her hands over her wrists. "I hoped that when I was able to get out of the room, the guy I thought was your boyfriend would help us get away from Joshua." She shrugged one shoulder. "I guess it worked out that way in the end. And I'm glad Joshua will pay for what he did."

Layla agreed. "Are you going to be okay?"

"I'll be fine. Joshua was on his way to being my ex before this. Now . . . I'm crossing him out of my future." Brandy slashed her finger through the air.

"He's the idiot," Jax assured her. "He didn't know how good he had it with you."

"You don't even know me." Brandy sounded down.

"I know you're willing to help Layla, not steal from her or try to use her. You never meant to hurt her. I believe that just as much as Layla does. So don't worry. The cops got Joshua and the paintings. You don't have to even think about him anymore. He'll be in a jail."

Brandy stared over at Joshua again. "Just when you think a guy is nice, they turn out to be something you never expected."

Layla bumped her shoulder into Brandy's. "Who knows? Maybe the third time's the charm."

"You'll forgive me if I'm a little gun-shy about trying again." She shook her head. "No. I think I'm going to focus on me and Abby. That's what's important."

"I hope you'll give Michael a chance to get to know you and Abby, too. It might be nice for Abby to know her uncle and have that one connection to her dad. He can tell her stories about Christopher and make him come to life for her."

"I will do that. She needs to know her father wasn't the sum of his mistakes. He was so much more." She hooked her hands around her knees. "I still wish that what I thought was real, was reality."

"It was real," Layla told her. "It took me a long time to understand that he didn't want to hurt us. He just wanted to love us and be loved by us. Was it selfish and destructive? Yes. But I don't believe he wanted to hurt either of us."

"That's the hard part, right? I thought we had the perfect family. I thought I was his one and only."

"You thought you were enough. So did I. And maybe when he was with me, I was. And when he was with you, you were."

"I wish he'd been brave enough to face us, so that we could get through the bad and figure out a way to go forward. Especially for Abby's sake."

"I wish that, too. I don't think I'll ever forgive him for leaving her." Layla wiped away a tear. It still hurt that he'd left Layla. But to abandon the baby he so desperately wanted . . . No. She couldn't let go of that.

"Thank you, Layla, for always being kind. You didn't have to be. You had every right to hate me. You have every right to blame me for this mess."

"I don't. Was I angry? Yes. Absolutely. But not at you. We both got hurt by the same man. Twice. Let's break that cycle."

Brandy grinned. "I'd like it if the next time we saw each other, it was simply a friendly chat. Two acquaintances catching up. Maybe over coffee and brownies."

"I'd like that."

"Do you need a place to stay tonight?" Jax asked. "If you're not comfortable staying here, there's an open cabin at the ranch. No charge."

Brandy shook her head. "I think I'll stay here, out of Layla's way."

"You're not in my way."

"But I've intruded on your life yet again."

"Again, not your fault. You were lured here because your asshole ex thought he could cash in on my work. I wonder if he planned to even share that money with you, or if he was simply going to take the payday and vanish from your life."

Brandy rolled her eyes. "Great. Something else to consider."

"Don't even give it any more thought. Or him," Jax advised. "Leave him wanting in your wake, broke and in jail. Because the attorney he needs is going to cost him a fortune."

Mason stepped out of the motel room. "Layla, we need you to inventory the paintings."

Layla stood, but Brandy grabbed her wrist. "They're really lovely. Truly amazing."

"Thank you." Layla walked into the room and winced at the paintings stacked and shoved against a wall.

"I know," Mason said. "We'll photograph each one of them, then return them to you because there is no way the Blackrock Falls PD wants to be responsible for this kind of liability if they're damaged or stolen from evidence."

"I appreciate that."

"So if you'll help the tech with the photographs, and let us know if anything is damaged or missing."

Instead of moving forward, she stared at the table in front of the windows where there were two tubes of paint and a brush.

Jax stood in the open door. "I suggest when we get the paintings back to the ranch you crate them and ship them to April immediately. I'll get you a top-of-the-line security system for the studio, though I'm thinking you may need a much more secure building, too. Whatever you need, I'll make it happen."

She appreciated Jax so much. "*I* should have taken precautions."

"Who knew some dumbass would come all the way here to steal your paintings. We won't be caught off guard the next time."

She looked at the craft paint on the table. "It's not even the right kind of paint."

Jax laughed. "Amateur." He rolled his eyes, like he'd have known what kind of paint to use.

It made her grin, too, and the stress of the last few days dissipated.

She walked right into his arms and held him close. "You are so good for me."

"You're the best thing that ever happened to me." He kissed her.

"Hey," Mason called. "This is a crime scene." He gave them a mock-disgruntled look until a smile broke through. "Come on. Let's finish this so you two can go home."

Jax cupped her face and kissed her again. "I like

the way that sounds. We should really find a place that *we* call home."

"Wherever you are is where I want to be." And since he was here, in Wyoming, she planned to stay, even if she hadn't actually made a plan.

Maybe that was because she was scared that this would all fall apart, the way things did with Christopher.

*But Jax is nothing like him. He'd never do anything to hurt me.* Either she believed that, or she didn't. And continuing this relationship meant she had to trust Jax, or they had no future. And that was unacceptable.

She loved him.

She wanted a life with him.

She wanted a family with him.

Jax brushed his fingers over her hair. "What is that look on your face?"

"We need to plan and build a life together."

His smile was open and happy. "Okay."

And just like that, nothing else mattered more than them. Everything felt right. The future looked bright.

# Chapter Thirty-Six

Jax stared at the woman across from him who'd come highly recommended by his sister Melody. "Your résumé is basically that you've worked at your family ranch your whole life." All of twenty-two years old, she'd never worked anywhere else.

Neither had Jax, so he didn't consider that a bad thing.

"Yes. That's right. And if I don't get away from them soon, I'll end up stuck there, under their thumb. They don't listen to anything I have to say. They bark orders at me all day. Nothing is ever good enough, even though I'm constantly having to fix or redo stuff because one of them didn't do it right. It's exhausting. Melody said you're fair, you let your workers do their job, and that I could do some of the fun activities with your guests." She looked so hopeful there'd be something more than mucking stalls, inoculating cattle, branding, feeding, fixing fencing, and the million other things you had to do on a working ranch.

"You'd like to work with the guests?"

She nodded. "Sounds like a good time to me. I'm good with people. I love kids and horses, probably more than adults a lot of the time." She seemed to catch herself. "I know my manners and how to deal with unhappy people who find fault in things just to pass the time." Sounded like she was talking about the family she needed space from.

"We do get a few of those throughout the season."

"I know the job comes with a lot of responsibility. I take that seriously. I'll carry my own weight. I can do that. I always have, even if it's not been appreciated."

He hated that for her. Here, they worked as a team. "Is there going to be a problem with your family if you leave them to work here?"

"That's my problem. And if I'm telling the truth, which I am about my skills, then the real reason I hope you'll give me a chance is because I am a hard worker. I always try to do my best, and all I want is for someone to see that, appreciate it, so I can end my day feeling like I accomplished something, not frustrated and angry and hurt that no one cared I busted my ass all day."

He liked her honesty. "I care." Jax wanted the people who worked at Wilde Wind to feel like this was their place, too. They weren't just employees but an extension of the family. "I don't want my employees leaving here unhappy or feeling like their contribution, big and small, doesn't matter. This place runs the way it does because the people care about the business and the animals we have here."

"I want to be part of that."

"And you understand that your duties will shift with the seasons. Work at the ranch slows down in the winter when we have fewer cabin rentals."

"Melody said I could pick up some extra hours at the bar if I'm not needed here."

"If you're okay with that, then you're hired. When can you start?"

She leaned forward in the chair, her hands on her thighs, hope in her eyes. "Now works for me."

"Good, because I have someplace to be and Zac could use your help with the fishing trip today."

"Really?" A bright smile lit her whole face, then it dimmed. "Um, full disclosure. I haven't done much fishing since I was a kid. But I can handle the basics, make sure the group stays together, take care of lunch, whatever else needs doing."

"Sounds good. Zac has been with us a long time. He knows the ropes. He can teach you. If there are any kids on the trip, make sure they wear their life vests just in case, and stick close to them so their parents can enjoy themselves, too."

She nodded enthusiastically. "No problem."

"Zac is probably in the green barn out back getting everything ready. Go help him after you fill out all this paperwork." He passed the papers to her, along with a pen. "Welcome to Wilde Wind Ranch. If for any reason you're unhappy here, you feel like you're not being treated fairly, someone says or does something you don't like, you come to me. I'll take care of it and do my best to fix it."

She held out her hand across the desk. "Thank you. I appreciate the opportunity. You won't be disappointed."

"I'll be sure to thank my sister for sending you my way. I think you're going to be a great fit here." Jax stood. "Now, if you're okay taking care of the paper-work and finding your way to Zac, I've got someplace I need to be."

He owed his sister a big thank-you for finding the last hire they needed for the ranch and taking that off his plate. The bar had one new employee. The ranch had two now. Which meant he didn't have to work sixteen-to-twenty hours a day.

He'd have more time to spend with Layla.

He could finally have a life. With her.

It had been four months since Layla arrived at the ranch. Before her, he'd have said love at first sight was something you only found in movies or romance books. Then he saw her and something inside him sparked. He needed to make her his. Because every time he looked at her, he thought, *Mine*.

He was definitely hers. Had been from that first moment when she stepped out of her car, wearing that pretty pink sundress, her hair gleaming in the sunshine, those green eyes filled with pleasure and awe by the view.

Every day they spent together felt like they got closer to what they both wanted, even as they simply let it be without talk about expectations and what came next as they settled into their relationship and they both worked on the logistics.

For Layla, that meant getting all the paintings she'd completed and recovered from Joshua's theft to April. Or more accurately, to the San Francisco gallery holding her upcoming Wyoming Wild show. All the paintings she'd done of the beautiful Wyoming coun-tryside. All the places Layla had fallen in love with and painted for show and sale.

He was so proud of her. He couldn't wait to attend the event with her. Because he wanted to be a part of her world, as much as he wanted her to be in his.

Which meant they couldn't stay in the cabin much longer. They needed a place that was theirs. Big enough for them and the future they wanted.

She needed a secure place to work and store the pieces she completed.

He'd found a great place to show her.

But first, he was going to show her some other great views before their appointment later. Not that she knew about his surprise.

He wanted to see her face.

He wanted to see if she was really and truly ready to commit.

If she wasn't, he'd just have to be patient until he persuaded her.

He couldn't imagine a life without Layla anymore. He loved her more than anything.

Now all he had to do was convince her Wyoming might not be the mecca of art, but it could be a good place for an artist to paint her masterpieces.

# Chapter Thirty-Seven

Layla stood in her studio and stared at the paintings on the three easels as well as stacked against the wall. The painting for the second commission Collin asked her to do sat drying. All the final touches had been done. She loved it. The stunning view, the vibrant colors, everything about it matched the view her customer wanted to bring back to LA with him.

She just knew he was going to love it as much as he loved the first one.

"Are you happy here?" That sexy, deep voice made her insides warm, her heart beat faster.

She hadn't heard Jax come in and glanced over, catching the steady way he stared at her. "Yes. I love the studio, my cabin, the hot cowboy who sleeps with me every night." She grinned at him. "Why? Is one of the guests not happy with their accommodations? I mean, I know I get very special treatment. The manager pays extra attention to me. Maybe one of the ladies who love looking at your ass in those jeans is jealous and hoping you'll come to her cabin," she teased.

Jax didn't even crack half a smile.

Her stomach knotted. "What's wrong?"

"Are you happy here?" Something in his voice changed, turned serious, and so did the look in his eyes.

She immediately reassured him. "Yes, Jax. Happier than I've ever been." She held her hands out to encompass the paintings. "Look at all the work I've done."

He stared at her. "Is that all? This is a good place for you to work?"

"My work makes me happy. This place makes me happy. *You* make me happy. If you can't see that, then I'm not sure what you're really asking me. What do you really want to know?"

"Is it enough?" He couldn't be asking her if *he* was enough. Jax had to know how much she loved him.

"Yes."

"Do you want more?"

She held his gaze. "Of you, always."

He shook his head and laughed under his breath. "This isn't going how I expected."

She raised a brow, unsure even more now. "What did you expect?"

"Honestly, right now, I don't know. You're always so . . ."

"What?"

"Sure in what you say."

"Then why are you questioning whether I'm happy here or not? I'd think that's obvious by the number of paintings I've done and the number of laughs, talks, wonderful moments, and amazing orgasms I've had with you." She thought that last part would lighten the mood.

Finally, Jax smiled. "You always find a way to surprise me."

"I'll keep trying to do that. I wouldn't want you to get bored."

He stepped closer. "That's just it. I have the best time with you."

"Wonderful. Let's go have some more." She stood, ready to go. "Where are you taking me today? You didn't really say, except that I should bring my camera."

He tilted his head and studied her. "How do you do that?"

She cocked her head. "Do what?"

"Just go with the flow. I come in here, desperate to know that you're where you want to be, and you so easily give me what I need to make it all seem all right."

She went to him and put her hand on his chest. "Everything is okay. Better than that." She wrapped her hands around his wrists, felt his pulse racing there. "So what is this all about?"

He touched his forehead to hers. "I want you to stay."

"I'm not going anywhere. Except wherever you're taking me today." She'd made no plans. She hadn't mentioned even a hint that she needed or wanted to be somewhere else.

Jax stood tall. His hands went to her shoulders. "While I've been hiring new people to free up my time, you haven't made plans to stay. At least none that you've shared."

"My cabin rental is open-ended. Month to month. I thought I could stay as long as I liked."

"You can. Of course. But this isn't permanent. It's not even truly ideal for you."

She hadn't wanted to presume anything, so she'd kept some things to herself until the timing seemed right. Like now. "I've been looking at properties nearby. Just, you know, browsing to see what's out there. What might work. Long term."

His eyes went wide. "You have? What about your California house? What if you miss it and want to go back?"

She shook her head. "The beach house is my past. I can't go back to living in those memories. I want to focus on making new ones. Maybe one day we can make that house ours for vacations or something, but right now, I'm where I want to be."

"With me?"

"Of course with you."

He kissed her softly. "Then grab your stuff and let's go exploring and find the inspiration for your next painting."

She went up on tiptoe, wrapped her arms around his neck, and kissed him, long and deep. "You make me feel like right here is where I belong."

# Chapter Thirty-Eight

Jax put his hands on Layla's shoulders, squeezed gently, and whispered in her ear, "Come back to me."

She startled and turned her head to look back at him instead of the stunning view in front of her. "What?"

"I called your name twice. If you stand here much longer, you'll grow roots."

She returned her attention to the grass-covered hills dotted with wild roaming buffalo and a winding river snaking through. They stood on the lookout he'd driven them to after taking her to three other prime scenic spots. She waved her hand out. "But look at this."

They'd been here for the last half hour after spending the last seven hours visiting the other locations he knew she'd love just as much as she did this one. "It's amazing. You've taken, like, twenty photographs. I think you got what you need to re-create this down to the last detail. But if we don't leave now, we're going to be late."

She turned and frowned at him. "Late for what? I thought this was our final stop."

"One more to go. A surprise. Actually two, if all

goes to plan, but we have to make it to the first one so we can tell everyone about it at the second place. So as much as you like this view, I have something else I want to show you, and I'm hoping you like it as much as I do." He was hesitant, unsure but hopeful. And anxious. So not like Jax at all. He hoped she didn't notice.

She slid her hands along his sides, squeezed, and grinned at him. "What's the surprise?"

"Come on. I'll show you."

She gave one more fleeting glance at the gorgeous view, then walked with him back to the truck. He helped her into the front seat and closed her door. She had her camera packed up by the time he climbed behind the wheel.

"So you're not taking me to another amazing location. From what I can tell, we started at the farthest point from the ranch and have been working our way back."

He chuckled under his breath. "You're not going to be able to guess."

"Are we going to meet someone?"

"Yes."

"A friend of yours?"

"No. Someone I asked to help me find something."

"What did you lose?" she asked, concerned.

"Nothing."

She scrunched her lips. "What is it that you want this person to find?"

"The life I want." His cryptic answers probably frustrated her, but he wanted to keep this a surprise.

"You have the life you want at Wilde Wind. You

love it there. Plus you have the bar. Please tell me you're not looking for another job."

"Actually, I am. Though it's not really a job, but something I want to be and do."

She eyed him. "You're not making any sense."

He took her hand and brought it to his lips and kissed the back of it. "Do you trust me?"

After all they'd been through, all they'd shared, he hoped he'd proven that she could rely on him always.

She didn't hesitate and answered, "Yes."

He breathed a sigh of relief because he knew trust didn't come easy for her. "Then just sit back, relax, and it will all be clear when we get there."

"Okay. But you're acting weird and it makes me nervous."

"Don't be. This is a good surprise. At least I hope it will be. I want you to like it. And I think you will, but I'm nervous about it, too, because maybe we should have talked about it first."

She put her hand on his thigh. "It's not too late. You can tell me what it is, and we'll figure it out."

He glanced over at her, then turned back to the road. "That's what I love about you. There's always a solution for us in your mind."

"That's what partners do, right? They work together."

"Absolutely. I love you. More than I ever thought possible. In a way that I didn't fully understand until you walked into my life. Mason practically fell in love with Lyric the second he laid eyes on her. It's like that for me with you." It had been a burning flame from the start. That was how he felt about Layla. She burned away everything in his past like a wildfire leaving the land ready for new growth and a bigger, brighter future.

It took her a minute to say anything. She stared at him, her eyes filled with wonder. "I love you, too. I never expected to love again. But you and I are so much more than what came before, and for me, it feels like an amazing gift."

He brought her hand to his lips and kissed it again, because he was driving, and hauling her into his lap and kissing her senseless the way he wanted to would end badly.

She smiled softly. "I want everything with you, but I've been trying not to get ahead of myself," she confessed.

He squeezed her hand. "You and me both. And I'm not trying to rush you into anything. I just want you to know that I'm serious about you, us, and a future here." He wanted that to be clear.

"I am, too."

He brushed his hand over her hair. "Okay." He took the turnoff to the right that passed one small house and dead-ended in a long driveway shaded by trees on both sides, hills on the right, and wide-open pastures on the left.

Her gaze scanned the landscape. "Where are we?"

"You'll see. It's just up ahead around the next curve." He slowed the truck so he could watch her out of the corner of his eye as the house came into view.

She scooted forward and leaned into the dash, gasping when the white three-story with the wraparound porch and solid wood front doors came into view. "Whose house is this?"

"Maybe mine." He stopped the truck and looked at her. "I hope *ours*."

The Realtor was waiting next to a silver sedan.

Jax rushed to add, "It's four bedrooms, four baths, with a huge attic space."

"With all those windows." She stared up at what was the third floor, though most of it probably had ceilings so low from the pitched roof that it cut down the usable space.

"As you can see by the weathered and chipping paint, the bowed and rotting porch steps, it needs some work. Someone started on the inside, thinking to flip it last year, so it's got new wiring, heating and AC, plumbing, and insulation and Sheetrock. But the kitchen and baths are all blank slates. It sits on twenty acres and has a huge barn and a shed on the property."

She undid her seat belt and shifted so she was facing him. "Do you want to start your own ranch?"

"No. We're about five miles from Wilde Wind Ranch. It's an easy drive even in the worst weather."

Her gaze went wide. "You want to buy this place for us?"

He needed her to believe it and want it as much as he did. He didn't care if it was this house, or another one. He just wanted them to be together.

"Yes. Wilde Wind is the family ranch. This place could be ours if we like it. Even if that's not now, but when you're ready. I've been thinking about buying my own place for years. I just never really had a reason that made sense when I didn't care that I still lived in the big house with my folks. There was plenty of space and they let me be an adult and do my own thing without interfering."

"With as much as you work, all you really did was sleep there."

"And now I sleep with you. And I like the way things are between us and being at the cabin. But looking forward, we need more space."

She glanced at the huge house. "This place is more than enough."

"Did I mention the twenty acres? Pick a spot. I'll build you a huge studio with state-of-the-art security."

She met his gaze. "This house, building a studio, that's a huge investment. For *us*."

He was ready to buy it for her, but if she wanted to do it together, it would make things a lot easier on him financially. "Do you want to go and look at it? We don't have to make a decision today. It's a lot of money, but I think it's worth it because this place looks like it has all the space we'll need for the future."

"Really?" She raised a brow and grinned. "We need four bedrooms?"

"Well, not right now." He gave her a sexy grin. "But if you want to fill a couple of them up, I'm happy to help." He leaned over and kissed her on the side of the head. "Come on. It's just a house tour." He hoped that would get her out of the truck.

He stepped out and walked to the waiting Realtor. "Thanks for meeting us so late in the day, Margie."

"My pleasure. This house has been on the market for a long time because it's unfinished. But for a buyer who wants to put their own stamp on it, it's a great place."

Jax hoped Layla saw it that way. "Margie, this is my girlfriend, Layla."

Margie shook Layla's hand. "He's told me all about you. I think you're going to love the attic space as well as the downstairs library. Both spaces get incredible light at different times of the day if you want to paint in the house until your studio is ready."

Layla gave Jax an astonished look.

"Of course I made sure you had space in the house to paint." He took her hand.

They followed the Realtor to the front door. "I'm just going to let you two go in and look around on your own. Because it's practically bare-bones, you'll be able to imagine what you want it to be." A thoughtful look came into her eyes. "Of course, if you're not able to see what the space could be, I'm happy to offer suggestions for the kitchen layout and where to put furniture, that sort of thing." Margie unlocked the door.

"I think we'll be okay." Jax let Layla walk in ahead of him.

She gasped and looked down. "Look at the floors. They're gorgeous."

"Hardwood throughout," Margie chimed in from behind them. "All professionally redone. Obviously the walls are a blank canvas. You'll need to put in the baseboards and crown molding if you want it." She waved her hand, to coax them to go explore.

Jax took Layla's hand and walked with her through the huge living space toward the back kitchen area. "I hate the fireplace," he said, hoping to get her to say something about the space.

"It's hideous." The rough stone was a mustard yellow,

cream, and brown coloration that ruined the feel and look of the whole room. "Nothing will make it better, except to tear it out."

"Agreed," Jax said, hoping this got them started on imagining the house of their dreams.

They walked into the kitchen area and stared at the old, outdated windows that were far too small for the huge space.

Layla went over and looked out them. "Looks like there used to be a pretty garden back here. With larger windows, you'd be able to see it. Maybe those big black metal-framed kind. Mix some modern in with the farmhouse exterior."

Jax liked that idea a lot and nodded his agreement. "The kitchen is big enough for a full set of cabinets against the back wall with the stove in the center. Put the fridge on the far wall. A huge island separating the kitchen and dining room area with a smaller table by the new windows."

"A white kitchen with dark countertops along the walls and the opposite on the island. Dark cabinets with a white countertop." Layla seemed to be trying to picture it with him.

"Maybe not black on the island, but a deep green or dark blue to add some color."

Layla grinned. "No. Lighter. The blue, blue of your eyes."

He hooked his arm around her shoulders and kissed the side of her head. "Whatever you want."

They walked through the rest of the first floor without much to say because the living space would come alive once they added furniture and their own personal touches. But when they got to the library, which was easily identifiable by the wall of wood bookshelves and a fireplace at the end of the room, Layla simply stood in the center, the light from the front windows pouring in over her. "I love this room."

"You love the light."

"I love the way this space feels. Cozy, even though it's spacious. I can almost hear the crackling fire on a cold winter's day."

"At least this fireplace isn't hideous." The smooth river rock in several shades of gray complemented the chunky wood mantel and felt right for the room. "One of your paintings above the mantel with a light spotlighting it will look amazing."

"We'll put *Moon* up there." Her simple statement said so much. She saw herself here with her painting up on the wall.

"We'll fill the house with your art, things we pick up when we travel together."

Her smile grew even wider. "Sounds like a plan."

They continued their tour of the first floor, noting the spacious bathroom space, the office that could easily be used as a guest room, then headed up to the second floor. They scoped out the three bedrooms to the right of the stairs, including the two bathrooms they shared. Then headed back down the hallway, past the stairs, to the large master suite.

"I love all the windows." Layla stared out the front ones, overlooking the yard and driveway. "The landscaping needs a lot of work. A lot more plants and flowers. But I love the huge trees."

"Check out the master bath." Jax could imagine a

tub under the window, shower at the far end of the room, double sinks on the other wall, a large built-in cupboard next to the door.

"It's almost as big as the one I had in my house. Plenty of space for us."

Jax pushed open the double doors in the bedroom. "The walk-in closet is the size of the bathroom."

"More than enough. Especially when we put in custom shelving, drawers, and hanging rods, that sort of thing. I want to see the attic."

They headed to the narrow stairs that led up to the attic space at the far end of the house by the children's rooms. When they opened the door and stared at the long open space, Layla sighed. "The kids would love this space. We'll put a TV, sofa, some chairs, their toys. Maybe we'll add a little kitchenette space with a small refrigerator and microwave for drinks and snacks. They can have their friends over and have a really cool space to hang out." She turned to him. "Do you see it?"

"All of it," he told her. "Come with me." He took her hand and went down both sets of stairs to the front door and pulled her onto the porch where the Realtor was waiting for them.

"So, do you like it?" Margie asked.

Jax squeezed Layla's hand, waiting for her to answer.

She kept her focus on him. "Confession time."

He raised a brow, his stomach tied into a knot of nerves. "What is it?"

"This is one of the houses I looked at online. Actually, it's the one I wanted the most. And now that I've seen it in person, I like it even more." She leaned into him, so Margie couldn't overhear them. "I love it. We should make an offer. I think it would be perfect for *us*."

"Yeah, about that *us* part."

"Oh. No worries. I'll totally pay my half. I want us to do this, everything, together."

He dipped his hand into his jeans pocket. "That's great. Because I want us to be together. Forever."

"Of course we will. I love you. You love me." She beamed. "And this place . . . we'll make it *our* home."

He went down on bended knee and held up the open velvet box to her, showing off the sparkling diamond ring.

She gasped and pressed her fingers to her lips. "Jax."

"You are my home. You're my everything. So be my wife, the mother of our kids, the one who is always by my side." He didn't have to actually ask the question because she was nodding yes all through that, but he did anyway. "Will you marry me?"

Tears slid down her cheeks. "Yes. Absolutely yes." She wrapped her arms around his neck as he rose to his feet and kissed her, long and deep, and with every bit of love he felt for her.

She broke the kiss on a laugh that brightened his heart. "Oh my God, I can't believe you asked me to marry you."

He held her close. "You seem surprised. But you shouldn't be. I love you. I can't live without you."

She pressed her forehead to his. "I feel exactly the same way."

He stepped away from her long enough to slide the ring on her finger. "Do you like it?"

She put her hand on his chest over his heart. "I love it. I love you."

"Look this way." Margie snapped a photo of them as soon as they did. She turned her phone and showed the picture of them smiling, joy making them both glow. "I got the whole thing on video, just like you asked, Mr. Wilde."

"Thank you." His phone pinged with the incoming video she sent him and another for the picture.

Margie beamed. "That was so special. I'm so happy for you both. You probably want to be alone. I'll leave you to explore the rest of the property. Just call me if you'd like to make an offer, or you want to see a few more houses."

Layla shook her head. "No. We want this one." She glanced at him. "Right? It's what you want, too?"

"I love it. I checked out the property the other day with a couple of the guys from the ranch."

"You were ready for all of this." She smirked at him.

"If we're going to start our lives together by buying a house, I wanted you to know I wanted it all. Mostly, you."

"You had me the second we met. Everything else is just stuff."

"Yeah, well, it's going to be a while before we can move our stuff in here. We need to hire a contractor to finish the house. An architect to design and build your studio."

She hugged him. "We'll get it done. But first, let's celebrate."

He took her hand and kissed the back of it right near the ring. "Oh, I have plans for that."

She raised a brow. "You do?"

"Trust me."

"Always."

Yeah, she did. And he would never let her down. He'd spend the rest of his life making her happy.

# Chapter Thirty-Nine

Layla walked into the Dark Horse Dive Bar with Jax, grinning so big her cheeks hurt. Their Realtor had made the offer to the homeowner, a figure below asking price, and the owner had accepted immediately. Next month, they'd own the place.

The second her eyes adjusted to the dimmer interior, she spotted the people gathered in front of them with a sign that said Congratulations!

Jax held up Layla's hand, showing off the ring on it. "She said yes!"

Tears gathered in her eyes as her parents came forward to hug her. *When did they get here?*

Her dad put his hand on her cheek. "You look so happy."

"I am," she assured him and her mom. "You need to meet him."

Her mom smiled warmly. "We did yesterday after we arrived and Jax showed us to the cabin next to yours. We spoke to him for a long time and had dinner with his parents last night. He seems like a good man."

"We're looking forward to getting to know him better," her father said.

She brushed away a happy tear. "How long are you staying?"

"A few days this time. We need to get back to your grandfather. He's sorry he missed coming, but he's not up to traveling. But Jax said there would be a guest room at your new place whenever we want to visit."

She stared over at him where he stood with his parents. "I can't believe he asked you to come for this."

Her dad put his arm around her shoulders. "He wanted you to have family here. Your brother wanted to come, but he had a project due. He plans to come see you next week. Jax already set up a cabin for him."

"I am so happy for you." April stepped in and hugged her next.

Donte, her husband, took her spot when April released her. "I knew he was going to keep you."

April brushed a tear from her cheek. "We saw the way you two looked at each other when you met. I really hoped you'd fall for him."

"I couldn't seem to help myself. I'm so glad I came to Wyoming. I can't imagine my life without him now."

Aria, Lyric, and Melody surrounded her in a big group hug.

"We get another sister," Aria announced.

"We still outnumber the boys," Melody chimed in.

"You and Jax." Lyric shook her head. "You belong together. And I can't wait to see the house."

"It needs some work," she confessed. "But as soon as it's ready, we'll have a big party. Maybe a wedding."

"I don't know if Jax is going to wait that long to marry you," Robin said, stepping into their group, her husband, Wade, beside her. "Welcome to the family."

One of the waitresses came by, passing out glasses of champagne to everyone.

Jax separated from a group of his friends and came over to join them. He put his arm around her shoulders, held her close, and kissed her on the head.

Wade held up his glass. "To Jax and Layla. May you have a long and happy life together. May you always have friends, family, and love that grows."

Jax clinked his glass to hers and everyone sipped and clapped for them. "Surprised?"

She pulled him down for a soft kiss. "Happy."

"Me, too. And that's what we'll be from now on."

# More from
# JENNIFER RYAN